PAT TRACY

D0017134

BURKE'S RULES

HARLEQUIN HISTORICALS®
$4.99 U.S./$5.99 CAN.

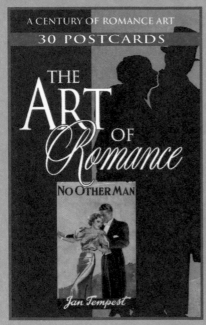

A CENTURY OF ROMANCE ART
30 POSTCARDS

THE
ART OF
Romance

NO OTHER MAN

Jan Tempest

The Art of Romance
is a beautiful
collector's
edition postcard
book published
in celebration of
Harlequin's 50th
anniversary in
North America.

This unique
collection includes
30 beautiful
postcards that can
be used as a
keepsake or shared
with friends.

Available in
February 1999
at your favorite
retail outlet.

ISBN 0-373-29046-2
9 780373 290468
50499

HARLEQUIN®
Makes any time special ™

PHARTIFC-C

"Listen, you. I'm bigger, more determined and meaner than you are!

"And there is no way that I am going to let you spend another night in this place. For better or worse, you're stuck with my involvement in your life."

Youngblood's statement sounded like a demented wedding vow.

"But you can't make me—" Jayne began.

"Sure I can. I'll just pick you up and take you where you should be."

"There are laws—"

"A respectable lady wanting to run a fancy girls' school can't afford to draw the wrong kind of attention to herself. It would be the kiss of death for your name to be linked with any unsavory gossip. I guarantee going to the sheriff in a misguided attempt to make me behave myself would unleash a flurry of wild rumors."

"That's coercion!"

"Highly effective coercion. Pack and be ready to go when I return."

Jayne just stared at his broad, retreating back in disbelief.

Dear Reader,

If you've never read a Harlequin Historical, you're in for a treat. We offer compelling, richly developed stories that let you escape to the past—written by some of the best writers in the field!

We are delighted with the return of Pat Tracy, who is known for her fresh and entertaining Westerns. Critics have described Pat's books as "sparkling" and "heart-lifting." In *Burke's Rules*, book two of THE GUARDSMEN series, a perfectly mannered schoolmistress falls for the "protective" bachelor banker who helps her fund her Denver, Colorado, school. It's great!

Be sure to look for *Pride of Lions,* the latest in Suzanne Barclay's highly acclaimed SUTHERLAND SERIES. Two lovers are on opposite sides of a feud in this passionate tale set in medieval Scotland. In Judith Stacy's new Western, *The Heart of a Hero,* a former bad boy enlists the help of the local schoolmarm in order to win custody of his niece and nephew.

Rounding out the month is *The Knight's Bride* by rising talent Lyn Stone. This is a heartwarming and humorous medieval novel about a very *true* knight who puts his honorable reputation on the line when he promises to marry the beautiful widow of his best friend. Don't miss it!

Whatever your tastes in reading, you'll be sure to find a romantic journey back to the past between the covers of a Harlequin Historical® novel.

Sincerely,
Tracy Farrell, Senior Editor

Please address questions and book requests to:
Harlequin Reader Service
U.S.: 3010 Walden Ave., P.O. Box 1325, Buffalo, NY 14269
Canadian: P.O. Box 609, Fort Erie, Ont. L2A 5X3

PAT TRACY

BURKE'S RULES

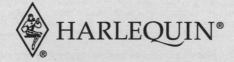

HARLEQUIN®

TORONTO • NEW YORK • LONDON
AMSTERDAM • PARIS • SYDNEY • HAMBURG
STOCKHOLM • ATHENS • TOKYO • MILAN • MADRID
PRAGUE • WARSAW • BUDAPEST • AUCKLAND

ISBN 0-373-29046-2

BURKE'S RULES

Copyright © 1999 by Pat Tracy

Printed in U.S.A.

Books by Pat Tracy

Harlequin Historicals

The Flaming #121
Winter Fire #188
Saddle the Wind #273
Beloved Outcast #333
Cade's Justice #392
Burke's Rules #446

PAT TRACY

lives in rugged Idaho. No longer a country mouse, Pat recently moved to the city of Idaho Falls, population 49,000, where she writes, practices karate and dreams of times when rough-and-tumble heroes had their hands full dealing with independent, lofty-minded heroines. Pat loves to hear from her readers: P.O. Box 17, Ucon, Idaho 83454.

The first category romance novel I read was *Corporate Affair*, a Silhouette Desire romance, written by Stephanie James. The characters, writing style and plot absolutely riveted me. Along with millions of other readers, I discovered both the romance genre and Jayne Ann Krentz, a brilliantly gifted author with several pen names.

This book is dedicated to Jayne Ann Krentz, Jayne Castle, Stephanie James, Amanda Quick, Amanda Glass and Jayne Taylor. Not only have you provided me with hours upon hours of magic, you answered a fan letter I wrote, asking about how one went about becoming published. You told me about Romance Writers of America, national and regional writing conferences, query letters and editors.

It's no accident that Burke's Jayne is book-smart, earnest and single-mindedly determined to accomplish a worthy goal. She's named for you, Jayne, and, I hope, represents the kind of stong, independent woman who deserves a "wounded wolf" with the courage to pursue a hero's quest. In taming the shrew and battling his inner demons, Burke finds his mate and recovers his soul. That's how it goes, right?

Chapter One

It was the hump that drew Burke Youngblood's attention to the man in a red flannel shirt and baggy coveralls, walking ahead of him on the Denver boardwalk. Burke mentally sifted through the Wanted posters tacked to his office wall, putting together names with distinctive physical characteristics. Thinking about the ugly pusses marring the black-walnut-veneered panels of his brand-new office was enough to sour his already grim mood.

He didn't know why his bank, the Denver First National and Trust, had suddenly been singled out as the most popular place for every man with a pistol and a larcenous desire to say, "Give me all the money in your vault." But he refused to have everything he'd sweated blood and tears to build stripped from him by men too amoral to perform an honest day's work.

He deliberately slowed his pace, keeping three yards between himself and the bandy-legged figure. Dangling from a dusty hat, a faded gray ponytail thumped against the red fabric stretched across the clearly visible hump.

"Pappy" Pikeman...no, Pickman. Burke pulled the name from the dozens he'd committed to memory. Pappy was a notorious, if aging, bank robber, specializing in dynamiting safes. Burkes's right hand drifted to the Colt .45 on his hip.

The man bearing a startling resemblance to Pappy paused on the corner. Across the street, where McClintock and Larimer intersected, rose the bank's new four-story structure, completed three months earlier. Burke also stopped, moving to the inside of the boardwalk so as not to block the pedestrian traffic that flowed in both directions around him.

The humpbacked man was peering into one of the French plate-glass windows. Burke still wasn't sure if he was trailing Pappy or someone who looked enough like the criminal to be his brother. Before the man entered the bank, Burke would know.

The anger that had been growing within him for the past few months climbed another notch. What was going on? If indeed Pappy Pickman was studying the building with robbery in mind, he would be the fourth thief in as many months to choose the First National and Trust as his target. It didn't make sense. There were at least a dozen other financial institutions in Denver with poorer security measures than he maintained.

Burke stepped onto the boardwalk and walked past the man raptly staring into the front windows. The brief glimpse he caught of the profile shadowed beneath the hat stoked his wrath. With a certainty he didn't question, he knew Pickman had joined the ranks of those who thought they could successfully steal from the First National.

Burke drew his .45 from its holster and shoved the barrel against Pickman's side. "Put your hands against the window."

He felt the shudder of shock that rocked the smaller man.

"What's going on?" The high-pitched protest bristled with outrage.

Burke leaned close and spoke through tightly clenched teeth. "I know who you are. If you want to see tomorrow, don't make any sudden moves."

"Don't shoot! Don't shoot! There's been a mistake!"

"You're right about that." Burke cocked the Colt.

"Reach into your pocket and take the gun out by its barrel."

"I ain't got no—"

Burke pushed the .45 deeper into his side. "Do it."

Uttering an oath, the man plunged his hand into the pocket concealed by the baggy coveralls. What came into view made Burke suck in his breath.

"I told you I wasn't packing a pistol."

Burke gingerly retrieved the stick of dynamite from Pickman's shaking fingers. "Now, we're going for a walk. Inside."

"Inside?" Pickman squeaked. "Ain't you gonna take me to the sheriff?"

"I might be willing to turn you over to Sheriff Donner after you answer some questions."

He turned pasty-colored. "I ain't answering no questions."

Burke spun the man around to face the doors closest to them. "Walk."

Pickman dragged his heels but managed to stumble forward. Burke eased the stick of dynamite into his coat pocket while keeping his gun pressed discreetly, but firmly, against his prisoner's ribs. They stepped in tandem through the glass doors.

The teller closest to the entrance looked up from the plump matron he was assisting. "Good morning, Mr. Youngblood."

"'Morning, Jamison." Burke nodded in the general direction of the customers standing in five short lines. If lowlifes like Pickman continued to view his establishment as their personal source of ill-gotten loot, the First National and Trust would soon be an empty shell of a building.

And, without your business, you'd be an empty shell.

The rogue thought stunned Burke. When had he started thinking of himself only as an extension of the banks he owned?

"Up the stairs," Burke ordered gruffly.

"Okay, okay, I'm going. Don't push."

They went up two flights. By the time they reached the top, Pickman was sweating heavily and wheezing. "Slow down. I don't see why you're in such an all-fired hurry."

Burke opened his office door and shoved his prisoner inside. "Better save what little breath you have."

Burke was surprised to find he had a visitor. Gideon Cade lounged casually in one of the chairs that faced the mahogany desk. Gideon got to his feet, eyeing Pappy with obvious interest.

Burke forcibly guided Pickman to an empty chair. "Sit."

"All right, all right."

"Is this where I offer to get the rope?" his friend drawled.

"If Pappy's feeling chatty, we won't resort to force."

"Knowing that your father is the president and owner of an eastern conglomerate of banks, I pictured him as being more of a dapper dresser."

Despite his anger at being the target of another robbery attempt, Burke grinned. "Allow me to introduce Pappy Pickman—not my father, but a low-down, bank-robbing scoundrel with the mistaken notion he could walk into the First National and help himself to some easy money."

"You can't prove anything," the older man grumbled.

"With a reward on your head, I don't have to prove anything," Burke replied. "Grab Pappy's picture off the wall, Gideon. It's the third one from the left in the fourth row."

Burke gave the directions without taking his gaze from Pickman.

Gideon sauntered to the cluster of Wanted posters that covered almost one wall of Burke's office.

"I never did care for all these ugly mugs staring at me every time I visited you, but I can see you've put them to good use. You've probably memorized the face of every outlaw within a five-state radius."

"Just about." Burke trained his Colt on the sweating

man. "Before I turn you over to Donner, you can satisfy my curiosity."

"Why should I? What's in it for me?"

Burke shrugged. "Is staying alive reason enough?"

Pickman's Adam's apple wobbled beneath his grizzled chins. "You're bluffing. No fancy-dressed banker is gonna shoot somebody in cold blood."

"I wouldn't count on that."

Sullenness tinged by fear clouded the prisoner's face. "I don't know why you're so riled. You got so much money, you wouldn't even miss the piddling amount I might make off with. It's not like it was personal."

"I happen to take being robbed very personally. Tell me why you chose my bank to hit."

Pickman's pale eyes shifted from Burke. "No special reason."

"I think there is," Burke said softly. "And, before I have you hauled off to the sheriff, you're going to tell me what it is."

Two hours later, Gideon and Burke were alone in Burke's office. Three security guards had transported Pickman to jail. He'd seemed eager to accompany them.

"Look on the bright side." Gideon tore Pappy's Wanted poster in half. You've got one less ferret-faced outlaw staring down at you."

Burke picked up the letter he'd received yesterday, holding the document so the bold seal of the United States Treasury was visible. "There is no bright side as long as the government is considering revoking my federal charter to mint U.S. coins."

"I can't believe they would let a few robbery attempts affect something as important as that charter. Hell, you own and operate the only privately held financial institution in the country with the equipment to print money and mint coins. The government would be crazy to shut you down."

"Representatives from another Denver bank insist their

facility would better serve the needs of the federal government.''

Gideon scowled. ''Let me guess, the Bank of Colorado, owned and presided over by Winslow Dilicar, has been suggested as a replacement.''

Burke laid aside the letter, pushed back his chair and stood. He went to the window that overlooked the congested street below, where buckboards, buggies and men on horseback vied for their place on the packed thoroughfare. ''Dilicar hasn't made it a secret that he wants that charter.''

''There's an arrogance about Dilicar that sets my teeth on edge.''

Burke pictured the dandified Easterner, whose facial expression habitually bordered on disdain. ''He's not one of my favorite people.''

''Emma doesn't care for him. He's been blackballed from our guest list.''

Burke felt a smile overtake him. ''That settles it. If someone as discriminating as your new wife doesn't care for him, he's snake excrement.''

Gideon chuckled. ''My wife is an excellent judge of character.''

''Except for that one memorable lapse when she married you.''

His friend's eyes sparkled with an inner light that made Burke uneasy. A smart man didn't let himself become as enamored as Gideon was with his bride. Bitter experience had taught Burke that the world was a dangerous place. A person had to be on his guard at all times. The delusion of romantic love invited disaster. The heart was a vital organ only so far as it pumped blood through one's system. All the rest was vain imaginings. A clear-thinking brain was the key to survival.

''You know how tenderhearted Emma is,'' Gideon said, warming to what was clearly a favorite topic. ''She's always concerned about the welfare of others. If she doesn't want Dilicar in our home, it's as good as saying he hasn't a redeeming quality.''

''She won't get an argument from me.''

A pause followed. For the first time, Burke wondered what had brought Gideon to his office. ''Would you care for a brandy?''

His friend shook his head. ''I can't stay much longer.''

More silence ensued. Gideon appeared restless. The man had been through a lot during the past four years. His younger brother and sister-in-law had been murdered, and he'd assumed the care of his young niece, while struggling to hold his freighting empire together. It astounded Burke that, despite the recent period of savagery, Gideon had lost his heart to his niece's tutor and married her.

The skin at the back of Burke's neck prickled. Until Emma Step had entered his life, Gideon Cade had been a ruthlessly logical man. But like Burke's brother, Logan, the freighting tycoon had sacrificed his cold-blooded rationality for the fiction of romantic love. The fallibility of two otherwise sane men made Burke distinctly uncomfortable. He could accept their physical craving for the women who'd joined them at the altar. It was the men's emotional weakness that disturbed him. As far as he was concerned, their declared love made them as vulnerable as newly hatched chicks.

Burke pushed his thoughts in a new direction. ''Has Hunter had any more problems with rustlers?''

''Not that I've heard. It appears your bank has claimed the honor of becoming a magnet to the area's lawless element.''

''Considering what Pappy told us, that's not likely to change,'' Burke said glumly.

''If what he said is true, you can count on every bandit within a thousand miles paying you a visit.''

In frustration, Burke shoved a hand through his hair. ''In effect, someone has put a bounty, payable in advance, on the First National.''

"Offering a free horse and fifty dollars up front to know thieves if they'll strike your bank is a powerful incentiv to men with no scruples."

"It's not going to do much good to keep foiling robber attempts. I've got to find the person paying the bribes."

"Do you have any doubt who's behind this?"

"Obviously Dilicar has the most to gain from the Firs National losing its credibility with the government. He' formally petitioned the treasury department to award th charter to the Bank of Colorado."

"And it's his newspaper that keeps printing article about the lack of safety at the First National."

Resolve settled in Burke's gut. "It's going to take irrefut able proof to convict a rich, respected businessman lik Dilicar of being guilty of anything illegal."

Gideon nodded. "Sounds as if the Guardsmen have new assignment."

Three men had formed the organization known as th Guardsmen. Burke Youngblood, Gideon Cade and cattl baron Hunter Moran had banded together to form an or ganization to protect honest, hardworking people whom lo cal lawmen seemed unable to shield from not-so-randon violence.

The Guardsmen refrained from exacting their own justic at the end of a rope or smoking pistol. Instead, they turne the thieves and murderers they caught over to authorities with the names of people who'd witnessed the crimes an would testify against the wrongdoers.

"Emma doesn't mind that you're still involved with th Guardsmen?"

Burke heard the edge in his voice and regretted it. H didn't begrudge Gideon his illusion of happiness.

"When I'm on Guardsmen business, she worries, o course."

Emma was the only outsider who knew the identities o the secret group's members. "Has she taken to nagging yo to quit? Wives do that, I've heard."

Amusement flickered in his friend's eyes. "Emma ended to nag *before* she became my wife."

"You have my sympathy," Burke said with an exag-gerated shudder.

"I don't need it. Emma's sweet nagging is one of the many ways she shows how much she loves me."

Burke shook his head. "You've got it as bad as my brother."

"Good," Gideon corrected softly. "I've got it good. Life has never been so worth living. Until now."

Until Emma, Burke heard him silently say.

A chill, having nothing to do with the threat against his bank, brushed Burke's spine. It made him nervous that a onetime cynic like Gideon Cade could crumble over a woman. Burke recalled an incident Gideon had related several months ago, an abbreviated account about climbing through a second-story window of his own home during a midnight rainstorm to woo his lady. That tale alone illustrated the asinine depths to which an intelligent man could plummet, if he believed he was in love.

"Be sure and give Emma my best."

"She's the reason I dropped by."

Surprised, Burke returned to his chair. "How so?"

"She has a favor to ask of you."

The chill paid a return visit. Burke rotated his shoulders. "What kind of favor?"

"It involves her friend Jayne Stoneworthy. You might remember her. She was one of the guests at our wedding. Anyway, Miss Stoneworthy is starting a school for young ladies and…"

Burke heard the drone of Gideon's voice as he would have heard the hum of a bee in the background. *Remember Jayne Stoneworthy?* He almost laughed aloud. Of course, he remembered her. Her image had hovered at the edges of his thoughts since that otherwise ordinary afternoon he'd first seen her.

Their paths had first crossed in the sanctuary of his home.

Before the school had burned down, he'd been prevaile
upon by the Hempshire Academy to open his private a
gallery for occasional student tours. One afternoon he'
strode into his residence and encountered a flock of gig
gling schoolgirls about to return to their school. His house
keeper had casually introduced their intrepid leader. *Jayn
Stoneworthy.*

It was hardly a momentous meeting. Midday, his hous
a-clutter with chattering girls. He'd been late for a meetin
with the Guardsmen and was in a hurry to make up for lo
time. Detached and impatient, he'd waited in his entr
Then he'd caught his first glance of her. His initial impres
sion had been that of a woman virtually hidden by a dar
cloak and unflattering bonnet. Buried beneath the flowin
folds of her cloak, she appeared to be slight of frame an
of average height.

Their gazes had caught. He'd found himself being po
litely investigated by a pair of intelligent green eyes th
evidenced no sign of feminine timidity. Something insid
his chest had tightened.

Then, amid a flurry of thank-yous, she and her charge
were gone. The encounter had lasted less than ten second
And yet, at odd times, her image infiltrated his thoughts.

He'd seen her again at Gideon's impromptu wedding t
Emma. His gaze had tracked her through the throng of wel
wishers. Evidently content to occupy the fringes of th
room, Miss Stoneworthy again had pricked his interest. Sh
certainly did nothing deliberate to draw his attention. Ther
were no soulful glances, no fluttering eyelashes, no co
quettish mannerisms to accentuate her feminine charm
Yet her quiet demeanor had made him want to draw close

She was hardly the kind of woman he ought to be at
tracted to. Oh, her dark-golden hair appeared beguiling
silky. Her green eyes, slightly tilted as they were, radiate
a tempting warmth. And her delicately shaped mouth in
vited the brush of his own lips to investigate their improb
able softness. Without the cloak, her shape was definitel

emale. Her modestly designed dress didn't conceal her osom's petite fullness, the sleek curve of her trim waist nd the gentle flare of her hips.

It was her expression, however, that of propriety rapped in the impregnable armor of chastity-until-arriage, that should have rendered her off-limits. Hers was e kind of innocent appeal that struck terror in the hearts f confirmed bachelors. Her virtue shone as brightly as her olden hair. The price of that virtue was, of course, mar-iage.

"So I would appreciate you dropping by."

Gideon's statement fell into Burke's thoughts with the oft splash of a stone sinking into a deep pool of water. *Drop by where?*

Gideon leaned forward in his chair. "Well?"

Not wanting to betray his distraction over a woman with whom he'd exchanged only the briefest greeting, Burke teepled his fingertips and frowned thoughtfully. "Could ou be a little more specific?"

Gideon's eyebrows knitted. "I thought I had been. Emma wants you to go to the Wet Beaver and check on ow Miss Stoneworthy is coming along."

Shock slammed into Burke. The Wet Beaver was a no-brious Denver brothel. What the hell was going on? Pro-ouncing the names of the teacher and the cathouse in the ame breath was akin to blasphemy.

"Coming along, *how?*" A cold rage built within him at he thought of Miss Stoneworthy selling herself several mes a night to any man with the coin to purchase her weet warmth.

"With her school, of course. Weren't you listening?"

"I must have missed something. Explain what Miss toneworthy is doing in a whorehouse."

"A *former* whorehouse," Gideon corrected. "It closed own, and she bought the building. Like I said, she's sunk ll her money into renovating it and turning it into a school or young women."

The tension that gripped Burke eased. ''That's crazy. N one's going to send their daughter to a place that was onc a house of prostitution.''

''I know it, and you know it. Unfortunately, Miss Stone worthy has no idea that the Wet Beaver was anything othe than a tavern. For obvious reasons, the former owner ne glected to disclose the fact. Anyway, she's running low o cash, and Emma's concerned about her. There's a long-lo uncle who's supposedly sending a bank draft to help ou but it hasn't arrived yet.''

''Using the bank draft for such an enterprise would b throwing good money after bad.''

''I agree. So does Emma.''

Burke regarded his friend quizzically. ''What precisel do you want me to do?''

''According to Emma, Miss Stoneworthy wouldn't hav bought the building if she'd known what it had been use for. She's not stupid, just naive.''

''But now that she does know—''

''That's just it, she doesn't,'' Gideon interjected. ''Emm only found out a short while ago.''

''How did that happen?'' Burke asked, fascinated by th amazing phenomenon of the prim Miss Stoneworthy own ing a brothel.

''I told her, of course. Anyway, Miss Stoneworthy need help, and Emma feels you're the best person to provide it.'

''Remind me what you want me to do,'' Burke said wai ily.

''Inform her that she has to move her school, find her new building and provide enough cash to cover her ex penses until she begins making money.''

Silence descended in Burke's office. He considered Gic eon Cade and Hunter Moran his two best friends. He woul risk his life for either man. But all things considered, Emm and Gideon were asking a hell of a favor.

''As I said,'' Gideon continued, ''I'll supply the neces

sary funds. Miss Stoneworthy is apparently a proud woman who won't let Emma help any more than she already has.''

''So, what you're asking is that I inform Miss Stoneworthy she's bought a whorehouse and find her a new building—with you underwriting all costs?''

''Right.''

Burke shook his head. ''I've got to ask, *why me?*''

''You're a banker.''

''And?''

''You lend money. Miss Stoneworthy will accept funds from you where she wouldn't accept a loan from a friend. Just visit her at the Wet Beaver.''

''She's living there?''

''Emma invited her to stay with us, but Miss Stoneworthy insists on remaining, even during the remodeling.''

''So, I walk into her place and say, 'I'm Burke Youngblood. This used to be a brothel, so you can't have your school here, after all. I'll help you sell this building. And, since I'm a banker, I'll lend you money to buy another place.''' There was no way to keep the mockery from his words.

''That's it,'' Gideon said, ignoring the sarcasm.

''I can't believe you're asking me to do something so crazy.''

''She's Emma's friend, and she needs help.''

''Which she won't accept from you?''

''But because she's sensible, she will accept a loan from a banker.''

''A sensible woman doesn't buy a brothel!''

''She just needs a chance, Burke.'' Gideon laughed ruefully. ''I know I'm asking a big favor. Just telling her she's bought a cathouse is bound to be ticklish, but once that's done, she'll be grateful for your assistance.''

It was the damnedest favor ever requested of him. The thing was, he couldn't say no to his friend. Judging from Gideon's slightly amused expression, he knew it.

''When's a good time for me to show up there?''

"I told Emma we could count on you."

"Did you?"

Gideon shrugged. "You know I would do the same for you."

What Burke *knew* was that his friend was so besotted with his new wife that she had him wrapped around her little finger.

"I'll take care of it." The skin at the back of Burke's neck started tingling again.

Chapter Two

A powerful knock rattled the front doors of Jayne Stoneworthy's new residence and school. She withdrew her head from the crate of books she was unpacking and sneezed twice. The workmen had left for the afternoon, and this was the first peace she'd had since they'd descended that morning with hammers pounding.

She looked toward the floral-etched glass panels installed yesterday. The shadowy figure of a man was visible. Perhaps one of the workmen had forgotten something. She weaved her way through the chaos of stacked lumber, sawhorses and sacks of nails. Two-by-fours of various lengths lay where they'd been cut. Even her upstairs bedchamber, the one area she considered habitable, had been invaded by the sawed-off portions of wood. The foreman's prediction that within two weeks the torn-apart great room would be transformed into a parlor, business office and three classrooms seemed overly optimistic.

Having accepted there was no way to look her best while immersed in the renovation project, Jayne didn't bother brushing the dust from her apron or tucking the tendrils of hair skimming her cheeks beneath her white kerchief.

She opened the glass-paneled door and looked up, then up some more, to fully take in the mountainous man standing before her. Roughly dressed, the gargantuan man resembled Paul Bunyan come to life. He definitely wasn't one of the workmen.

"May I help you?"

"Oh, that you can, girly-girl." His black mustache and beard rippled as his booming voice filled the room. "I quenched my thirst at the Plucked Turkey. Now I'm itching for some sweet female comfort."

Though certainly the largest, this wasn't the first man to arrive with the mistaken belief the saloon she'd recently purchased was still in business.

She craned her head to gain a better view of the jovial face revealed beneath a battered brown felt hat. "You've come to the wrong place."

He walked through the doors, leaving them open behind him. She tried to hold her ground but would have had better luck trying to block a mud slide.

"I see things are in an uproar. I don't mind a little dust." Thick fingers closed around her waist, whisking her through the air, he plunked her onto the long bar counter carved from the trunk of a pine. "No need to apologize. So you ain't fixed for cavorting. With that yeller hair of yours and those big green eyes, I can overlook you needing a bath." He raised a massive arm and sniffed. "Truth be told, I'm not so fresh myself."

"I do not have *yeller* hair. It's light brown."

"Naw, you're wrong. Your hair's as yeller as a shiny gold nugget."

"No, *you're* wrong," she said briskly. "I want you to leave."

He gazed at her with such dopey goodwill she couldn't be angry. Even so, his interruption was putting her behind schedule. She had a dozen things to accomplish before her head could hit the pillow that night, not that she planned on getting much sleep. Since moving in, she'd learned that the street came alive after dark with boisterous men converging upon the nearby saloons.

"Listen…" She broke off. "What's your name?"

"Newton Timothy White. Most folks call me Newt. Maybe you heard of me. I found a vein of the prettiest gold you ever did see. My mine's The Lucky Lasso, on account of I always wanted to be a cowboy, but never could find a horse big enough to carry me, for long anyway."

"Well, Miner Newt, pay attention."

Grinning sappily, he leaned forward. "Sure thing, pretty filly."

"This building is no longer a saloon. There's not a drop of liquor on the premises and even if there were, there's nary a 'girly-girl' to serve it."

The man's features sagged dramatically. She was put in mind of a hound dog. She doubted this affable, if somewhat inebriated miner, represented a threat to her safety.

"Ya mean this here ain't the Wet Beaver anymore?"

She nodded. "Several weeks ago it became the Stone-worthy School of Tutoring for Young Ladies."

The miner's bushy eyebrows climbed to the outer reaches of his broad forehead. A vibrant red blush swept the portion of his face not carpeted by his lush mustache and beard.

He ripped the hat from his head, mangling it between gigantic hands. "I'm beggin' your pardon, miss. I had no idea the Wet Beav—" He broke off, his blush deepening to purple. "I mean to say, I… Oh, Lordy, you've got to forgive me. I didn't mean any offense, honest I didn't."

Jayne scooted forward and jumped down from the bar. Newt's reaction was similar to that of others who'd visited the building in the mistaken hope of sharing a drink and some conversation with a dance hall girl. It astonished her how differently the male population of Denver treated her when under the misapprehension that she served drinks in a saloon. Even more amazing was that a few words could transform her in their eyes from a notorious sinner like Belle Starr to a respectable personage akin to Betsy Ross.

"It's all right, Mr. White." She wondered how long it

would take him to pull himself together and depart. There was that list of chores.

"No, it ain't," he said morosely. "I never in my life have disgraced myself with a lady. If my sainted mother knew what I'd done, she'd turn me over her knee for a good paddling."

Jayne doubted even his saintly mother had a knee big enough to turn him over it. She patted his arm and tried to usher him to the door. "We won't tell her. It was an honest mistake."

He continued to maul his hat. "I should have knowed right off by looking at you that you weren't no good-time gal. Why, it's as plain as the sparkle in your green eyes that you're a lady, right down to your brown leather shoes—even if you are lookin' a mite worse for wear."

If she was offending the sensibilities of wild and woolly miners, it was time to pay attention to her appearance. "Mr. White, why don't you visit another tavern? I'm sure there's lots of…um…'good-time gals' who'll help you spend your gold."

He frowned. "You're not supposed to know about such women."

"Don't be silly, how could I *not* be aware of them? What with their fancy clothes and big-feathered hats, they're impossible to miss."

"You're supposed to *pretend* you don't know about them."

"All right, we'll just say you're going for a walk." She pulled experimentally on his arm. Nothing happened. "You are going, aren't you?"

"I don't like the idea of you alone here. Some other feller might come along and make the same mistake I did. You could be in big trouble, Miss…" He paused, his rough-cut features solemn. "What's your name?"

"Stoneworthy." What on earth was she going to do with a three-hundred-pound knight who preferred plaid and denim to shining armor? "Actually, this has happened before, and I've been just fine."

His expression remained disapproving. "I'll fix that. What did you say the name of your school is?"

She obliged him by repeating the information. He headed for the doors that had remained open throughout their confrontation. It disturbed her that any passerby could have overheard the ridiculous exchange with her uninvited visitor. If she wanted to establish a successful school for young ladies, she would have to be more careful about such things.

He stepped across the threshold. "I'll be back."

"You will?"

He nodded gravely. "I'm going to fix it so you won't be bothered by any more no-account, low-life drifters like me."

"You're not a drifter. You're a miner with your very own gold mine."

"I should be strung up and shot for insulting you."

"That seems a bit harsh." Really, he was taking this too much to heart. "Cheer up, Mr. White. You've got a dozen wheelbarrows of gold dust to spend." She frowned. "Though, in good conscience I must recommend you consider your future and deposit your newfound wealth in a bank."

He shuffled booted feet the size of watering troughs. "That's what my mother would say. Don't worry, I've already done it."

"Well then, good day to you." Even though he stood directly in front of her, she waved goodbye.

His palm came up, and he wriggled huge, sausage-sized fingers. "I'll be seeing you, Miss Stoneworthy."

The boardwalk buckled beneath his weight as he ambled away. For the life of her, she couldn't imagine how Miner Newt thought he could assist her.

She stepped through the open doors, turning to lock them. Without warning, a man moved in front of her. A small shriek sprang from her throat. Tall, lean and grim-lipped, this new arrival projected none of Mr. White's affability. Wearing a black dress coat, pristine white shirt and snug-fitting black trousers, the intruder radiated an aura of sophisticated hardness.

Her gaze flew to his face. Whereas the miner's features looked as if they'd been carved by a dull ax, this man's countenance had been chiseled with the precision of a sculptor's hand. Angular, strongly defined cheekbones, narrow lips and deeply set brown eyes created a visage without inherent tenderness. Thick black hair, combed severely back, added to his formidable expression. Handsome was too benign a word to apply to a face of such harsh contours. Yet his features were imbued with a bold, almost savage beauty.

Recognition dawned. Standing before her was none other than Burke Youngblood, owner and president of Denver's largest bank. They had met briefly on two previous occasions. The indelible impression he'd left during those fleeting encounters had followed her into her dreams.

She had no idea why one of Denver's most powerful and wealthy men stood on her doorstep. It seemed prudent to inquire. "Uh, may I help you?"

Burke took in the bedraggled appearance of the woman he'd agreed to check on. After overhearing her naive exchange with Newton White, Burke felt obligated to teach her an unforgettable lesson that would irrefutably demonstrate the danger she'd placed herself in by moving into a former whorehouse. "I'm certain you're the perfect person to…help me."

Mr. Youngblood's gritty voice performed some kind of dark magic on Jayne's inner tickings. She licked her suddenly dry lips. The banker's expression bordered on carnivorous. "Are you sure you have the right place?"

Only as the question emerged did a horrible inkling of what might be about to transpire unravel within her. Surely not, she told herself. A man of Burke Youngblood's wealth and reputation wouldn't—

"I'll be in exactly the right place when we go upstairs, find ourselves a bed."

Like jagged bolts of hot lightning stabbing the earth, three thoughts struck Jayne. Burke Youngblood did *not* remember her from their previous meetings, he expected much more from a dance hall girl than friendly conversation and...and he was no gentleman!

She raised her chin. "You've come to the wrong place."

Something elemental flashed in his eyes. "We won't know that till I'm there." His glance took in the room's torn-up condition. "It's a little drafty down here, but if this is where you want to do it, I'm game."

Heat crawled to her cheeks. After being raised by her late aunt Euphemia, Jayne had a good idea what "it" was. The spinster had waxed with vigorous zeal upon the subject of men's lusts.

Without conscious thought, Jayne's gaze drifted to Mr. Youngblood's lower anatomy. To her inexperienced eye, it appeared Euphemia had been on the right track, which would explain why disrobing was required to facilitate actual...er...linkage.

"The view's likely to be more interesting without my trousers on."

His husky observation shocked Jayne from her reflections. An even deeper blush singed her face and throat. What a time for her thoughts *or* gaze to wander! "*You've* made the mistake. This is no longer the Wet Beaver. I bought the building to—"

Without signaling his intent, he swept her into his arms. "You talk too much."

Before she could react, he was striding toward the stairs. Stunned by the unexpected turn of events, she tried to twist free.

He slung her over his shoulder. Her field of vision shrank

to the bobbing floor and an upside-down view of his lean backside.

With an audible whoosh the air bounced from her lungs. She looked over her shoulder and was greeted by the sight of her posterior pushed up alongside his face. One wide palm rested proprietarily upon her upthrust bottom. Incensed by his familiarity, she pounded his back with her fists. The jarring blows should have had him howling for mercy. Evidently, the banker had a high tolerance for pain. He didn't miss a stair as he took them two at a time.

"Well, well, what have we here?" he drawled with maddening calm. "An ample-sized, unmade bed, waiting for us to get acquainted."

He tossed her onto the disheveled bedding. Jayne bounced twice, then rolled to her side, scrambling to reach the edge of the mattress and freedom.

"Where're you going?" Restraining hands pulled her to the center of the bed. "You must be new at this. The exercise is supposed to come between the sheets, not on top of them."

"There's not going to be any exercise." She slapped his renegade hands. "The tavern went out of business. I bought this building to use as a school for young ladies. *Now let me go!*"

She counted the seconds before her explanation had Burke Youngblood on his knees, pleading that she accept his apology.

"You can't expect me to believe that." He straddled her hips and pinned her hands. "No sane person would buy a brothel and try to turn it into a school for respectable girls."

Jayne's thoughts reeled. *Brothel?* She'd bought an obscure, run-down tavern, not a house of ill repute.

When the man's harsh face a scant inch from hers, his dark, glittering eyes promised danger.

"Am I going too fast? Do you like your customers to take it slower?"

"Mr. Youngblood—"

"So you know my name...." He brushed his mouth against her startled lips. "If that's how you like it, I'm willing to slow down."

"You're not listening," she began again, desperate to make him understand his mistake before it was too late. "I'm not what people call a...uh...'good-time gal.' I'm a respectable teacher and businesswoman."

"Some men might like the fantasy of having a virgin or a Sunday school teacher in their bed, but I like my women bold. If you're going to pretend to be someone, try Cleopatra or Delilah."

"Cleopatra? Delilah?" she sputtered, astonished by his preferences. "They're two of the most treacherous women who ever lived."

"You're not supposed to criticize your customers' tastes," he chided. "I know what's the problem. You want your money in advance, don't you?"

Burke reached into his coat pocket and extracted a roll of bills. He'd already pushed Miss Stoneworthy further than he'd intended, yet he refused to back off until he'd put the fear of doom into her. The mildly panicked look in her vivid green eyes indicated she still didn't grasp the full significance of the danger she'd placed herself in by living in a cathouse.

"Let's see, what's the going rate for an hour in your bed?"

"Marriage, you insufferable clod, now get off!"

She surprised a chuckle from him. "Marriage? That's a mite steeper than I planned." He peeled off a bill and returned the rest of the money to his pocket. "Ten dollars should cover it."

"Ten dollars!" she cried. "I've never been so insulted in all my life."

He leaned across her and placed the bill on the nightstand. "What do you expect when you entertain customers dressed like a charwoman?"

When he'd agreed to Gideon's request, there had been

no way to anticipate events spinning out of control like this. But when Burke had overheard Miss Stoneworthy's cavalier treatment of the rough-and-tumble miner, Newton White, he'd decided she needed to find out what happened if a man without scruples had only one thing on his mind. Who better to play such a part than himself?

"I'm dressed for work, not entertaining, you dimwit!"

"Keep insulting me, and I'll take back the ten. You'll have to settle for five dollars. I've got my standards where such things are concerned."

Her flushed face glared up at him with enough righteous fury to send him to Hades. Why not steal a kiss? he wondered. After today's debacle, she wouldn't let him within a hundred feet of her. He might as well gain a little satisfaction for his troubles.

"You mule-headed dolt, I'm *not* in the business of selling myself. I'm a respectable woman!"

"Are you telling me I've made a mistake?" he asked, surprised by the peculiar tenderness her impassioned objection stirred. What possible attraction could exist between himself and a protesting virgin?

"Hallelujah! The voice of reason has finally penetrated the pea-sized organ serving as your brain. No matter what this place used to be, it's now the Stoneworthy School of Tutoring for Young Ladies."

"You almost had me convinced until you made that rude remark about my brain." He tugged the white kerchief from her hair. "No school of refinement would let you within a hundred miles of its students."

She sucked in her lower lip. Meaning to claim it for himself, he bent his head.

"I'm not usually rude," she muttered. The moistened lip slid free.

"Neither am I."

He wove his fingers through silken hair that lay like a river of spilled gold on the pillow, taking the kiss. Female heat, wet and beckoning, drew the tip of his tongue into the sweet cavern of her mouth. She stiffened and pushed against his shoulders.

It was ridiculous to be disappointed by her resistance. He was taking what she wasn't offering—a moment and kiss stolen from time. He groaned with unexpected need. Mingled with sawdust, her womanly taste and scent honed a sharper edge to the hunger surging to life.

Enough... He'd trespassed further than he had any right. She shifted beneath him. New need erupted. He tried to end the kiss. His mouth refused to cooperate. His hands were getting restless. He had to stop. Now.

Struggling for control, he raised his head. "I'm sorry."

She shifted again. "You will be."

He wasn't sure he heard her right. The blood thundered in his veins with the fury of a herd of stampeding cattle. Her wet lips invited more insanity. If he didn't start breathing again, he was going to black out.

"I didn't mean for things to go this far," he said hoarsely.

"Save the apology."

He felt more than saw the blur of movement. One moment he had heaven and bliss rolled into one package beneath him. The next instant, a thunderbolt of pain exploded in his skull. The beguiling woman with green eyes splintered into a whirlwind of spinning stars, then disappeared into blackness.

Chapter Three

Jayne felt Burke Youngblood stiffen and then go lax, collapsing on top of her. The cut-off two-by-four slipped from her fingers and thudded to the floor. Her face was pressed against his chest. The faintly musky masculine scent she inhaled was unfamiliar, yet oddly stirring.

Resisting a sense of light-headedness, she tried to squirm from beneath his pinning weight. It took several minutes of concentrated wriggling before she slithered to freedom. Unexpectedly, the experience left her feeling an uncanny kinship with a worm trying to create a narrow passageway through an apple. Anyone attempting to take a bite from Burke Youngblood's dense hide, however, surely risked a broken tooth.

Her relief at gaining her freedom lasted half a second. Off balance from her exertions, she toppled to the floor. Her inelegant landing had her skirts around her ears and her bottom smarting from the jarring impact. When the world righted itself, she blew her bangs from her eyes. A broad male hand with hair-grazed knuckles dangled over the side of the bed.

Jayne scrambled to her feet. The foreign invader lay facedown upon her rumpled bedding. Though built upon leaner lines, the felled beast was nearly as tall as Newt White. Almost everything about the banker was black. His thick hair, jacket, trousers—even his hand-tooled boots. And his heart, she added silently, stalking to the foot of the bed. The brute hadn't even possessed the courtesy to remove his boots! The high-and-mighty financier clearly had no respect for women. He'd more than deserved the blow to the head she given him.

Shouldn't he be coming to about now?

She circled the bed. He lay perfectly still with his face pressed against her pillow. A terrible foreboding chilled her. Was he...dead?

She took an unsteady step forward. Surely, an astonishingly virile specimen of manhood such as Youngblood couldn't be killed by a forceful whack to the side of his head.

She inched closer. Would a judge consider that an adequate defense? "I'm sorry, Your Honor. I truly thought a man built upon such rugged lines would have a stronger head. I didn't hit him all that hard, you see...."

Gingerly, she shook his shoulder. Nothing happened. Was he breathing? Gathering her courage, she clutched the sleeve of his jacket, tugging and pushing until she gained sufficient momentum to roll him onto his back.

An cry of distress escaped her. At his left temple a bluish-colored lump swelled. From it, a tiny trickle of blood oozed down his cheek. It was foolish to feel remorse for defending herself against him, yet a pang of guilt smote her. Aunt Euphemia had always accused her of being too tenderhearted, but surely one was entitled to feelings of regret when murder was involved.

You haven't killed him. He's merely been rendered unconscious, the inner voice of reason suggested.

Jayne desperately wanted to believe that voice. She leaned forward, bringing her cheek close to his eerily tranquil face. His relaxed features were a jangling contradiction to the fires that moments before had ignited his gaze. The faintest whisper of breath from his slightly parted lips feathered across her sensitive skin. *Thank God...* He was alive.

She drew back. It wasn't that she thought the world would be a better place with him in it. It was just that she didn't want to be a murderer. A perfectly natural sentiment, she assured herself.

He needed to be revived. The most logical way of doing so was to throw a bucket of water in his face. Unfortunately, she had no wish to drench her bed linens and mattress. Sighing at having to forgo the sight of him sputtering to consciousness, she went to her dresser and opened a drawer. After withdrawing a handkerchief, she poured water from a pitcher into a basin and dipped the cloth into it.

Burke opened his eyes. It felt as if someone had taken a hammer to his skull. Throbbing pain radiated from the left side of his head. His gaze focused on a framed, hand-stitched bit of fabric tacked to the wall across from him. "Dumb asses and men are best driven by whips." He squeezed his eyelids shut before opening them again. The daunting message remained.

Wincing, he turned his head. A pink embroidered pillow blocked his vision. "A smart woman calls no man master."

He groaned. *I'm dead, and this is hell.*

"You're not dead...." Open relief coated the observation.

He turned his head again. Holding a white cloth, Jayne Stoneworthy approached with hands extended.

"Not yet. Of course, whether or not that continues to be the case depends on what other acts of violence you intend to unleash."

A look of contrition filled her green eyes. "I refuse to feel guilty about hitting you. I had every right to defend myself."

Someone should warn her to stay away from poker tables. That she obviously did feel some remorse for knocking him unconscious was written plainly across her earnest features.

"What did you use?" He tried to sit up, then fell back against the mattress. An oath hovered behind his clenched lips. He'd wait until he was alone to set it free. "I feel as if I had a run-in with a railroad tie."

"Actually it was a piece of wood left by one of the workmen."

"I deserved it," he admitted grudgingly. "I didn't have you pegged as the kind of woman who could defend herself if backed into a corner."

"Well, you were wrong."

"What's the cloth for?"

She glanced at her hands. "I was going to wipe away the blood on your forehead and place a cool compress against your wound."

He pressed his fingertips to his head. They came away sticky and crimson-colored. "You really whacked me."

She flushed. "You deserved it."

"We've already established that." He waved her toward him. "Proceed with your ministrations. I'm certainly in need of them."

Wariness tinged her gaze. "Do you promise to behave yourself?"

Her question startled a laugh from him. He flinched. "Miss Stoneworthy, rest assured you've relieved me of the slightest urge to get on your bad side."

She didn't draw closer. "You know who I am?"

The answer to that question could wait. He wanted her gentle tending. "My head's pounding so hard, I'm not sure what I know."

His words caused her to fly into action. She was at his side, bending over him, lightly dabbing his forehead. He groaned, more from the pleasure of her touch than discomfort. His eyelids lowered. Not only would she make a bad poker player, clearly the woman diligently attending his injury had a soft heart. She would probably give her last nickel to some down-on-his-luck trail bum. Charity and generosity were attributes that might get one to heaven. They were a real liability when running a business.

The cloth grazed a sensitive spot. He grimaced. On the

other hand, she did pack a wallop. Maybe there was a future for her in business, after all.

"I'm trying not to hurt you."

"I'm tough. I can take it."

Her soothing caress and the fabric's damp coolness made the pain seem almost worthwhile. How long had it been since he'd shared physical contact with a woman based on receiving innocent comfort?

"You're being surprisingly...stoic about this."

He opened one eye. He shouldn't have been surprised by her closeness. Finding her face within kissing distance, however, shot unwelcome shards of desire through him. The building pressure did nothing to ease the throbbing in his head. He cursed his unexplainable susceptibility to Miss Stoneworthy, wondering if the blow he'd suffered was partly responsible for his uncustomary lack of control. Considering her incendiary effect on him, "stoic" was the last word he would use to describe his reaction.

A myriad of emotions swirled in her gaze. He identified confusion, concern and that ever present look of wariness. "Considering my behavior, I'm lucky you're bothering to patch me up."

She withdrew the compress. Maybe he shouldn't have reminded her of what had precipitated her attack. She eased herself from the bed. Only when she moved away did he realize she'd been sitting beside him. As she went to the water basin on the dresser and wrung out the cloth, her straight back, slender waist and the gentle curve of her hips held his fascinated attention.

The scent of sawdust laced with a whiff of lilac water lingered. Sawdust and lilacs... He bit back a cynical laugh. That the hardly exotic combination of fragrances should tie his stomach into knots proved he wasn't his usual self.

She returned to the bed and sat down, reapplying the folded material to his injury. Now it was her breasts that claimed his attention. Manfully, he tried to ignore their soft presence. She was being excessively kind. He'd deserved the violence she'd wreaked upon him.

She leaned closer. The gray material of her gown outlined twin swells of bliss. He imagined them uncovered, exposed to his hands and mouth. Disgusted by his lustful contemplations, he slammed his eyelids shut and tried to think virtuous thoughts. Not a single noble idea popped into his head. How long had he been on this downward path to hell?

"How do you feel now? Is the pain easing?"

She had to be kidding.

"I'm feeling downright chipper." Even though it was the last thing he wanted to do, he pushed away her hands and sat up. "I think I'll start every day with a blow to the side of my head."

"No doubt your surliness is a result of your injury." She slid away from him and stood. "May I point out that, had you not acted in a most ungentlemanly manner, you would not be suffering at the moment."

He rose to his feet. The room swayed. *Ungentlemanly?* He'd been an out-and-out blackguard. He allowed the shuddering waves of pain to roll over him as he adjusted to being vertical. His quick scan of her bedchamber revealed half a dozen rude sayings about the nature of men, ranging from lace-bordered wall hangings to hand-sewn pillows. The one that caught and held his attention was a green satin cushion with gold tassels that read "A prudent woman guards her private furrow, lest she awakes to find it plowed."

"Miss Stoneworthy, no jury would convict you for hitting me with that plank of wood."

"I know," she said quickly. "I wasn't sure you did."

"Have I given you cause to think I'm an imbecile?"

Her damnably enchanting chin raised. "No, you've only given me cause to believe you're an unprincipled...lecher."

Laughing at her prim, disapproving expression wouldn't

help his head. Nor, inexplicably, did he wish to hurt her feelings. Obviously she felt she'd fought off the devil incarnate to preserve her virtue.

"There's something we need to clear up. I don't make a habit of visiting brothels, or forcing myself upon unwilling females."

"This isn't a brothel."

"It was, and because of that, it's never going to be a respectable school for young women. I dropped by this afternoon because Gideon Cade asked me to check on you as a favor to his wife. When I got here, I overheard that miner trying to buy your favors. It was obvious you didn't understand what a dangerous situation you were in. Had he not accepted your explanation, you could have found yourself upstairs in bed with him."

"Which is just exactly where I did find myself with you!"

"Because I wanted to show you that you can't set up housekeeping in a brothel and not suffer the consequences."

"Stop calling this a brothel. It was a tavern that—"

"Not a tavern," Burke Youngblood interrupted with a cold finality that made Jayne want to hit him again. "It was a house of prostitution."

"But it can't have been!"

"Lady, just saying something won't make it so."

She wanted to hate the man towering above her. She certainly hated his calmness in the face of the horrible disaster unfolding before her. His insufferable superiority grated. He acted as if he had the answer for everything. He was arrogant, condescending *and* a shameless reprobate.

"Now that you've delivered your news, you can leave." She wanted to be alone. She'd poured all her money, except the bank draft Uncle Clarence had promised, into remodeling this building.

Reeling from the banker's revelation, she thought back to the day when Emma had tried to tell her something about the tavern having a bad reputation. Clearly her friend had found out about the brothel's tawdry past but had been too much of a lady to come right out and say what the problem was.

"Do you have any brandy?"

Jayne's thoughts came crashing back to the present. "There are no fancy women *or* alcoholic spirits on the premises."

"Too bad," he drawled, gingerly touching the bruise on his forehead. "You look as if you could use a drink."

"So do you," she snapped, "but, that doesn't alter the fact I have no alcohol."

"No demon rum for Miss Stoneworthy, do I have that right?"

Sensing he was secretly laughing at her, she scowled. "If you want to ingest vile liquor, there are any number of saloons to accommodate you."

"I'm not sure I can make it that far."

Despite her intentions, reluctant sympathy surged within Jayne. "Perhaps you ought to sit down. Are you feeling dizzy?"

He shook his head, then groaned. "Maybe sitting is a good idea."

Even though she knew she had every reason to abandon him to his misery, Jayne took his arm and escorted him to a chair. She plucked the green cushion from his downward descent and absently handed it to him.

"Perhaps a glass of water would help."

"I wouldn't turn one down."

She didn't understand why the sight of him running his lean fingers through the gold tassels on one of Aunt Euphemia's embroidered cushions caused a tickling feeling inside her. She tugged at the pillow. "If you're feeling faint, you should put your head between your knees."

He eyed her balefully. "I have no intention of fainting."

"No one *intends* on swooning. It just happens." Why wouldn't he release the cushion? The last thing she wanted

was for him to read one of Euphemia's pithy observations
about the failings of men.

"Well, it's not going to happen to me," he virtually
growled. His gaze fell to the neatly sewn letters on the
pillow, and his fingers ceased their idle stroking. "I assume
you've heeded the advice contained in this message."

She had no intention of discussing the condition of her
private furrow with Burke Youngblood. She had yet to find
an easy way to explain her late aunt's dismal opinion of
the male gender. Euphemia, often absentminded and generally kind, had been rebellious of all masculine authority.
She considered all pants-wearing members of the human
race mentally deficient.

The older woman believed, with a passion that could
foment a revolution, that males were completely inferior to
females. She cheerfully expounded to anyone willing to
listen that a woman was sufficiently strong and capable of
living her own life without enduring the tyranny of any
man.

"It's my late aunt's stitchery," Jayne confined herself to
answering.

He tossed aside the cushion and turned his head to take
in more of Euphemia's creations, ranging from a hand-
painted plate that read "A good man is more rare than
sweet-smelling elephant dung" to a plaque of varnished
wood proclaiming "The hands that rock the cradle haul the
water." His roving inspection settled finally upon a painting of a scantily clad Grecian woman winning a footrace
against three nude Greek runners.

Beneath the vividly colored picture, poking up from
crumpled newspapers that lined an opened crate, was a
twelve-inch statue of a nude female racer that Jayne hadn't
yet convinced herself to display, even in the privacy of her
own bedchamber. As Mr. Youngblood reached to extract
the figurine from the rumpled papers, she hoped he didn't
notice the startling resemblance she bore to both the runner
in the painting and the statue. When she'd posed for the

projects, she'd been fully clothed. Aunt Euphemia's artistic eye, however, had rendered her niece otherwise.

She wished he didn't seem so fascinated with the statue. The way his gaze caressed it greatly disturbed her. Since she'd scarcely envisioned anyone, other than herself, ever viewing the marble figure, she was unprepared for the hot wave of self-consciousness that flowed through her. Having him examine a female nude, especially one of her likeness, was excruciatingly embarrassing.

"Do you suppose you can walk downstairs unassisted?"

He returned the full force of his dark eyes to her. He looked exactly as he had moments before she'd whacked him. Maybe she ought to have kept that piece of two-by-four close by.

"I might need a shoulder to lean on."

She doubted it, but would do virtually anything to get him out of her room and away from Aunt Euphemia's statue. "Let's give it a try."

He carefully returned the statue to the crate. She braced both hands against his arm to steady him as he rose. He hadn't taken more than two steps before he changed things so that his arm was draped around her. She suffered the familiarity and urged him forward. Slowly they made their way down the stairs he'd flown up two at a time. Though he wasn't putting much weight on her, she was pressed tightly against his side. When they reached the jumbled confusion of the main room, she waited for him to release her.

Several moments passed with no action on his part. She frowned. Was he exhausted and about to lose consciousness again?

"I never realized before just how much I like the smell of sawdust mingled with lilac water."

The husky observation made no sense. "I beg your pardon?"

"Never mind. I suppose you're waiting for me to let go of you."

"Can you? I mean without falling down?"

He chuckled, then audibly sucked in his breath. "You're probably going to insist we find out."

"Not if you're too woozy to stand unassisted."

"Ah, Miss Stoneworthy, you appear to have a much more forgiving nature than your aunt."

Jayne suppressed a smile. "If you'd tried to have your way with Euphemia, she would have shot you through the heart."

"She was an expert with pistols?"

Was it her imagination or had he just hugged her? "Actually, archery was Euphemia's sport. It would have been an arrow that dispatched you."

"Poison-tipped, no doubt."

"No doubt," Jayne muttered absently. "Is there someone I can contact to see you home?"

"I'll make it under my own power." The pressure of his embrace eased. "But maybe I should rest before I try."

He swept debris and sawdust from a chair and sat down.

"I could fetch a doctor."

"There's no need." Youngblood stretched his booted feet before him. Despite his travails, he appeared surprisingly sound. "I wouldn't turn down a glass of water, though."

She'd been so busy trying to make him disappear, she'd forgotten about getting him a drink. "I'll be right back."

Counting the seconds until she could see the last of him, Jayne entered the room that was being transformed into a kitchen. She primed the pump at the wet sink, blessing the fact that the previous owners had installed it.

When she returned to Youngblood, Jayne found him studying his chaotic surroundings. "Here you go."

He accepted the glass and drank deeply. "How much is all this work costing?"

"More than I want to think about."

"Selling it while it's like this will limit your buyers and lower your selling price."

She rubbed her eyes. The idea of selling the building for which she'd had so many plans made her want to pound the wall in protest. Being a quitter was more repugnant than being the fancy woman Mr. Youngblood had thought her.

"You do realize you can't have your school here?"

"Yes." She hated it when someone pointed out the obvious.

"Do you have enough money to manage?" he pressed, "until you find a buyer?"

The personal nature of his question irritated her. She had no intention of discussing her finances with a man who a short while ago had tried to buy his way into her bed.

"I'm expecting a bank draft that will take care of my immediate needs."

"Before coming here, I had our bank records checked and learned you have an account with us."

A very small one, she thought wryly. "Yes."

"When you receive the bank draft you're expecting, I'll personally handle the transfer of funds to your account. Just inform the teller who you are, and he'll show you to my office."

She bristled. "That's hardly necessary."

"Gideon Cade asked me to look after you, as a favor to his wife."

"Well, *I* didn't ask you," Jayne said curtly. "How are you feeling? Did the water help? Do you think you're strong enough to leave?"

"I have the impression you're trying to get rid of me."

Perceptive man. "I have a lot to think about."

"Don't be too hard on yourself. Everyone makes mistakes."

"Even you?" The question slipped out before she could stop it.

He inclined his head. "I make it a habit to avoid mistakes."

Overbearing, conceited, pompous... She choked back the uncomplimentary but entirely accurate adjectives bubbling behind pursed lips. He sat in a shadowed corner so it was difficult to judge if the color had returned to his face. No matter what his condition, though, she wanted those long legs striding down the boardwalk.

She forced a conciliatory smile to her lips. "There was that itty-bitty mix-up about you thinking I was a fancy woman."

That wasn't what she meant to say! She'd been about to bid him a firm farewell.

"There was no error."

"Hmm, yes, well...." It took a moment for his statement to penetrate her scattered thoughts. "What did you say?"

"There was no mistake. I remember you quite clearly from our previous encounters. I knew you weren't a prostitute."

He didn't look as if he were joking.

"But you acted as if you thought... That is, you said..." She mentally reviewed his despicable behavior until the moment she'd brought him under control with the blow to his head. "You carried me upstairs, threw me on a bed and pounced on me!"

"All for a good cause. You needed to be taught a lesson."

That he should sit composed before her after making such an outrageous statement, left her momentarily speechless.

"It was obvious from the way you handled the miner," he went on, "that you had no idea of what a dangerous situation you were in. But we've already had this discussion," he finished matter-of-factly.

Comprehension and anger grew. "But I thought you believed I was a good-time gal."

"In that getup?" he gestured to her grimy apron. "You're dressed for the poorhouse, not a cathouse."

"But then...." Abruptly, she did understand. He'd known all along who she was and had deliberately made his obscene proposition in order to…. "What kind of lesson were you trying to teach me?"

After they cleared that up, she really had no choice but to hit him again. Perhaps she ought to invest in a firearm, after all. No judge would punish her for shooting Burke Youngblood. There had to be something in the law about extreme aggravation making it permissible to pepper a scallywag's hide with buckshot. *And,* she was aggravated.

"This is the West. There's a breed of man out here who acknowledges no law other than his own. He sees something he wants, and he takes it."

"Give me back my glass of water." She grabbed the drink and plunked it on a nearby table. Nails rattled and dust flew. Even as she battled to control her temper, the cold brutality of Youngblood's words caused goose bumps to skitter across her skin. "I've proved I can take care of myself."

"You got lucky."

Her hands clenched into tight fists. "No, you're the lucky one. If I'd known you had something on your mind besides a sordid interlude in my bedchamber, I would have hit you so hard you never would have wakened!"

"Calm yourself. If anyone should be offended it's me."

"What?"

"Do you think I'm the kind of man to buy a prostitute's services?"

"Yes, that's exactly the kind of man I think you are. Because, other than your money, you have *nothing* to recommend you." She drew a deep breath. "And another thing, what gives you the right to take it upon yourself to teach anyone a lesson? Do you go around Denver acting out disgusting charades for the benefit of lesser mortals, or was I special? Just how feebleminded did I have to appear to warrant your interference? But then, perhaps you amuse yourself by storming into women's bedchambers so you can issue uncouth propositions. Is that your principal means of entertainment?"

"Which question do you want me to answer first?"

As nothing else could have, his lazy drawl demonstrated his indifference to her fury. A red haze fell over her eyes. Three two-by-fours propped against a nearby wall caught her attention. *Too unwieldy.* She glanced to her left.

"If you're considering violence again, I suggest you think otherwise."

Her gaze swung back to him. "You *kissed* me!"

"Yeah, well, I apologize for that. Things got out of hand."

"Is that all you have to say?"

"Do you want to hear it won't happen again?"

"Of course I do!" Several seconds ticked by. She drew herself to her full height. "Well?"

"I'm thinking."

"There's nothing to think about. I have no intention of ever speaking to you again." She searched for something more scathing to say. "I'm going to withdraw my money from your bank."

"That will be a blow."

The soft-voiced mockery had her wishing for that gun. *"Get out."*

He slowly uncurled to his intimidating height. "You're upset."

She ground her teeth.

"Once you've cooled down, we'll put our heads together about the best way to unload this property. Depending on what you get from its sale and the size of the bank draft you receive, I'm sure we'll find another building that will suit you."

"There is no *we.* As of this minute, we have no connection."

"Sure we do."

The man was a dense as an old leather boot. "I beg to differ."

His dark eyes flashed. "Beg all you want, but the fact

remains that my best friend is married to your best friend. I intend to honor his request to look after you.''

''You're an overbearing, tyrannical, pompous blockhead.'' It was as liberating as removing a corset to speak the words aloud. ''I'm not a charity case to be passed about. I'm fully capable of taking care of myself.''

He looked around the room with exaggerated interest. ''Oh yeah, buying a brothel proves that.''

''*You've* proved you're a mannerless cur. There's no way you can force me to accept your assistance.''

He stepped toward her. ''Watch me.''

''You don't scare me.'' She regretted keenly the trembling of her voice.

''Are you sure?''

She had the awful feeling she'd pulled the tiger's tail and was about to be eaten alive. And there wasn't a whip in sight. ''I've never b-been more sure of anything in my life.''

''You interest me, Miss Stoneworthy.''

As would a pork loin? His look was definitely predatory. ''Don't come any closer.''

''Ah, now you're being sensible.''

''S-sensible?'' She'd never stuttered in her life, until now.

''I wanted to see that look of panic in your beautiful green eyes upstairs. It took you long enough to realize some men won't dance to your tune, though a very sweet tune it is.''

''You're not making any sense.'' She stopped retreating when she felt the bar pushing against her back.

''I'm making 'man' sense.''

Aunt Euphemia, wherever you are, everything you ever said about men is true. They're incomprehensible, barbaric creatures who should be living in caves, or trees, or under rocks.

She raised her palm. ''If you touch me, I'll knock you unconscious again.''

"With your bare hands?"

She raised her chin. "I'll tell Emma on you."

He rolled his eyes. "What kind of threat is that?"

"She'll tell her husband, and he'll…beat you up."

It could happen.

"You've got me shaking in my boots."

She wished *she* were big enough to take him on. His quivering lips betrayed his amusement at her puny arsenal of threats.

A ferocious pounding had Jayne almost jumping out of her skin.

"Damn, just when things were getting interesting," Youngblood growled.

She pivoted and raced to the door, throwing it open in grateful anticipation of greeting her unknown rescuer. There stood her cheerful miner, bless his heart, all seven feet of him. She'd never dreamed a big galoot could look so beautiful.

"Hello, come in." She reached for his arm. "It's good to see you again. How have you been?"

He beamed down at her. "I'm doing mighty fine, Miss Stoneworthy. I told you I would be back, and here I am."

"Yes, indeed, you did." *And you're big enough to flatten a grizzly, let alone one insufferable banker.*

Newt looked past her. "I see you got company. How do, Mr. Youngblood?"

"Hello, Newt."

Drat, from the miner's respectful tone, there probably wouldn't be any bloodshed. She sighed. "You know Mr. Youngblood?"

"I sure do. I wouldn't put my money in any other bank but his. The First National is as safe as if St. Peter himself were guarding it."

"It's been robbed three times," she pointed out waspishly.

"Yep, but they didn't get away with any money."

"That's right, your money's safe with us." The banker

surprised Jayne by heading toward the door. Hooray, he was finally leaving.

He pointed to the plank of wood the miner carried. "What do you have there, Newt?"

The miner held up the board into which uneven letters had been burned. "I had this sign made up at the smithy's for Miss Stoneworthy so everyone will know this ain't a cathouse anymore, begging your pardon, miss."

In disbelief, Jayne stared at the words branded into the wood.

"The Miz Stunworthee Skull of Tootering fer Yung Laddies," Youngblood read aloud, pronouncing the catastrophically misspelled words correctly.

"Do you like it?" Newt asked, his voice brimming with pride.

"How thoughtful of you to make it," Jayne answered weakly.

"Don't mention it. I'll grab a hammer and some nails and put it up."

Jayne rubbed her forehead.

"It doesn't matter." Youngblood pitched his voice so it reached her ears alone. "The sign won't drive off any prospective business. You'll be out of here by nightfall."

Her head jerked up. "No, I won't."

"There's no way I'm going to let you spend another night in this place."

"You have no say in anything I—"

"Shut up, Jayne," he said softly.

Newt returned with the hammer. If she gave the command "attack," would he use it on the banker?

"Won't be but another minute, Miss Stoneworthy."

"Thank you."

"Pack up a few of your things," Youngblood continued, "I'll take you to a hotel. Tomorrow we'll get serious about finding you a new building."

"Listen, you—"

Energetic hammering muffled her protest. In the subsequent silence, Youngblood leaned closer.

"No, you listen. I'm bigger, more determined and meaner than you are. You might not like it, but I've taken an interest in you and, for better or worse, you're stuck with my involvement."

His statement sounded like a demented wedding vow.

"But you can't make me—"

"Sure I can."

"There are laws—"

"A respectable lady wanting to run a fancy girls' school can't afford to draw the wrong kind of attention. It would be the kiss of death for your name to be linked with any unsavory gossip. I guarantee going to the sheriff in a misguided attempt to make me behave myself would unleash a flurry of wild rumors."

"That's coercion!"

"Highly effective coercion. Pack and be ready when I return."

She stared at his broad, retreating back. Good heavens, her life had just been taken from her control.

Aunt Euphemia, it's far worse than you supposed. Some men are more primitive than any ancient beasts who ever stalked the earth.

Newt poked his shaggy head inside. "You want to make sure I got the sign straight?"

Chapter Four

Jayne went to her bedchamber's open window and pushed aside white curtains to look at the street below. From her second-story vantage point, she saw that dusk was settling over the shops, taverns and passersby. Burke Youngblood had not returned and made good on his outrageous threat to collect her as if she were a shipment of cabbages.

Despite the coming night's warmth, Jayne shivered. The banker's decisive manner appeared intrinsic to his nature. It seemed foolish to hope his bold declaration had been vainly uttered. Yet hope she did, clinging to the possibility that good sense had prevailed over his rash statements, and he intended to leave her in peace.

She let the curtains slip through her fingers and turned. The sturdy dresser blocking her locked bedchamber door had required relentless pushing and prodding to budge.

Burke Youngblood had scarcely entered her life, and he'd already caused her a great deal of trouble. It was as Aunt Euphemia said. A man might appear in the guise of offering help, but he usually ended up becoming a burden.

Jayne surveyed her barricaded domain and, pronouncing it impregnable against any invasion, went to the bed and picked up an unwieldy drawer. Because she'd gone to all this work to keep him out, he probably wouldn't come. That was one of life's ironies. Expected calamities rarely occurred, while ones that couldn't be foreseen arrived with bass drums.

Burke stood on the boardwalk across the street from Jayne Stoneworthy's ill-fated school. He'd seen the curtains flutter moments ago and recognized her profile at the bed-chamber window. The vagueness of her outline frustrated him. He wanted to prove that she wasn't the elusive creature who'd been teasing the edges of his thoughts. She *was* real. And damned if he didn't want to unravel the mystery of her effect upon him.

He took a slow drag on his cheroot and contemplated the second-story window. What on earth had possessed him to carry her upstairs and throw her on that bed? When he'd stepped inside the building, his purpose had been clear, to teach her that she couldn't take up residence in a former brothel and open her door to any man who knocked.

Somewhere along the line, he'd crossed the edge of reason and pushed things beyond the bounds of decency. He wanted to blame her for the fiasco. His decision to treat her like a saloon girl had been sound. By all rights, she should have been terrified for her safety. When he'd backed off, she should have been grateful for the time and effort he'd taken to demonstrate her precarious situation and humbly thanked him. Then she should have cheerfully agreed to vacate the premises.

He hadn't backed off....

Burke scowled. He would have, if she'd played her part correctly. As twilight deepened, so did the grimness of his mood. For better or for worse, he'd issued an ultimatum. Unless a demand was enforced, it was worthless. The question of the hour was, did he intend to back up his words?

A primitive quickening surged. He couldn't believe how much he wanted to barge into her bedchamber and insist she follow the wise course he'd charted for her. It wasn't his nature to act impetuously. That this woman made him want to abandon caution did more than surprise him. He was shocked by his desire to stretch out his arm and use the considerable resources at his command to bend her to his will.

No, not bend. He wanted her to admit her folly and yield to his superior wisdom, so he could rescue her and her fledgling school from ruin.

And then?

He chose not to think that far ahead. The memory of sharing a bed with her soft body twisting beneath him was too raw to permit long-range planning. He would proceed one step at a time. First, she had to be dislodged from the Wet Beaver.

Burke studied the second-story window. Beneath it, a narrow ledge spanned the building. He guessed the plank's width to be twelve inches. The conversation he'd had with Gideon several months ago returned. At the time, Burke had thought his friend had lost his mind to engage in such hotheaded theatrics as scaling a wall during a rainstorm.

Even in his youth, Burke hadn't been hotheaded. His thirtieth birthday was behind him. It was a little late to entertain rash thoughts about climbing buildings and traipsing across narrow ledges.

His gaze lowered to the smoldering tip of his cheroot. He definitely wasn't hotheaded. The same couldn't be said about the blood flowing through his veins. Imagining Jayne Stoneworthy in an old-fashioned nightgown with her incredibly kissable lips tilted toward him made him hot all over.

He flicked the thin cigar to the boardwalk and ground out the flame. Evidently the certainty that he was about to make an even more colossal fool of himself wasn't sufficient reason to prevent him from proceeding.

He strode determinedly across the street. Some things couldn't be stopped. He was going to find out what it was about Miss Stoneworthy that agitated his restlessness and prodded a streak of protectiveness he hadn't known he'd possessed. He didn't delude himself that the answer would come easily.

He *did* delude himself that he could navigate the skinny ledge without breaking his neck. No way was his cemetery headstone going to read "Here lies Burke Youngblood, cut down in his prime as a cathouse he did climb."

Jayne had a passionate aversion to people who failed to keep their word. She balefully regarded the dresser wedged against the door. It had taken a lot of hard work to put it there. The least Burke could do was show up, pound futilely to gain admittance and then crawl away with his tail between his legs—fitting retribution for terrorizing her this afternoon.

A blur of movement drew her glance to the open window where a man's booted foot suddenly appeared. Before she could react, the rest of him emerged through the opening. He uncurled to full prominence. *Burke Youngblood!*

As if her thoughts had delivered him to her bedchamber, he loomed tall and foreboding—scowling, dust-covered and holding a long-haired gray cat in the crook of his arm. The hardness of his expression was so at odds with the soft feline he cradled that she was struck momentarily speechless.

His gaze went to the dresser blocking the entry to her room. "That's the first predictable thing you've done since I met you."

"How dare you invade my bedchamber!"

"Save the maidenly outrage for later."

That sounded ominous. "I don't foresee there being a later between us."

"Then you're shortsighted." He shoved the bundle of gray fur toward her. "Is this yours?"

She automatically accepted the bedraggled feline. "I don't have any pets." The cat, a big one, was surprisingly relaxed and limp-boned at being held by a stranger. "Did you climb all the way up here, carrying him? He must weigh ten pounds.''

Burke's lips turned downward in obvious disgust. ''I didn't start out with him. He joined me on the way up and used my back for a ladder.''

''Uh, well, that's interesting.'' She tried to hand the animal back to him. ''Since he isn't mine, you can take him and go.''

''I'm not taking him anywhere, and when I leave it's going to be through that door with you beside me.''

Claws dug warningly into Jayne's arm. She realized she was squeezing the cat and eased her grip. ''I thought that by now you would have come to your senses where I'm concerned.''

He arched a dark eyebrow. ''Did you?''

Needing the freedom of her hands to express herself, she sat her furry burden on the rumpled bed. ''If you'll look at the situation logically, you'll see that my problems are none of your concern. This afternoon, in heat of our debate, things got out of control. We both made some imprudent statements.''

''Did we?''

His enigmatic expression revealed nothing about what he was thinking.

''As a practical, coolheaded businessman, you must agree I'm right.''

''Which would make me...*wrong?*''

''Umm...'' It had been her observation that men didn't like admitting when they were wrong. ''Let's just say that you were overzealous this afternoon in seeing to my welfare.''

''All right.''

She blinked. Never in a million years would she have expected him to be so reasonable. ''You agree with me?''

He shrugged. ''I can see where I came on a little strong.''

A little strong? A cavalry troop charging into battle

would have exhibited more restraint. "I suppose that's all that needs to be said."

"Since I have no intention of climbing back out the window, you won't mind if I move that dresser?"

The sudden change of subject caught her off guard. Her gaze swung to the massive piece of furniture. "Of course not. But let me assist you. It's extremely difficult to maneuver."

"That's all right. I can handle it."

And he did. She scarcely had time to appreciate his display of muscular strength before the deed was accomplished.

He opened the door. The cat bounded down the stairs. Instead of imitating the feline's speedy departure, Burke propped his shoulder negligently against the door frame and studied her with disturbing intensity.

"So what have you decided?" he asked.

"About this place?"

"For starters."

She looked around regretfully. "I suppose I'll have to sell the building and find another."

"That could take a while."

"July is almost gone," she'd said unhappily. "I'd hoped to open my school for a fall session."

"It's going to be tough to make that deadline."

"I know. The only bright spot on the horizon is the bank draft I'm expecting from Uncle Clarence."

It seemed odd to share her feelings with a virtual stranger. And yet something about Burke's implacable strength encouraged a confidence or two. Despite his shocking lack of manners, she sensed in him an astute mind capable of untangling complex problems. What would it be like to call such a man friend and benefit from his store of knowledge?

The direction of her thoughts astonished Jayne. The last thing she wanted or needed was an ally as domineering as

Burke Youngblood. At the first opportunity, he would become a tyrant.

Loud male voices poured through the window. Jayne winced. She was getting used to being awakened during the night by rowdy revelers.

Burke rubbed his jaw. "After I left today, I did some checking."

"Checking?"

"About possible sites for the kind of school you want to open."

He had her undivided attention. "And?"

"I might have found something that will work for you."

When he failed to elaborate, Jayne assumed he'd devised a new way to torture her. He was going to force her to pry the information from him. Pride tempted her to send him on his way without making any inquiries.

Strange, she hadn't realized before that an overabundance of pride was a flaw with which she had to contend.

She thought she detected a hint of amusement in his dark eyes. He knew, blast his black heart, that he'd baited his hook with an irresistible lure. Her desire to maintain control over her life warred violently against the untenable situation in which she'd inadvertently placed herself. No one was going to send their daughter to a school that had formerly been a brothel.

From the street below, another spate of rude laughter filled her chamber. Postponing the moment of surrender, which was how she viewed soliciting any information from him, she walked to the window. It appeared that, even after she rid herself of Burke Youngblood's presence, another raucous night would prevent her from getting a decent night's sleep.

She stared down at the street. Wild and woolly men seemed to come alive after dark. While under the influence of intoxicating spirits, they weren't reticent at whooping their nighttime jubilation at the top of their lungs.

Her gaze dropped to the narrow ledge. It was a miracle

that Youngblood had reached her in one piece. She frowned. Technically speaking, she supposed the safe arrival of Burke Youngblood in her bedchamber ought not to be termed a miracle. It should be called a catastrophe.

She turned. It was time to forget pride. She would pump him for all the information she could drain, get him to vacate the premises *and* maintain control of her destiny.

"I'm very interested in hearing about the building you've found."

She was shocked at the physical and emotional distress the moderately expressed words caused. Her skin burned, her throat tightened and her hands shook. Her discomfort sprang from more than the simple act of swallowing her pride. Something about making herself vulnerable to this man sent out a war cry that she don a full coat of armor.

Somehow, on a battlefield utterly alien to her, she and Burke Youngblood had become engaged in a compelling conflict, the scope of which was shrouded in mystery. For a panicky moment, she wanted to run. Reason intruded. Surely it was only her imagination fostering these fanciful images of swordplay, of victors and losers, of…absolute surrender.

"I'll show you the building in the morning."

She rubbed her forehead. It made sense to see the location by light of day, but she was uneasy about spending more time in his disturbing company. "All right."

"Have you packed the things you'll need to stay at a hotel?"

The blandly asked question made her head snap up. She'd assumed he'd forgotten his demand that she sleep elsewhere. This was it, the one issue upon which she wouldn't compromise. It was one thing to accept business advice from him. She had to draw the line, however, at letting him dominate her personal life.

She drew a deep breath. "Mr. Youngblood—"

"Burke," he corrected quietly, straightening from his casual stance at the doorway. "Since we're going to be working together to get this school of yours established, we might as well be on a first-name basis.''

Again she experienced the sensation that he was taking over, but calling him by his first name was no grave hardship. ''*Burke,* I'm not staying at a hotel.''

He stepped toward her. ''I know you'd rather remain here, but it's Friday night. The saloons are brimming with miners, cowpunchers, gamblers and fancy women. Tomorrow will be even worse. This building happens to be sitting in the middle of all the excitement. You aren't safe here, Jayne.''

''I haven't had any trouble.'' She tried to ignore the music, laughter and quarrelsome voices that kept intruding upon their conversation.

''It's blind luck that trouble hasn't already found you. Be sensible. Cut your losses and spend the night where you know you'll be safe.''

''I'm not going anywhere until you explain why you're determined to involve yourself in my life.'' She hadn't planned on demanding an explanation for his forced entry into her world, but she needed to know what was motivating his sudden concern for her and her school.

A half smile slanted his narrow lips. Her heart performed a most peculiar maneuver—something between a flip and a twist.

''I guess I have been a little high-handed,'' he drawled.

High-handed? Again she was put in mind of a military confrontation. Forget the cavalry. He'd thundered into her sphere with the jarring force of barbarian hordes sweeping across ancient Europe.

Doubting he would appreciate the comparison, she searched for words that wouldn't further inflame his domineering tendencies. ''You've been acting as if you were the most tyrannical of fathers.''

He flinched, but the smile remained. ''Believe me, I have no intention of acting like your father.''

Jayne decided he was deliberately trying to charm her.

She hardly knew how to react. No man had ever focused this form of attention upon her. It was disheartening to discover that recognizing his ploy didn't free her from his magnetism.

"I can't believe you take this kind of interest in all Denver's fledgling businesses," she pressed determinedly.

"I'd be lying if I said so," he admitted. "Do you always know the reasons behind everything you do?"

"Of course. One can't blunder through life."

"Ah, so I'm dealing with a woman of logic."

"You're dealing with a woman who wants to know why you're willing to invest time, effort and money on her behalf."

"I assume the suspiciousness I'm detecting is based upon your late aunt's dire warnings about accepting favors from men."

"Aunt Euphemia's philosophy about the male gender has nothing to do with this. Credit me with enough intelligence to recognize you could very well have an ulterior motive for assisting me. I have no intention of placing myself under your influence without knowing what you expect in return."

Jayne knew she was pink-cheeked, but she needed to know what lay behind his sudden desire to help.

"I approve of your cautious attitude. A number of men might expect certain favors in exchange for their help. A wise woman pays attention to such things. I assure you, though, I have no ulterior motives."

His eyes held an almost whimsical expression that weakened her resolve to challenge him. She was amazed by the degree of energy it took to withstand his charm. "Trust has to be earned."

"Life's taught me the same lesson," he said quietly. "The reason I'm willing to put my resources at your disposal are twofold. First, I have this character quirk of rooting for underdogs."

Even though she fit the description, she didn't appreciate

being compared to a four-legged animal. "There has to be more to it than that."

"There are dozens of businesses I've supported through their uncertain beginnings. My basis for consideration is that the owner be absolutely committed to his course and willing to pour all his time and energy into his enterprise. You possess that determination, correct?"

She stared at him, trying to gauge whether his offer carried hidden strings. She was uneasy at accepting his help and just as uneasy about losing it. "There's nothing I want more than to establish my school."

He nodded. "I thought as much."

"I want to make it clear, though, that ours is to be a strictly business relationship. I'll repay all monies advanced, with interest."

His eyes held an alarming gleam. "I wouldn't have it any other way."

"About my spending the night in a hotel." She would resist any unreasonable authority he chose to exert. "I have no intention of —"

Two gunshots fired in quick succession startled a shriek from her. Only when Burke's arms closed around her did she realize she'd hurled herself at him. His scent, at once familiar and mysterious, teased her senses. The security of his embrace, unwelcome as it was, had her heart hammering against her ribs. *No,* it was the sound of gunfire that had her palpitating.

"You were saying?"

His deep voice rumbled in her ears. It became imperative to return some distance between them. She pulled free. He made no effort to restrain her.

"I was saying that I have no intention of staying more than a couple of nights at a hotel. Since I'm repaying all the money you're advancing me against my uncle's bank draft, I refuse to squander my limited resources."

"Again, I applaud your wisdom."

She looked for a sign of amusement in his gaze, but

found it unreadable. "I would appreciate your waiting downstairs while I gather my things."

"I've seen ladies' unmentionables before."

"Such comments will end our association before it begins."

He shrugged. The casual gesture was at odds with the subtle tension he radiated. She looked into his eyes and wished she could be blessed with the ability to read his mind. Was he as he portrayed himself, a banker and businessman, interested only in helping her establish her school? Or did he hope to extract a hidden payment from her in the future?

A shiver stole down her spine. She couldn't pretend that feeling his strong arms close around her moments before had been a loathsome experience. His rugged masculinity touched something inescapably feminine within her.

"Only time will prove whether you can trust me." He moved to the doorway, then paused, looking over his shoulder. "I'll wait downstairs."

Left to her confused thoughts and the mayhem floating up from the street, Jayne resisted the impulse to call out that she'd changed her mind. Only a fool would reject Burke Youngblood's help.

She fetched the valise she'd stored beneath her bed, deciding she felt like the sovereign of a small kingdom forced to accept aid from a more powerful principality. If she wasn't careful, her borders would be breached and her authority to act usurped. It was a history lesson she'd taught countless times.

It didn't take long to pack her personal things. Descending the stairs, she was struck by the unpalatable realization that Burke had gotten his way without resorting to force. He'd used logic to sway her. Logic and the sound of blasting guns.

I think I could be in a bit of trouble, Aunt Euphemia.

How did one deal with a man of power and remarkable persuasiveness who'd mastered the skills of applied charm and reason?

Very carefully, a distant voice seemed to caution.

Chapter Five

It wasn't surrender. By linking forces with her pushy benefactor, she was exercising good sense. Jayne joined Burke at the bottom of the stairs. Burke... It unnerved her at how quickly she'd begun to think of him by his first name.

"That didn't take long," he observed, hardly more than a shadow in the muted light provided by a single low-burning oil lamp. He stepped forward. "I'll take that for you."

He reached for the valise. She was tempted to make an issue of carrying it herself. True wisdom, however, lay in knowing which battles to wage with the overbearing banker. She released the handle without comment.

His palm curved around her elbow as he guided her to the door. "Do you have the key?"

"Of course," she replied, resenting being treated like a child.

"Wait here while I douse the lamp."

Evidently giving orders was as natural to him as breathing.

Moments later a cloak of darkness claimed the room's interior. Sufficient light from an outside street lamp filtered through the front windows and glass door panels. He had no difficulty making his way back to her. His unerring approach had her fumbling to get the key in the lock. She attributed her uncustomary awkwardness to his disembodied presence and the almost palpable tension he projected. Mentally, she commanded the stubborn key to turn.

There was an audible click. In the room's subsequent stillness, her sigh of relief was clearly heard. A strong arm came around her, crowding her into a tiny pocket of space. It took a half second to comprehend that he was turning the knob and shoving open the door. In that minuscule fragment of time, her heart stopped beating, and her stomach curled into a tight ball.

She couldn't get across the threshold quickly enough. It did nothing for her peace of mind to realize her knees had been reduced to insubstantial globs of melted butter. She wanted him to cease his disturbing behavior, but she didn't know precisely what he was doing to annihilate her composure.

Just existing, taking up space and breathing were not things she could order him to stop doing. As much as she chafed under his unsettling effect, she intuitively understood that the problem was with her, not him. She was the one who'd temporarily lost her bearings. Therefore, it was up to her to find them. And she would. Just as soon as she put some desperately needed distance between herself and the worrisome Mr. Youngblood.

He followed her through the door. She shoved the key into his free hand, refusing to deal again with the tricky lock—anything to avoid having him pressed up behind her.

He said nothing as he saw to the task. Looking beyond his broad shoulders, she stared at the beautifully etched glass panels she'd purchased in a moment of extravagance. Leaving them for the new owner saddened her.

"This building you found, do you recall if its doors are the same size as these?"

He returned the key. Her fingers curved around the piece of metal, warmed by its contact with his flesh. She slid the key into a pocket.

"Offhand, I can't give you the exact measurements. Do

you have a preference for certain-sized doors?'' he inquired blandly.

Despite his neutral tone, there was no missing the soft humor tinging his deep voice. ''I just had those glass panels installed. If there's any way to take them with me, I intend to do it.''

''You have excellent taste.''

She braced herself against the unexpected pleasure his compliment sparked. The street's noisy hubbub penetrated the cocoon of intimacy that had embraced them. Miners and cowpunchers poured from brightly lit saloons. Harpsichord music from different establishments collided in jangling bursts of discordant clatter. Loud voices, male and female were raised in drunken laughter, song and angry tones, crafting a sinful chorus of raucous notes. It was as if she and Burke had stepped into a world of violent sounds.

''Stay beside me.''

He didn't have to tell her twice. She pressed closer. He still carried her satchel. His free arm curved around her shoulders. For once, she wasn't disposed to assert her independence. It was an alien sensation to feel in need of protection from someone bigger and stronger than herself. Yet being sheltered by him was strangely satisfying.

They surged forward, weaving their way through the tumultuous celebrants milling along the boardwalk. The summer night was ripe with raw, loosened energy that seemed to pulse between the roving clusters of drunken men.

''Hey now, watch where y'er going!''

The slurred shout erupted from a small, roughly dressed man who stumbled into the path of several wranglers swigging drinks from earthen jugs.

''Naw, runt, it's you who better watch what you're about.''

''Who you calling runt, skunk face?''

''Wylie, you gonna let that dwarf get away with calling you skunk face?''

''What do you think?''

"Oh, hell." Burke's arm tightened around her as he placed himself between her and the brewing trouble. With her nose pressed against his side, she couldn't see what was going on. But she heard plenty—oaths, grunts, dull thuds of fists striking and connecting, along with wheezing groans.

Jayne had never been caught in a flood, but she felt as if she and the banker had been sucked into a wild tide of churning water. Someone barreled against Burke. Still in his protective grasp, she was jostled from the tight crook of his strong arm. Her fractured field of vision was filled with a turbulent sea of men who'd abandoned reason and were bludgeoning one another. Flailing arms and pounding fists sent bodies hurtling in every direction.

The majority of combatants didn't seem to care whom they engaged in fisticuffs. Anyone crossing their path appeared to be fair game. Someone else rammed against her and Burke. One second she was tucked by his side, and the next she sailed backward into a hostile current of battling ruffians.

"Jayne!"

She heard Burke's hoarse shout above the surging fury and tried to get to him, but two hooligans materialized from the writhing mass of brawlers and commenced trading blows. Like an avenging warrior, Burke moved between the pugilists. He tossed them apart and charged toward her, still securely gripping her valise.

Jayne's heart thumped against her ribs. She'd never inspired a heroic rescue before. His boldness took her breath away. He closed the distance between them. A look of fierce determination stamped his rugged features. Goodness, he looked capable of slaying a fire-breathing dragon on her behalf.

From the corner of her eye, she saw a rush of motion. The image of a wildly swinging brown jug flashed. Hot pain and exploding rainbows converged in her brain.

* * *

"Jayne, can you hear me?"

Burke's voice penetrated the vortex of throbbing pain churning inside her skull. She tried to open her eyes. The right one refused to cooperate. The left lid flickered, then gave up the effort. Tears flowed freely. Lying very still and not moving her head seemed her most prudent course.

There was a subtle disturbance in the air current around her. Something wet and cool was gently applied to her forehead. It felt wonderfully soothing. She almost sighed her pleasure.

"Come on, open your pretty green eyes and say something rude so I'll know you're all right."

"It hurts too much," she mumbled. It registered that she was lying upon a soft surface, and the sounds of riotous battle had been silenced. "What happened?"

"I messed up."

His tone was bitter with self-reproach, which made no sense. "Are you blaming yourself for our being swept into that drunken mob?"

"Not entirely." His voice was closer. Whatever she was lying upon dipped toward the husky sound. "If you had done as I suggested earlier, you'd have been settled in a hotel room when the fight broke out."

"You suggested nothing," she felt compelled to point out. "You took it upon yourself to *order* me to accompany you."

"Then I should have been tougher about enforcing that order," he said gruffly. "How does your head feel? You took a hard blow."

This time she thought she detected a note of concern in his voice. Obviously, the jug that had plowed into her had scrambled her senses. "I feel as if one of those huge draft horses stepped on my face."

"Damn, I'm sorry I didn't get to you in time."

"It wasn't your fault. Those brawlers should be locked

up so they can't attack decent folks who are minding their own business.''

''The law expects decent folks to be safely tucked in their own beds, not walking the streets late at night.''

Tucked in their own beds… The phrase brought immediate clarity to Jayne's resting place. A pillow that smelled like sunshine cradled her head. She ran her palms along crisp sheets. At the freedom of movement and smooth friction of her bare arms against the bedding, several alarming realities slammed into her. She wasn't fully clothed. Surreptitiously, she investigated her state of dishabille beneath the blankets.

Her dress was gone. So was her corset and… She wriggled her toes. Her stockings remained, but her shoes had been removed. Indignation spiraled. Someone had reduced her to her chemise and pantalettes. That someone had better *not* be the man who she now realized was sitting beside her on the mattress.

''If the pain is too much, I can fetch a doctor, Jayne. Some laudanum would take the edge off the hurt you must be feeling.''

Hot, suffocating rage made her flesh burn. ''I'm sure drugging me would suit your purposes perfectly.''

It took herculean strength to get the words past her tightened throat. Embarrassment and fury rose within her. Just when she'd relaxed her guard, the cad had shown his true colors. And they were as black as his wicked, lecherous heart.

''Do you care to explain that statement?''

Through the self-imposed darkness of her closed eyelids, she heard the barely banked anger beneath the calmly voiced question.

''Don't bother acting offended, *or* innocent.'' She drew the blankets to her chin. ''I know exactly what's been going on.''

''Do you?''

"I'm not some innocent young miss to have the wool pulled over my eyes."

"Aren't you?"

"And don't try to intimidate me with those surly two-word questions of yours. It won't work."

"Won't it?"

She ground her teeth. New pain radiated in her skull. "It's perfectly obvious what evil designs you've had in mind for me all along. And if you say, 'Is it?' I swear I shall blacken your eye."

"Will you, indeed?"

She knew he'd deliberately crafted the three-word question to drive her insane. Unfortunately, it didn't appear the trip would be all that far. She felt pushed to the outer boundaries of reason. One more sarcastic remark from him would complete the journey.

"Where am I?"

"I assume you would like a more specific answer than Denver."

Her hands curled into fists. *Composure,* she breathed. It was essential that she retain control of her roiling emotions. So far as she could determine the fiend hadn't taken advantage of her unconscious state. At least, she didn't think he had. Could a woman tell if she'd been ravished?

Surely, a barbarian the likes of Burke Youngblood would leave telltale evidence of his lovemaking. Euphemia's graphic explanation of a how a man physically invaded a woman's body would cause a twinge or two, wouldn't it?

Jayne's eyes remained sealed shut beneath the damp cloth that rode low on her forehead. She concentrated intensely, focusing on the critical juncture between her thighs. If there was any discomfort there, however, it was obliterated by the throbbing in her head.

Unable to trust the messages her body was sending, she took comfort in logic. If Burke Youngblood had had his evil way with her, would he have taken the trouble to redress her in her chemise and pantalettes? She considered the question. He was a man of complex layers. He disguised his carnal nature behind the facade of a self-controlled businessman, but he had a devious side. He might restore her clothing to lull her into a false feeling of security.

She forced herself to draw another steadying breath. Now wasn't the time to panic. She would have an accounting of his actions, and then she would deal with the repercussions—after she killed him.

"Tell me the worst of it," she instructed.

"The worst?"

"Yes, I need..." She swallowed. "I need to know how bad things are."

Burke saw that Jayne was becoming more agitated with each passing moment. For the life of him, he couldn't understand why. She was safe from the violence that had broken out on the boardwalk. True, she'd been struck a hard blow, but he sensed the emotions making her voice tremble had little to do with her physical aches. Her color had been normal when she'd regained consciousness, but now she was flushed.

Guilt burrowed deeply inside him at failing to shield her from the vicious mayhem that had erupted around them. The fundamental tenet of being a man was to protect those weaker than himself. He'd placed Jayne under his care, and he'd let her down.

How did a man apologize for failing to safeguard the woman under his protection? Gall burned the back his throat at having to acknowledge to her and himself he'd failed.

He decided to postpone the bitter reckoning. "Backing up to your earlier question, you're in bed."

"Whose?" she virtually croaked.

He'd damned well been tempted to put her in his own. But at the last minute, sanity overrode the crazy temptation, and he'd carried her into one of his guest chambers. Under the circumstances, he doubted she was in the mood to appreciate his clear thinking.

"You're in one of the guest bedrooms of my home."

He could almost feel the increased tension radiating from her.

Her hand went to her forehead. She pulled off the cloth. "When I open my eyes, I expect you to have removed yourself from this bed."

"Be reasonable. If I'm going to take care of you, I have to be close by."

Crescent-shaped lashes fluttered, then lifted above one green eye. She'd couldn't have made her anger any plainer than by fixing her gaze upon the white plaster ceiling instead of him.

"Do not speak to me of reason, sir. I want you off this bed. Now."

Perhaps it was best to humor her. The faint lines of tension marring her forehead had to be adding to the soreness of her bruised cheek and the puffy eye that remained swollen shut.

"I'll rinse out the cloth." He leaned forward to retrieve it.

Her fingers tightened around the material. "I do not wish for you to apply a damp cloth to my brow. I do not wish for you to speak soothing words. I do not wish for you to care for me in any way."

Gently, he extracted the mauled fabric from her grip. "Well, that's too bad, because that's exactly what I intend to do."

He rose from the bed and headed for the pitcher of water. Obstinate, there was no question Jayne Stoneworthy was that. He should have been put off by her disagreeable temperament. After all, women were supposed to be sweet-tempered and obliging. What did it say about him that he found her intractability as appealing as her lively intelligence and lithesome curves?

He submerged the cloth in cool water. A vision of himself and Jayne similarly submerged in a translucent pool of water jackknifed into his mind. The image was of them locked in a lovers' embrace.

He wrung out the cloth with more force than necessary and wondered if there was an ailment he'd never heard of that made grown men lose their minds when they reached thirty. When he'd walked into the Wet Beaver and over-heard Newton White trying to buy Jayne's services as a prostitute, Burke and his common sense had taken wildly divergent paths.

He shook his head, reminding himself that he didn't be-lieve the myth of love at first sight. His brother, Logan, and Gideon Cade might have been sucked into the romantic mire that had them blubbering their undying loyalty to one woman, but Burke had his rules to protect his heart against those rules. Other men might confuse their basic needs with sentimental yearnings, but that was one mistake he would never make.

Seeing his brother become engaged to the conniving Ro-beena Stockard had proved to Burke that a man couldn't be in love *and* clear-thinking. The memory of the shocked betrayal that had etched Logan's face when he'd discovered Robeena in the bed of another man still haunted Burke.

It still tormented Burke that he'd been the man in bed with his brother's fiancée. The scheming temptress had de-cided a more secure future lay with the richer, more estab-lished Youngblood brother.

Burke was smart enough to know that all women weren't as treacherous as Robeena. When a man gave away his heart, however, he also gave away his reason. The night his brother had walked out of his life without allowing Burke to explain the scene Robeena had engineered had been the night he'd vowed to keep his own heart under lock and key. He'd thrown away that key so long ago, he doubted even the most diligent search could recover it.

Burke faced Jayne. There was peace of mind in knowing that the strange feeling of protectiveness she evoked from him had nothing to do with a debilitating sentiment like love.

"I don't know why you're upset. Earlier today, I was lying in bed, and you were tending me."

"That was entirely different."

His lips curved, and he grimaced. No good could come from being charmed by her sassiness. It annoyed him that her gaze was still riveted to the ceiling as she continued to blatantly shut him from her field of vision.

"I was responsible for your injury. Not, of course, that you didn't deserve it," she interjected quickly. "Placing a compress on your head was simply the Christian thing to do."

He leaned over and laid the folded cloth on her forehead. "And the difference between then and now *is?*"

"You know the difference!"

"As far as I'm concerned this conversation has taken place in Greek. Do us both a favor and spit out what you have to say."

"I most certainly did not take advantage of you in your unconscious state and remove your clothing, sir!"

Burke rubbed his hand over his mouth. Damned, he knew she'd notice sooner or later that he'd shucked off her dress, petticoats and corset.

"My actions were just as Christian as yours," he shot back without compunction. "If I'd been trussed up in one of those whalebone contraptions, I'd sure as hell hope you would pop me free of it so I could breathe."

The image was ludicrous, but Burke preferred charging to retreating.

"It can't have escaped your notice that a woman can breathe quite satisfactorily in a corset."

"As long as she isn't exerting herself."

"I was unconscious. One can't be less active than that."

"You needed all the air you could get, and I made sure you got it."

"So it's your assertion that you removed my clothing strictly for medical purposes?"

"What other reason could I have?" he asked, daring her to accuse him of impropriety as it occurred to him what was provoking her agitated manner. He didn't know whether to laugh or feel insulted that her opinion of him was so low that she thought him capable of taking advantage of an unconscious woman.

"It's an established fact that no man is capable of subduing his bestial appetites when in the company of an unclothed female."

Burke's mouth fell open. *"What?"*

"It's a quirk of nature, I suppose," she said with a long-suffering sigh. "But it's a weakness all men share. They are simply unable to subdue their animal lusts when confronted by exposed feminine flesh."

Burke's face grew hot. After he removed Jayne's corset, his gaze *had* strayed to the creamy skin exposed above her camisole, and he admitted the rosy peaks of her breasts revealed through the sheer garment had held his attention, while her subtle female scent had sent hot blood pounding. And yes, he'd been tempted to peel away the almost transparent fabric that separated him from the vision his fevered brain fashioned. That he'd restrained himself ought to earn him some kind of heavenly reward.

It was galling, however, to endure haughty censure in the here and now. "Not all men are slavering wolves. Some of us manage to 'subdue our lusts.'"

"Are you saying that you didn't…er…ah…"

A contrary streak he hadn't realized he possessed made him hold his tongue. She'd brought up the subject. Let her put into words her imagined grievance against him. He doubted she could.

"Did you place your…" She broke off.

Burke could feel the sweat on his brow. Her soft, unsure voice made his skin burn and grow tight. He *was* losing his mind. He was in the presence of a prissy woman who thought of him as a depraved beast, and he was regarding her as anything but a damsel in distress. His breaths were sharp and shallow, and his heart was pounding too fast.

"Sir, I need to know if you removed and then restored the undergarments I have on."

He was forced to admire how she'd phrased the delicate but damnably insulting question. "And if I did?"

"I want to know this very minute, did you have your way with me?"

"What way would that be, Jayne?"

"You fiend, you know what I'm talking about. Answer me!"

All at once, Burke felt ashamed. It was hardly Jayne's fault that whenever he looked or thought about her, the demands of his body took on a wild life of their own.

"I know what you mean, but I've got to tell you it's damned insulting when someone thinks you're capable of attacking a helpless woman."

She reached for the cloth on her forehead. "I've made no accusations. I've only asked for answers. You must admit it's highly suspect that you took me to your home, placed me in a bed and removed my clothing."

"Not all of it. You're still fully covered," he pointed out sharply. "But in answer to your question, I did *not* take advantage of you. If I had, you would know it."

"I thought as much."

"Did you?"

Her low opinion of him made his anger simmer. One lousy proposition to teach her a much-needed lesson, and she was ready to think the worst. So, he'd slung her over his shoulder and carried her upstairs, tossed her onto a bed and taken a kiss. That didn't give her the right to label him a satyr.

Burke shoved his fingers through his hair in frustration. That his actions *did* warrant her suspicions rankled what was left of his eroded patience. He still couldn't believe he'd pushed things as far as he had. The loss of his usually rigid control shocked him.

"Aunt Euphemia was quite frank in her discourses about the violent means men employ when coupling with women."

Struggling against the urge to employ a little violence himself, Burke scowled. "Sounds as if she was some kind of self-proclaimed expert on men."

"I don't know that she was an expert, but she was most firm in her conclusions."

"I'll just bet she was."

For the first time since she'd come to, Jayne turned her head toward him. The delicate eyebrow above her unswollen eye shot up. "Good heavens, what happened to you?"

"What do you think happened?" Feeling grossly maligned, if not by his reluctant houseguest, then by forces beyond his control, Burke shoved his fists to his sides. "I had to fight my way through a wild mob to get to you."

Chapter Six

Jayne gaped at Burke in astonishment. Instead of a measly little mob, he looked as if he'd fought his way past the Four Horsemen of the Apocalypse. Until now, she'd avoided looking directly at him. Hearing from his own lips that he hadn't taken advantage of her, however, gave her the courage necessary to actually meet his gaze.

Several dark bruises marred the harsh planes and angles of his face. His lower lip was cracked, and his left eye showed signs of swelling. Gone was the tailored black coat. His dress shirt had one sleeve torn off, exposing a naked, well-muscled arm. Blood and smudges of dirt stained the garment's once pristine whiteness. It was untucked and bereft of all buttons.

An expanse of firmly sculpted, darkly furred chest held her spellbound. She swallowed. Against her will, she was fascinated. She'd never seen a man's uncovered chest before. His startling state of partial nakedness made her stomach clench.

"There was the little matter of a mob standing between us," he said, answering her earlier question about what had happened to him.

"You look dreadful." She meant his face, of course. His upper torso appeared splendidly fit.

"Neither of us are looking our best." He pulled forward

a carved mahogany chair and straddled it, resting his folded arms along its back. "Under the circumstances, checking an unconscious woman into a hotel in the middle of the night would make a shambles of her reputation."

A flush warmed her skin. He *had* been looking after her best interests, and she'd suspected him of the most vile act.

"Please accept my apology." Not choking on the words was a victory.

"For what?"

"For thinking that you might have... Well, that is..."

Jayne winced at her incoherency, then raised her chin. Just because she was a virgin and intended to remain so didn't warrant a timidness of speech from her, especially with as worldly a person as Burke Youngblood had proved himself to be. She would speak as boldly as Euphemia would have in a similar situation.

"We both know for what I'm thanking you. I'm aware of how difficult it must have been to restrain your bestial urges when you unclothed me. I'm grateful you didn't place your male member within my person."

Intrigued, she watched a tide of red climb from his chest to his hairline. Clearly her frankness embarrassed him. The heat burning across her own cheeks testified to just how delicate a subject they were discussing. The air in the bed-chamber thickened with awareness. She affected what she hoped was a matter-of-fact expression.

"You have a straightforward way of putting things."

Jayne clung to her facade of sophistication. "My aunt raised me to be an independent, free-thinking female."

She cleared her throat. It was best to conclude this discussion and not begin another until she was fully clothed and in a vertical position. "Thank you for delivering me safely here."

"You're welcome."

More silence loomed. "Uh, I would appreciate my clothing being returned to me as soon as possible."

He rested his chin on his crossed arms. "Why?"

She blinked at him in confusion. "Because I wish to be on my way."

"Where?"

As much as she'd detested his two-word questions, she found his one-word queries even more annoying. "It's obvious I must leave."

"You're thinking of appearances," he surmised.

She nodded, then winced. She was getting a crick in her neck from lying on her side and conversing with him. "It will be better for both our reputations when I'm gone."

He rubbed his jaw thoughtfully. "This afternoon that was true."

"And tonight, too," she added quickly.

"Tonight things are different."

She didn't like the sound of that. Tired of lying down, she made sure she had a firm grasp on the blankets and sat up. The throbbing in her head increased. "The hour of the day hardly makes a difference."

What was he thinking as he continued to stare at her? That she looked like a pummeled gargoyle?

"Earlier this evening, no one would have remarked upon you taking up residence in a hotel for a few days. Now with your face looking as if you've been street-brawling, you would call undue attention to yourself. Until the swelling goes down, the only prudent course is to remain out of sight. Staying here as my guest is the perfect solution to your dilemma."

His words struck with the pounding force of a hailstorm. Yet she couldn't dispute his statement's validity. Any parent of a prospective student seeing her in her present, disreputable state would expect an explanation for her appearance. Even after explanations had been rendered, seeds of doubt would be planted about her standards.

"I can't stay here." He had to realize that much was true. "My reputation would be in shreds."

"Only if the local gossips got wind of it."

Jayne bit back a cynical laugh. Denver had a healthy

network of garrulous women who seemed to know everything that went on in town. "Believe me, word would get out. It always does."

"My staff is paid to be circumspect. I guarantee your privacy. The minute you leave the premises, though, anyone who knows you and catches a glimpse of your face will be curious about what you've been up to."

Her hand went to her cheek. "Um, do you have a hand mirror?"

An oval looking glass hung above the pitcher and washbasin, but there was no way she could peer into it with Burke sitting across from her. She refused to wrap herself in a blanket and parade before him.

"I'll fetch you one." He got to his feet. "Let me reassure you about one thing."

"What's that?"

"Despite my bestial urges, you'll be safe in my home."

What was she supposed to say to that?

He continued to stare at her. Against her naked skin, she felt her loosened hair against her back. The unruly mass had fallen free from its anchoring pins. Never in her life had a male seen her with her hair down.

"You're right to be suspicious of men. We do have…urges, but a few of us have scruples. Nothing will occur between us that you don't want to happen."

Dumbstruck, she could think of no suitable response.

"I haven't had much experience with innocent females, but I recognize one when she crosses my path." He cocked his head. The action further separated the folds of his shirt, exposing a greater expanse of chest. "I'm glad you appreciate bluntness, because I'm going to be completely honest."

Perhaps it would have been better had she been more restrained in her manner of speech. In her attempt to come across as sophisticated, she'd freed him to speak with greater boldness.

"I did get hot and bothered when I was peeling off your

gown. You have a beautiful body. But there's more to you than your enticing curves. I like the way your mind works, even though you're prone to lecturing. When you're no longer a guest in my home, I plan to see you socially.''

''But you said ours was to be a strictly business relationship.''

''I've decided we will have two relationships. One professional, one personal.''

''*You've* decided? I certainly have some say in transpires between us.''

Complacency claimed his bruised features. ''Naturally.''

''Well then, we'll maintain only a business association.''

Her declaration failed to rattle his overconfident expression. ''I have no problem conducting both business and pleasure with you, Jayne.''

''*Pleasure!* You said you recognized an innocent female when you saw one.''

Unadulterated mischief leaped into his eyes. ''There are respectable ways for gentlemen and well-bred females to share simple pleasures. I could escort you to dinner and the theater. There are picnics, church socials and Saturday-night dances at the Grange.''

''But you're not interested in those things.'' Visualizing him at a church social was as impossible as imagining a panther at a tea party.

''When you know me better, you'll discover my interests are varied.''

That might be, but she remembered too well the feel of his hands on her body and the imprint of his lips and tongue when he'd swept her into the dark whirlwind of her first kiss. Burke Youngblood was not a man to indulge in the innocent pastimes he'd just described. With a woman's infallible intuition, she knew that when he spoke of pleasure, he meant the most basic, primal way a man and woman could interact. Picnic, hah!

''After what's happened between us, it's understandable that you're not ready to trust me,'' he continued smoothly.

Too smoothly. "Only time and more traditional encounters will allay your suspicions. I'm a patient man."

She wet her dry lips with the tip of her tongue and pondered his casually proclaimed plan to… Goodness, it almost sounded as if he meant to court her. Her heart took a peculiar lurch. With his masculine chest brazenly exposed, along with a naked, well-muscled arm *and* his rugged looks, Burke seemed more dangerous than an innocuous word like "suitor" implied.

She shook her head. What was she thinking? He didn't wish to court her. No, his was a more base interest, one he'd made no effort to camouflage. Her suspicions about his true motives, however, failed to extinguish his pull upon her.

Aunt Euphemia had warned that even the most sensible woman could lose her bearings when a smooth-talking man appeared on her doorstep with flattery and candy. Jayne might not presently have a doorstep, and Burke hadn't presented her with sweets, but his flattering words and interest had already made alarming inroads in her original resistance toward him.

"I don't see how you can expect me to remain here as your guest after everything you've said."

"On the contrary, if my intentions were dishonorable, I would hardly be so forthright in expressing my interest."

She, who'd always counted upon her ability to think clearly, found his logic oddly seductive. She was tempted to accept his invitation. Drawing attention to herself that portrayed her lacking in character would end her school before it began. And appearing in public with a battered countenance was bound to cause destructive comments.

She'd already compromised her hopes of success by purchasing a former brothel for the venture. From now on, she had to be scrupulous about her reputation. Being hidden at Burke's residence until her appearance was once more respectable seemed an ideal solution to her predicament—as long as she didn't have to ward off any advances in the middle of the night, of course.

"You believe none of your servants would disclose that I'm here?"

"My staff have been with me for years. During that time they've given me no reason to doubt their loyalty."

"Do you often have female guests whose presence they conceal?"

Instead of offending him, the question brought a half smile to his lips. "When we know each other better, you'll have the right to inquire about my private life."

"Since you admire my honesty, you should appreciate hearing that we're not going to know each other any better. I intend to leave here as soon as my bruises fade. As for picnics, church socials and the theater, I'll be far too busy to engage in such frivolous activities."

She and Burke might be virtual strangers, but she sensed he was a proud man, too proud to pursue a woman who clearly expressed her disinterest in him. Aunt Euphemia always said one of a man's greatest weakness was his vanity.

"You focus on what's important to you. I'll concentrate on what's important to me."

With that cryptic remark he left the room.

He didn't seem particularly distressed by her rejection. Was it because his interest wasn't that deep, or because he didn't believe any female could resist him? Perhaps she was the first woman immune to his compelling virility.

Are you immune? The rude question materialized without warning. She wanted to dismiss it, yet couldn't. Something about Burke made her heart beat faster and caused an unfamiliar sensitivity to her skin. Staring into his eyes for an extended length of time made her stomach go fluttery.

Oh, he was dangerous, all right. Dangerous to the independent future she'd mapped for herself. It was a good thing Euphemia had warned about the pitfalls that could make a sensible woman stumble. With her guard up, Jayne knew she could resist Burke. The man hadn't been born who could fill her sharp mind with fantasies of becoming his personal slave for life.

No matter how often he offered to escort her, she would rebuff him. He'd presented a business agreement, and she would accept only that. No flowers, no candy, no dinner invitations, no moonlit strolls and no kisses.

Unfortunately, the thought of his taking her into his arms and kissing her again made her toes curl. It was a shame being independent meant she had to abstain from the heart-stopping feeling of having his mouth molded against hers. She sighed. Some sacrifices were harder than others. She wondered when she'd turned into a sensualist.

There was a tap at the door frame. In walked Burke. His rumpled black hair, bristly jaw and state of half-nakedness made her mouth go dry. In the few minutes they'd been apart, he seemed to have grown in stature and energy.

"Here's the hand mirror."

She accepted it and glanced at her reflection. The shock of a blackened, swollen right eye greeted her. A bluish bruise marred her cheek. She looked hideous! That Burke had demonstrated any continuing interest in her wasn't a testimony to his vanity. Good grief, the man must be blind to find anything about her features the least appealing.

She cleared her throat. "You're right. I can't go into public."

"I knew you would see it my way."

"How long does it take for a black eye to heal?"

"Not long. You can plan on staying one to two weeks."

"One to two *weeks!* I can't be idle that long. I have a building to purchase. It's bound to need remodeling. There are books to order, correspondence to attend to and—"

"Things needn't come to a standstill because you're here. The middle of the night, though, isn't the best time to hash out these kinds of details. Get some rest. Tomorrow will be soon enough to tackle your problems."

She hadn't thought about the lateness of the hour. There

wasn't anything she could do until morning to resolve the
uncertainties plaguing her. For better or worse, she would
be Burke's guest for the rest of the evening. Taking prag-
matic stock of her situation, she reconciled herself to being
so for perhaps the next two weeks.

Somehow, she would make the best of things.

"You're being very kind, Mr. Youngblood."

"After referring to my—I believe you called it 'male
member,' you can surely bring yourself to call me by my
first name."

"Thank you, *Burke,*" she said, irritated that he wouldn'
let her retreat behind a wall of formality.

"It won't benefit you to believe my actions are based on
kindness. I've made my interest in you clear. Are you ready
to admit that you're not as unaffected by me as you pretend?"

His presumption shocked her. She'd been very carefu
not to betray her reluctant fascination with him. Since she
had every expectation of exterminating her unwilling
awareness, he need never know that she was, even for a
moment, attracted to him.

"I've given you no encouragement to view me as any
thing other than a hardworking business associate. You
have my gratitude for your efforts thus far, but my primary
goal is to become free from any dependence upon you."

"You only *think* that's your goal."

His reply momentarily made her doubt her own feelings
Her resolve hardened. No man was going to lecture her
about the workings of her own mind. "No doubt you'll tell
me my real goal."

"As with any woman cast adrift in the world, you seek
security."

She couldn't refute his statement. "I believe I said vir
tually the same thing."

He shook his head. "Financial stability doesn't mean you
can't associate with men."

"On the contrary, for a single woman wishing to safeguard her reputation, that's exactly what it means."

"Are you saying that you've never had a male friend, a suitor or a beau?" His attitude was one of skepticism.

"Avoiding emotional entanglements with the opposite sex is the only prudent course for a woman on her own."

"I assume your aunt, with her great knowledge of men and their carnal natures, influenced your opinions on this subject."

"Aunt Euphemia was wise beyond the century into which she was born."

"Just how many lovers did she have?"

"None!"

"How did she acquire her vast wisdom about men? One husband is hardly a basis to condemn the entire male gender."

"My aunt never married."

"Somehow that doesn't surprise me."

His dry tone made her want to do something to wipe the smug smile off his face. "She was engaged to be married upon six different occasions."

"If six suitors abandoned her at the altar, no wonder she was bitter."

Jayne ground her teeth. "You're mistaken. It was my aunt who called off each union. You see, even though she had a perfectly sound notion about the deplorable character of men in general, she allowed herself upon occasion to hope that certain individuals might possess exemplary attributes."

"Let me guess. None of them measured up to her high standards?"

Jayne nodded. "For the most part, they were affable and successful gentlemen. Unfortunately, none of them possessed the intellectual and spiritual sensitivity Euphemia required for a lifetime companion."

"Good grief."

"So, you see, my aunt gave each man an opportunity to win her, despite his inherent male flaws."

"You mean she put them through their paces and, being mere mortals, none of them measured up to sainthood."

"Euphemia was a Renaissance woman. She would have been miserable shackled to an ordinary sort of man."

"From some of your earlier remarks, I gather you share her views."

"I have no desire to marry, if that's what you mean."

"We agree upon that, at least."

The comment left no doubt that his wish to socialize with her was based upon lustful inclinations. Her breath hitched in her throat. Standing before her in his present roughed-up state, Burke Youngblood incited yearnings of which, until now, she'd been blissfully ignorant.

"Nor am I the kind of woman to entertain thoughts about establishing an unsavory liaison with a man." That had to be made clear.

The half smile returned to his lips. "For a woman who doesn't indulge her physical appetites, you sure think about them a lot."

More warmth steeled across her cheeks. "You flatter yourself."

He grinned rakishly. "I would grow old waiting for you to do it."

"I believe you were leaving...."

He ignored her unsubtle prompting and continued to regard her with maddening cheerfulness. "Here's the situation. We're going to have a mutually satisfactory business relationship. I'll invest in your school and make sure it gets off to a sound start. You'll pay me back with interest. And, on a personal level, we'll become good friends."

"To what purpose?" she asked in alarm.

"Does there have to be a purpose for friendship?"

"When one person is a man and the other a woman, there certainly does. Neither of us has an interest in marriage. And I'm completely serious about not forming an unsavory attachment.''

"There you go, thinking about getting me into bed again.''

Jayne's mouth fell open. "Such talk as that—''

"Such talk as that,'' he interrupted briskly, "is what we'll exchange. There will be no mincing of words between us.''

"This is America. No kings, remember? You'll *not* tell me what to do.''

"Fine, we'll be equals.''

In frustration, she studied his composed features. "You're deliberately agitating me.''

"I'm deliberately trying to get past your prejudices against men and any relapse on your part to stilted, insincere maidenly speech.''

"I am a maiden!''

"It's not a permanent condition. There's hope for you yet.''

"Oh! You have a perverted sense of humor.''

"Do you honestly think God put you here on earth to remain a virgin?''

"I honestly believe He *didn't* put me here to become your paramour!''

Burke rubbed his jaw. "Yeah, you're probably right about that.''

"Well then, this conversation is at an end.'' She was going to watch him every step of the way. He wanted to loan her money. Fine. Any ideas of hanky-panky he might be harboring were going to remain mere thoughts. Unfulfilled fantasies. Wishful longings. On *his* part, she reminded herself stoutly. "There's something you should know.''

"What's that?''

"I'm not the kind of woman to be courted.''

"That's convenient. I'm not the kind of man to participate in such an asinine ritual.''

"I bid you good-night, then.''

"I'll bid you the same." His formerly amused expression deepened to one of reflection. "Nothing will happen between us that you don't give permission to happen."

"Is that your way of telling me I'll be able to sleep tonight without worrying about you invading my bed?"

"I couldn't have said it better myself."

Despite his arrogant remarks, she believed him. "Thank you."

"You've given me something to think about."

She eyed him curiously. "What's that?"

"What does a man do with a woman who refuses to consider marriage and won't conduct an affair?"

"That's easy. He leaves her alone."

"Wrong answer, honey."

Honey? "Not if he's listening."

"Oh, I'm listening." He crossed the room and turned down the lamp.

The gathered shadow that was Burke moved toward the lit hallway.

How could foreboding and excitement well up within a person in the same moment? "Burke…"

"Yes?"

"I don't believe in love, not the romantic kind that supposedly occurs between men and women."

"That's something we agree upon."

The door closed with a soft click. Another option of where she could have spent the night tumbled into her thoughts. Without question, Emma Cade would have taken her in.

Had she deliberately ignored the possibility of staying with her friend so as to remain in Burke's company? Staring into the darkness, Jayne sensed that in matters involving the banker, she wasn't as objective as she'd fooled herself into believing.

The potential for trouble was certainly at hand.

She rolled to her side and comforted herself with the knowledge that Euphemia had raised her to resist any man's lure. And as soon as she found out precisely what his lure was, she was going to nip it in the bud.

Chapter Seven

The next morning, Burke grimly surveyed the scrambled eggs, ham and gravy-smothered potatoes his cook had prepared. Burke's displeasure had nothing to do with the meal served by his housekeeper, Margaret Bailey. It was eating his breakfast alone that was causing his frown. According to Mrs. Bailey, instead of venturing downstairs to share the morning repast, Jayne had requested that a tray be sent to her chamber.

When his housekeeper delivered the message, he had been unprepared for the disappointment that cut through him. No doubt, Jayne was self-conscious at having anyone, even his servants, view her battered countenance. Under the circumstances, her feelings were understandable. What he didn't understand was why the schoolmistress's absence affected his mood.

Burke bit into a warm soda biscuit. As he chewed, he noticed a dollop of honey on the china plate. The glossy pool was the same color as Jayne's hair. He recalled its silken splendor spread across her bed pillow and he shifted on his chair. Sinking his fingers into the tousled mass of silk was a memory he would carry to his grave.

It wasn't his custom to lie awake for hours thinking about a particular woman. The real source of his restlessness, surely, centered on saving his bank. And it was that concern, combined with a lack of sleep, that was making him short-tempered, not Jayne's absence from the table.

Burke cut into the slice of ham. When he proved Dilicar was behind the robberies, he would again enjoy uninterrupted sleep. His behavior would return to the familiar boundaries framing his logical nature. There would be no aberrations such as trying to teach Jayne his infamous lesson, or climbing through her second-story bedroom window.

He speared the ham and thrust it into his mouth, chewing without tasting it. She'd had every right to be outraged at his behavior. And yet, in the heat of the moment, it had seemed the most reasonable thing in the world to terrorize Jayne into recognizing her perilous, unprotected state.

Last night's conversation returned. Remembering his words to her he cringed. What had he been thinking to suggest it was possible for a man and woman to be friends? He didn't believe that for a minute. Perhaps a married man could have a friendship with a married woman. He considered Emma Cade a friend. But between a single man and single woman... It might be possible, if there was no physical attraction. He swallowed the ham. Such was definitely not the case between him and Jayne.

She wanted him to think the attraction was all on his side. Something in her gaze, a fleeting flare of female awareness, however, made him doubt that. If she felt no desire toward him, she wouldn't be so wary, so bent on spelling out her resistance. Or was that wishful thinking on his part? A man might tell himself any number of lies to experience the feminine fire that shone softly in Jayne Stoneworthy's solemn green eyes.

He reached for a goblet of water and drank deeply. Though he didn't like the way she filled his mind, crowding out concerns about saving his bank's charter, he told himself he needn't be troubled by the anomaly. Of course, she occupied his thoughts. A desirable woman had moved into his home. That he'd removed her outer garments, seen her in her female underpinnings, and that she'd slept under his roof was bound to affect him.

He returned the goblet to the pristine white tablecloth. How long had it been since he'd engaged in sex? Months, he reflected dourly. He'd told her he didn't pay for female companionship and had been insulted at her presumption he would. The cold truth was, he did barter for sexual release—not in brothels, but with sophisticated women who understood that he would reward them with jewels and other baubles for sleeping with him.

He might tell himself such gifts were unnecessary. But the subtle exchange allowed him to remain emotionally unencumbered. He gave pleasure. In turn, he was pleasured—physically. A civil transaction that satisfied both parties. Odd, how empty those encounters now seemed.

Burke pushed back his chair and stood. Making love to Jayne wouldn't be an empty experience. There was a fearlessness about her, an animation of personality, and zest for living that she would surely share with her lover. His blood heated at the image of her sweetly generous lovemaking.

He tossed the linen napkin to the table. The woman didn't believe in taking lovers. Nor did she believe in sly transactions that put her body on the auction block to the highest bidder. She didn't appear to believe in the holy sanctity of marriage, either, which should have cheered him. It didn't.

Jayne had created a life that precluded allowing any man access to her lithe form. *Bravo, Miss Stoneworthy, for your celibate destiny.* As he turned from the table, his words from last night drifted to him. She'd been right to ask what purpose it would serve for them to become friends. His answer had boxed him into a corner from which there was no escape. He shook his head. It was hard to believe he invariably won at chess, but then, when he played, he thought with the region above his waist.

If Jayne did agree to accompany him in the social pastimes he'd listed, he would be forced to live in a state of perpetual, unsatisfied sexual arousal. Surely he was smart enough to spare himself that hellish fate.

He turned to the doorway. There was no decision to make. For whatever reasons the schoolmistress appealed to him, he was damned well going to squash his attraction. In good conscience, he couldn't try to seduce a virtuous woman, driven by necessity to seek shelter in his home. When she was no longer his guest, it still would be dishonorable to slake his physical appetites with her.

Why had he let his mouth run away with him? *Not* acting on his outlandish words held no appeal, but that was what honor obliged. She'd done something to him, he thought darkly. Somehow she'd broken through a layer of control he'd thought impregnable. Last night, he'd felt reckless, prodded to sample the lady's charms. Hell, he'd been feeling…playful.

How did she do that, make him feel protective, possessive *and* lighthearted? The playfulness she'd stirred was utterly foreign to his temperament. He was a serious man with a serious problem. He had no time for the kind of bedroom antics the prim schoolmistress sent tripping through his thoughts, especially since neither he nor she felt inclined to marry. With her moral objections to conducting an affair and her reputation to preserve, she was the last female on earth he should try to entice to his bed.

The irony wasn't lost on him that he couldn't remember another woman ever tempting him as much as Jayne. It was a good thing he was a man of superior self-discipline. Otherwise, they would both be in trouble. Confident of his ability to resist the prickly but beguiling schoolmistress, he stepped from the room.

Oomph…

Rushing down the hallway that Burke's housekeeper had directed her to, Jayne plunged into a solid figure that seemed to come from nowhere. To keep her balance, she raised her hands to his chest. "Excuse me!"

Two strong palms anchored her shoulders. She didn't

need his steadying influence, but it seemed churlish to jerk away.

"I beg your pardon." She attributed her breathlessness to her hurried pace. She uncurled her fingers from the lapels of his black jacket. "I didn't mean to run you down."

"I thought you'd decided to have breakfast in your room."

The contusions marring his face failed to lessen his rugged appeal, Jayne thought. Instead, an aura of dangerous charisma edged his features. It wasn't fair. While last night's brawl sharpened Burke's already lethal attractiveness, she was left looking like a lump of white dough run over by a wagon.

"I finished. The meal was delicious. Your cook is marvelous."

She knew her voice was too highly pitched, but lodged somewhere in his brain was the memory of how she looked in her chemise and pantalettes. Contemplating that made her skin burn and her pulse flutter.

"It occurred to me, however," she began, determined to propel this conversation to its conclusion, "that we should organize our day."

His eyebrows rose. "*Our* day?"

"There's so much to do and so little time to accomplish it. I've made a mental list of things for you to attend to this morning, but I really should write it down. I was hoping you could provide me with pen and paper."

His hands still rested upon her shoulders. If she restricted her gaze to his chin, she found she could hold on to her thoughts better. Odd how, even after seeing a person several times, one observed new details about him. Burke's well-defined jaw was slightly squared. She'd failed to notice before the slight cleft bisecting his chin. The unexpected urge to press her fingertip into the small crease mystified her.

"The library is the best place to conduct business."

If she weren't standing so close, it might occur to him

to lower his hands. She stepped back. "As I said, I have things mentally organized. It's just a matter of putting everything on paper."

The weight of his touch disappeared. Assuming he would take her arm to guide her down the hallway, she braced herself for the renewed contact. But he moved aside and gestured for her to proceed. She absolutely was *not* disappointed by his oversight. It was just that things would be easier if he remained somewhat predictable.

There was no reason to feel self-conscious that he followed behind her. And yet, she wondered if his disturbing gaze was affixed upon any particular part of her anatomy, and what that part might be.

They passed several open doorways. She caught glimpses of a parlor, a sitting room and the elegant gallery she and her students from Hempshire Academy had visited before the school had burned. Each chamber was plushly appointed with exquisitely carved furniture, brocade upholsteries and velvet draperies. Crystal chandeliers, freshly cut floral bouquets and heavy silver candelabra also abounded. She marveled at the costly oasis he'd created for himself. The three-story, red brick mansion with its six white columns could easily have accommodated a family of ten. One man calling the palatial edifice home revealed both the extent of his wealth and his need to preen.

As he stepped ahead and gestured toward the doorway on her right, however, she admitted there was nothing pretentious about him. Burke Youngblood strode through the halls of his home as unselfconsciously as he might have traipsed along a mountain trail. He moved with a masculine grace she hadn't realized even existed.

He wore another black dress coat that accentuated his broad-shouldered, lean-hipped physique. Knowing that the jacket that he'd worn last night had been torn from him during the wild brawl, Jayne wondered if his wardrobe consisted entirely of white shirts, black dress coats and matching trousers. He probably had them lined up in a neat row, with another row of polished black boots standing at attention beneath them.

Grateful they'd reached their destination, she entered a large chamber lined with tall shelves filled with leather-bound volumes. Being in a room populated abundantly with books always made her pulse race. She resisted the urge to draw closer and read the titles. Once her school was established, she hoped to instill within her students a love of literature.

Tearing her gaze from the leather spines, she scanned the chamber. It was appointed as she would like to arrange her office. Two padded maroon chairs were situated across from a wide, beautifully polished desk. She didn't think she'd ever envied anyone as much as she envied him this library.

He pointed to one of the chairs. "Have a seat."

She complied and smoothed the folds of her gray skirt. The housekeeper had returned the gown that morning, cleaned and pressed. Her substantially battered valise had provided fresh undergarments. The bath she'd enjoyed earlier left her feeling almost normal. She resisted pressing her fingertips to the side of her face, just as she suppressed the vanity that made her want to avert her swollen cheek and blackened eye from his inspection.

Burke Youngblood was a business associate, nothing more. Since she had every intention of keeping him so, she would have to get over the self-consciousness she experienced in his company. Now was an excellent time to focus his attention upon opening her school. She should be grateful for the morning sunlight pouring through the parted maroon draperies, just as she should be grateful that her beleaguered face repelled him.

Burke withdrew a volume from a shelf, then pulled open a desk drawer and retrieved several sheets of paper, along with a pen. He handed her the book first, then the other materials. "Now you can make your notes."

She accepted the items. His coolness was unmistakable.

Euphemia had maintained that men gravitated toward women based solely on their physical appearance, which was why her aunt had advised against wearing clothes that would accentuate Jayne's female attributes. Other than getting a good look at her damaged face, no other reason existed for Burke's frigid disinterest.

Jayne told herself that his fickleness didn't come as a disappointment. She was relieved to be spared his unwelcome attentions during her brief stay in his home. Yes, that was exactly how she felt, relieved. And, if she did experience a tiny pang of regret, it was only because no man had ever gazed at her with the same hot intensity Burke Youngblood had.

She neatened the papers and laid them on the leather book resting on her lap, then wrote the numeral *1*. "The first point I wish to settle is that you will keep an accurate tally of the funds you advance me."

Burke sat behind the desk and withdrew a pen from the inkwell. "That's the kind of detail you don't need to remind a banker to attend to."

Jayne nodded in satisfaction. Good, he was looking at their association in business terms. "As I've said, I'll shortly be receiving a bank draft from my uncle. He's sent several letters, the most recent indicating he plans on giving me twenty-five hundred dollars."

Burke whistled softly. "That's pretty generous."

"I know." Jayne looked up from her notes. "You can't imagine how shocked I was to discover I even had an uncle, let alone that he planned on sending such a large amount of money."

"Wait a minute, you didn't know you had an uncle?"

"I thought Aunt Euphemia was my only relative. Evidently Uncle Clarence and my family had a severe falling out shortly after my father made him a loan. I don't know the particulars, but in all the time I was growing up, my uncle's name was never mentioned."

"That's the way families treat black sheep."

"You're probably right," Jayne said thoughtfully. "From Clarence's letters, he wants to make restitution for a wrong he apparently feels he caused my parents. When I answered his first note, I assured him that he needn't repay me. But I did look forward to meeting him."

"You turned down his offer?" Burke asked, his tone mildly skeptical.

"His debt wasn't to me. I didn't want him to feel that the only way I would reestablish a family connection was if he paid me."

"I'm sure he considered your attitude refreshing." Burke settled back in his chair. "It's been my experience that, when a long-lost, *rich* relative shows up, family members generally anticipate a financial windfall."

Faint mockery coated Burke's observation. Jayne wondered if he had always been so cynical, or if a cataclysmic life event had rendered him so coldhearted. The foolish urge unfurled within her to reassure him that everyone didn't have an ulterior motive for his actions, that selfishness and greed were not at the core of every decision made. Then she recalled her own suspicions of *his* motives for offering assistance and realized she was the last person to sermonize about trusting others.

"Uncle Clarence wouldn't let me decline the money. From his correspondence, I gather he's a wealthy Philadelphia businessman."

"What trade?"

"He's never mentioned the source of his livelihood. My impression is that he's retired and watches over various investments."

"Has he given you a date you can expect the bank draft?"

"His last letter indicated I could receive it any time." It was strange. Before she'd known about her uncle and the money he intended sending, she'd been managing adequately. But, once she knew he planned on mailing it, it seemed as if she had a desperate need for the sum. She never would have splurged on the glass-paneled doors without the promised draft. Nor would she have placed that additional order for more textbooks. "So, there's nothing to prevent us from proceeding," she said brightly, fearing Burke might be having second thoughts about advancing the loan. "I want to reestablish myself in another building as soon as possible."

"This evening we'll visit the place I've located. If you approve, we'll start the renovation immediately."

At the word "we," warmth suffused her. Since her aunt's death, Jayne had felt terribly alone. Even though they were only business associates, it was comforting to know she was no longer completely on her own. She knew her feelings were inconsistent with how she'd been raised. Independence should have meant everything, and Burke's inclusion of himself in her affairs should have been a curse. But, even though she recognized the paradox, she couldn't banish the inexorable lifting of her spirits.

"Do you think it's going to require much remodeling?" She dreaded the thought of enduring another round of workmen wreaking havoc.

"The previous owner ran a small general store with living accommodations above. The business proved so profitable, he's moved to bigger quarters. It won't be difficult to add interior walls for classrooms."

Even though Burke spoke lightly of the project, it sounded daunting. She wished she could close her eyes and will the school into existence. "I can hardly wait to see it."

Burke leaned forward, resting his elbows on the desk. The barely checked enthusiasm reflected in Jayne's eyes tugged at his resolve to keep his thoughts on business. Her simmering excitement kindled a primitive awareness within him.

He struggled against the powerful urge to remove the desk's barrier and draw her hands into his, just so he could partake of the warmth she radiated. He knew, however, that holding her hands would not appease the sensual tension tightening his skin.

His gaze went to her mouth. "I'm impressed you recognize the wisdom of waiting until dark to venture out."

"After looking into the mirror this morning, I'm not remotely tempted to show my face in public."

You're achingly lovely.... The words hovered dangerously close to being spoken. He gritted his teeth and cursed Gideon Cade for asking his damned favor. It was hard to believe that, twenty-four hours earlier, his life had been running smoothly. Well, maybe not smoothly, not with the robberies plaguing him. But he'd been able to be in a room with a woman and have his brain function. And he'd also been able to control his body sufficiently so as not to embarrass himself.

They were just talking. More than six feet separated them. And, thankfully, so did the barrier of his desk. "You had a list to discuss?"

Her green eyes became even brighter. He smothered a groan, willing her to dim the feminine vibrancy she seemed to have no idea was exciting him.

She looked at the paper he'd given her and began writing industriously. "I've contacted four women who live in town to serve as instructors. They have academic backgrounds, are married and would like to earn extra income for their families. I need to draft and mail letters telling them about the new location for the school."

Burke began his own list. "You'll want those letters posted soon."

"Yes. I've already mailed correspondence to sixty families in the area with daughters between thirteen and eighteen years of age, informing them about my school."

He looked up. "That was a sizable undertaking."

"Loutitia Hempshire provided the names. Even though her records were lost in the fire, she was able to recall most of her students."

Jayne placed the end of her pen between her lips and

made a delicate sucking gesture. Burke shifted uncomfortably, reminding himself that the woman had no idea she was torturing him. That was the trouble with innocent females. They acted provocatively without realizing it.

"How many girls do you plan on instructing?"

"Thirty would let me meet all expenses, along with making a profit."

"Did you mention where you planned on holding your school in the correspondence you sent out?"

A rosy blush stained Jayne's cheeks. "Uh, it was just a preliminary letter. The mailing occurred before I'd settled up on a particular building."

"Considering the place you chose, I'd say that was a stroke of luck."

"Uh, yes."

Risky area for conversation. Talking about the brothel was bound to trigger memories of his outrageous actions when he'd slung her over his shoulder, carried her upstairs and tossed her onto that unmade bed. Damn, why couldn't he forget her elusive feminine scent and the sweet taste of the kiss he'd stolen?

Because both the scent and taste are branded into your brain.

"What's the next item on your list?"

It wasn't a croak. He cleared his throat and found himself counting the seconds until this meeting was over. He wondered if he were losing his mind. Surely, preferring dealing with the odoriferous likes of Pappy Pickman to conversing with lovely, sweet-smelling Jayne was an indictment of his deteriorating mental processes.

Chapter Eight

Jayne took a final glance of her reflection in the bedchamber mirror. She tried not to notice that, instead of fading, the bruises appeared to be getting more vivid.

Their first evening meal had passed in relative silence. Darkness had settled. It was time for Burke to keep his promise and show her the building he'd found. She wanted to believe the thrill of anticipation she experienced was due to their destination. Honesty compelled her to admit, though, that it wasn't the prospect of viewing a wooden structure that was making her heart race.

She descended the first tread on the stairs. He stood in the foyer below, dressed in black. His expression appeared watchful. Her stomach trembled. His innate strength heightened her fierce awareness of him.

Was this how Persephone had felt when forced to join the lord of the underworld? The fanciful question struck Jayne as she reached the last step. She tried to dismiss the eerie feeling that she was surrendering to a force stronger than herself.

"It's warm outside. You won't need a shawl or cloak."

The chill stirred by his deep voice seemed to contradict the claim.

"Then I'm ready."

He offered his arm. She stared at the black sleeve before

gingerly resting her fingers against the smoothly textured fabric. Beneath the civilizing layer of material, she felt the raw power at his command.

They walked in silence down the hall. The sensation persisted that he was taking her to his own private world. Only the lightest touch connected them. Had they been joined by handcuffs, she doubted she could have felt more bound to him. The pads of her fingertips had never been so sensitive. Through them, she sensed the subtle flexing of male muscle and sinew.

When they stepped into the moonlit night, she glanced toward his rigid profile. Paradoxically, the darkness imbued him with warring auras. On the one hand, he looked invincible enough to overcome any imaginable threat. Conversely, the sheer force of his masculine strength posed its own danger. Despite the results of last evening's altercation, she didn't doubt he was well suited for the role of protector. But if he chose to use his power against her, to whom could she turn for protection?

A coach and driver awaited them on the street. With a swift economy of motion, he assisted her into the vehicle and called out directions before joining her on the opposite seat. The inner carriage lantern cast him in shadows. No longer could she endure the tense silence that had reigned during the dinner they had shared.

With a determination born of nervousness, she smiled. "You have no idea how excited I am to see the building you've found. From how you've described it, it sounds almost perfect. Do you anticipate any difficulty engaging carpenters? With all the construction going on, I've found qualified workmen are in short supply."

Abruptly her mind went blank of innocuous remarks. She resented his tranquil bearing as he sat across from her in the gently swaying carriage.

"I don't foresee any problems hiring competent carpenters. Denver's growing so fast, it's attracting hundreds of building craftsmen."

"Oh." Silence descended between them. She assured herself it was only her imagination making it seem his pensive gaze was anchored to her mouth. Something about the carriage's weak light, no doubt, fostered the illusion.

When the vehicle came to a halt, Jayne said a silent prayer of gratitude. Again, she endured his casual handling as he assisted her down to the boardwalk. She considered the row of buildings spread out before them. The neighboring shops consisted of far more respectable businesses than those at her school's present location. There wasn't a tavern or saloon in sight on either side of the tree-lined street. The district even boasted the new style of gas lamps that had begun to spring up across town.

"You'll notice it will take only minor adjustments to the door casings to accommodate the glass panels from your place."

He was right.

Beside the front entry, charmingly designed oval windows caught her attention. There were three on each side of the entry. "It's more lovely than I could have wished for."

He fished a key from his pocket. "Let's go in and see what you think."

He unlocked the door and walked in. She didn't stray far into the darkened room, but he strode boldly forward, quickly lighting lamps sitting atop large barrels. The main area had been emptied of merchandise and also stripped of shelves and display counters. Despite planks of missing wood from the walls and floor, a feeling of exhilaration stirred. The high ceiling and generous interior dimensions would permit large and airy chambers.

"You're right. This room could easily accommodate the four classrooms, parlor and office I want." Her words echoed in the vacant space. She moved carefully across the floor, which was littered with broken glass, piles of dirt and debris and wadded clumps of newspaper.

"The upstairs consists of two bedchambers, a sitting

room, a kitchen, equipped with a coal stove and running water, and a necessary."

The features he described made relocating even more desirable. For weeks she'd searched for a building in which to have her school, but everything, except the tavern, had been beyond her means. She feared the cost of this building was also beyond her limited resources.

"The upstairs apartment was left as neat as a pin. It won't take much to clean up this mess and make the changes you need."

She turned to him. "You don't have to sell me. I love it and the neighborhood. It would be absolutely perfect, but..."

"What?"

"I don't think I'll get enough from the sale of the Wet...er...the tavern to pay for something this size, with all its amenities."

He pushed back his jacket and slid a hand into his pocket. "Haven't you heard of a mortgage?"

Jayne frowned. "Of course, but no bank will issue a mortgage to a woman with my meager funds."

"You're forgetting whom you're talking to."

"I know to whom I am speaking," she replied. But did she?

Protector or menace?

The words played a game of chase through her jumbled thoughts. She reminded herself of the fine line separating a personal relationship from a professional one. "I've made it clear I'm not asking for any special favors."

"Because you're not willing to offer special compensation in return?" The question shimmered with casual insolence.

"That's right."

"If I loan you the difference between what you get from the sale of your present building and what this one costs, it will be because it's a sound business decision."

She'd always considered herself a fairly trusting person. Why was it so hard to trust him?

Because Burke Youngblood affects you differently than any man you've ever known. Nor was it just his physical effect making her so uncomfortable. He possessed some peculiar kind of male magic that corrupted her thoughts. Standing a few feet from him in a room of darkened corners, she was struck by the bizarre urge to draw closer and run her palm across his faintly stubbled jaw. Should she take such an outrageous liberty, she doubted he would remain so coolly aloof. What *would* he do?

The thought of his taking her into his arms and kissing her made her knees tremble. When he'd fastened his mouth to hers before, the event had been so hurried she'd scarcely had time to absorb the myriad of feelings rushing though her. Besides, she'd been defending herself, which had afforded little opportunity to analyze the queer phenomenon of being kissed.

She fiddled with her reticule drawstrings. "You know as well as I do why I'm uneasy about our business dealings."

"Because I'm a man, and you're a woman?"

She straightened. "That's right."

"Relax, Jayne, I'll spell out our agreement in black and white in the form of a legal document that will keep our association strictly professional. And we'll sign the agreement before witnesses."

She was grateful no document would ever require her to put her lascivious thoughts on paper. If Burke discovered that in the space of a day and a night he'd managed to sway a lifetime of moral teachings, she would die of mortification—not that she would ever act upon those licentious yearnings.

As long as Burke kept his hands and his lips to himself, she was safe in his company. From his formal behavior throughout the day, it was obvious she needn't fear any additional inappropriate behavior on his part.

"I can only say that I love this building and would like nothing more than to have my school here."

A hard half smile edged his narrow lips. He stepped forward. "Then let's shake hands, *partner*."

Her palm was engulfed by his warm, unyielding grip. The subtle friction of flesh sliding against flesh sent a hot flush careening through parts of her she'd scarcely realized even existed.

She briefly closed her eyes, recalling Euphemia's embroidered message on the gold-tasseled pillow. For the first time in her life, Jayne felt that furrow's tingling presence. She blushed profusely.

Truth be told, it was probably Burke Youngblood who should be bolting his bedchamber door at night.

"Do you suppose shooting him would get his attention?"

It took a moment before Gideon's question to Hunter Moran penetrated Burke's thoughts. His head came up sharply. He and his friends had dismounted and were watering their horses at the rocky shoreline of a fast-running stream. Juniper, foxtail and piñon pines shot up in varying heights between the enormous granite boulders sprawled across the rugged landscape. Yellow rabbit brush, crimson Indian paintbrush and white prickly poppies were among the pungent wildflowers growing in the dense mountain grass.

"He's so far gone, a dozen bullets peppering his hide wouldn't get his attention." Hunter jerked the red neckerchief from his throat, pushed back his tan Stetson and mopped his brow. "I'd say he hasn't heard a word we've said for the past ten minutes."

"Maybe he's not interested in the subject," Gideon suggested.

"Yeah, trying to connect the robberies at his bank with Dilcar is bound to be boring." Hunter retied the scrap of red fabric around his neck.

Burke wanted to toss Gideon and Hunter's joking words back at them. Unfortunately, they were right. His thoughts had drifted. No, not drifted. They'd flown with arrowlike directness to Jayne Stoneworthy. She'd been living with him for almost two weeks. Without a doubt, that span of time represented the most frustrating days and nights he'd ever experienced.

It didn't do much for his pride to admit he'd stayed away from her during the daytime because he didn't trust himself to be alone with her. The more he was around the school-mistress, the more susceptible he became to her eccentric charms. On a couple of occasions, he'd come close to claiming her cultured little mouth in a straightforward kiss that would have probably earned him another whack on the head.

He'd ordered his assistant, Owen Gardner, to oversee the move from the Wet Beaver, the sale of that property and the renovation of the new building.

Burke didn't want to think about the frustration he endured each night as he lay awake, hard and aching, visualizing the chaste Jayne Stoneworthy nestled snugly in the second-floor bedchamber he'd provided her. Nor did he want to think about her recent insistence that, now that the discoloration had faded from her bruised face, she should move into Agnes Sawyer's Boarding Domicile for Single Females.

Imagining his home without Jayne made his heart chill. Even though he hadn't spent much time with her, having her there satisfied him in a fundamental way he couldn't explain. Despite the inner turmoil her presence caused, knowing she soon would be gone made the future bleak.

He wasn't sentimental. But somehow, when he thought of Jayne, he pictured her awash in colors similar to the wildflowers carpeting this high mountain valley. Maybe it was the enthusiasm that vibrated through her when she spoke, or the sparkle in her eyes when she quoted one of her late aunt's derogatory observations about the male gender, or maybe it was simply the way she *was*.... Direct, fearless and unapologetically independent. Whatever the elusive qualities forming the character and person of Jayne Stoneworthy, he found himself wanting her more than he'd ever wanted another woman.

When she left, she would take the color with her. He would be reduced to existing in the lifeless shadows that formed his world. Why hadn't he realized the dreary dimensions of that world before Jayne had entered it?

"We've lost him again," Gideon muttered.

"When he drifts off, where do you suppose he goes?"

The amused speculation lacing Hunter's question penetrated Burke's reflections. Damn, pondering the merits of Jayne Stoneworthy was becoming a habit. He should be thanking his Maker she would soon be gone.

"I'm listening." Burke tried conceal his impatience with himself. "I was thinking about what a waste of time it was to ride out to Sutton's ranch."

"The rumor Sutton put Corbett Baldwin on his payroll was worth checking out. If Baldwin's here, it isn't for the piddling wages a wrangler earns."

"Gideon's right," Hunter said. "An outlaw on the run doesn't plant his butt in a saddle to chase steers."

Frank Sutton had a history of hiring guns for his operation. He'd used underhanded methods to acquire additional grazing lands for his ranch and made lots of enemies. The man craved the kind of protection a professional packed in his holster. Corbett Baldwin wasn't a typical bodyguard, though. He'd been connected with a string of stagecoach robberies all the way to Mexico. It wouldn't take much to tempt him to try his hand at robbing banks.

Burke scowled. "With rails joining boomtowns springing up overnight, it's too damn easy for a criminal to hop a train and put a thousand miles between himself and any lawman on his trail."

"I know," Gideon agreed, "but according to Sutton, he hasn't hired Baldwin."

"I've heard he fancies himself a lady's man," Hunter drawled. "And he isn't too particular about whether or not the lady's willing."

"I'm sorry you joined me on what turned out to be a wild-goose chase." Burke reached for his horse's reins and led the animal toward the road that would take them back to Denver. "Who spotted Baldwin, anyway?"

"Nat Walker," Hunter answered.

No one said anything as they guided their mounts from the streambed up the grassy incline.

Nat Walker was Hunter's foreman, levelheaded, honest and hardworking. He'd done his share of traveling, and if he said he saw Corbett Baldwin riding across Sutton's range, the odds were Nat Walker was right.

Damn...

"You're not in this alone, Burke." It was Hunter who broke the momentary silence.

"We know your charter's on the line," Gideon added. "And we're here to make sure you keep it."

Not for the first time, Burke realized the bond between himself and these two friends was as strong as that of brothers. They'd faced death together and protected each other's backs. The partnership they'd formed, combining the assets of Hunter's sprawling cattle ranch, Gideon's freighting empire and Burke's network of banks made them three of the richest men in the state.

However, it was respect and friendship that formed the bedrock of their association.

When they reached the road leading to town, Burke decided to share an idea that had been bouncing around in his head. "This might sound crazy, but I've decided to cut down the number of armed men I've got posted."

"With that bounty out there, your place will become an even more tempting target," Gideon said reflectively.

"Which means you want to invite another robbery?"

Burke had always admired Hunter's quick mind. "If Corbett Baldwin's in the area and thinking about accepting that bounty, he's a bigger threat than Pappy Pickman. If I catch Baldwin, though, he'd know who was paying him.''

"That's a couple of big 'ifs,''' Gideon observed. "You would have to capture him alive *and* get him to talk.''

"But you're right about Baldwin being the kind of man who would know, going in, the name of the person fronting the money to pull a job like robbing the First National,'' Hunter said approvingly. "It's an audacious plan. But if you cut the number of guards, you're bound to snare someone in your trap.''

"And that someone could be the person to lead us to Dilicar.'' Gideon slapped his leather gloves against his thigh. "Hunter's right. It's an audacious scheme, but damn it, Burke. It could work.''

As he saw his friends' determined expressions, Burke was strangely humbled by their unswerving loyalty.

"Uh, I'm sorry if I seemed a little distracted.''

"No doubt the woman you've got living with you has something to do with your lack of concentration,'' Gideon said blandly.

The casual statement hit Burke with the icy impact of a plunge into a frigid mountain lake. His gaze snapped to his companions. "You're mistaken.''

"Am I?'' Gideon asked. The male amusement in his eyes made Burke want to shove his friend down the embankment they'd walked up.

Hunter squinted toward the red ball descending behind jagged granite peaks. "It's getting late. We'd best head back.''

The three men mounted. Burke cleared his throat and held up his hand. "Sometimes a man finds himself needing to protect a lady's reputation,'' he said by way of apology for his abruptness. "I seem to be in that position.''

"Been there,'' Gideon said. "Hurts like hell, but it's worth it.''

Burke knew Gideon was referring to Emma. Again it

rubbed him wrong that his friend was so open about his feelings for his new wife.

"I haven't *been there,* as you put it. Nor do I plan on going. This is a temporary thing, nothing like what happened between you and Emma."

"Too bad," Hunter said with maddening cheerfulness. "Of the three of us, I'd say Gideon is the happiest."

Burke found it ironic that several months ago Hunter had speculated about how it would feel to be married to the right woman. Gideon and Burke hadn't had any interest in the topic, and Hunter's foreman, Nat Walker, had ridiculed the idea of there being a *right* woman for any man. Now both Gideon and Nat were married. Jayne was living in his home. Yet Hunter continued to remain miraculously free from any female entanglements.

It was a strange world.

"I am happy," Gideon said evenly. "I'm blessed with the most beautiful, most intelligent, bravest, most loyal woman on earth as my wife."

Both Hunter and Burke groaned.

"Give it a rest," Burke snarled.

"Yeah, have some pity on us bachelors," Hunter chimed in.

"You won't be bachelors forever," Gideon said.

Burke scowled. "I'd just as soon you cursed me as say something like that—or shoot me. It isn't natural for a man to be so content."

Hunter laughed. "You're just contrary, Burke. I wouldn't mind some sweet-smelling, soft-talking woman making me the center of her world."

"A man in love is a fool," Burke responded dourly.

"How do you figure that?" Gideon asked curiously.

Burke was more than happy to supply him with the festering answer. "The first thing a man loses when he thinks he's in love is his ability to think rationally."

Gideon scratched his jaw. "I can't argue with you there."

His friend's honesty startled Burke. "You admit I'm right?"

"Yeah, what of it?"

"You know better than anyone a man can't afford to waste his time mooning over a bit of fluff in skirts. It's a cold, hard world. A person has to be on guard. Besides, the notion of falling in love is something women make up to trap men into marriage."

Hunter shook his head. "Even though it's not something I've personally experienced, even I know love is real. Look how happy Gideon and Emma are. And look at Nat. He's been walking on air since he and that pretty seamstress tied the knot. Even Gideon's butler has mellowed since he took a wife."

"Emma and I *are* happy," Gideon said emphatically. "And we share a hell of a lot more than what transpires in our bedchamber. I expect my feelings to be the same when we're decrepit old-timers hobbling around with canes."

"Love is sentimental hogwash," Burke maintained stubbornly. "The best way to enjoy a woman is temporarily. Nothing beats variety."

"Who are you trying to convince, us or yourself?" Hunter asked.

"What do you mean?"

"Well, it's been months since you've escorted any of your fancy women around town."

"That's right," Hunter said. "If I didn't know better, I'd say you've reformed your wild ways, Burke."

Ordinarily his friends' good-natured ribbing didn't bother him. It made him uncomfortable, though, to realize they were right. It had been months since he'd been with a woman. It didn't cheer his mood to realize that the only female he wanted to be with was Jayne.

Gideon had a suspicious gleam in his eyes. "Has your turning over a new leaf got anything to do with your houseguest?"

Burke shifted his position on the saddle. "That subjec is off-limits."

"So you said, but the woman in question happens to b my wife's best friend, and I was the one who asked you t check on her. I had no idea at the time, though, you in tended to take such a *personal* interest."

"Who else knows Jayne's living with me?" Burke de manded. He had to know if he'd compromised the school mistress's reputation.

"Aside from your servants, no one besides me and Hun ter."

"How did you find out?"

"I caught a glimpse of her going up the stairs as I cam out of your library this morning."

Burke pulled his hat down over his forehead. "That in formation goes no further than the three of us."

"My wife is bound to find out sooner or later."

"Better later," Burke snapped. "There's a good reaso Miss Stoneworthy accepted my hospitality."

"I'm sure there is. My question is why you issued th invitation?"

Burke remained silent.

"Emma is quite attached to Miss Stoneworthy. May inquire what your intentions are toward the lady?"

"My *intentions?*" Burke asked, astonished by Gideon' gall.

"That's right."

"They're none of your damned business."

"Maybe not. But I can't help wondering how a refine woman such as the Eastern schoolmistress fits in with you preference for a casual string of female companions."

Burke had pondered the same riddle. "As you're awar Miss Stoneworthy and I share a business connection. I' following through on your request that I help get her scho started."

"When I asked you to get her out of the whorehouse, wasn't thinking of your home as an alternative."

"I always thought Miss Stoneworthy was a fine-looking lady. She didn't strike me as the type to trade her favors for—"

Burke swung around on the saddle. "Shut up, Hunter."

The rancher's steady stare increased Burke's discomfort. "If it's just business, why are you acting like you've got a rattler in your boot?"

"The first sign of a man falling in love," Gideon said, "is he gets short-tempered."

"No chance in hell of that happening," Burke coldly informed his friend. "I've made it a policy not to be governed by mawkish sentiment, which definitely includes falling in love. I've got three rules against it."

Hunter looked amazed, then hooted.

Gideon shook his head. "Now, I've heard everything—rules against falling in love."

"They're good rules," Burke said defensively.

Hunter grinned. "What are they?"

"Rule number one—only an imbecile gives his heart to a woman. Rule number two—marriage is a lifelong prison sentence. Rule number three—always remember rules one and two."

"If you follow them, you'll end up a bitter old man."

"A bitter, *lonely,* old man," Gideon added.

"I'll end up sane and happy, thank you."

Gideon cleared his throat. "Well, good luck. Keep me posted on Miss Stoneworthy's debts. I'll reimburse you as you go along."

"There's no need for that. I've decided to cover her expenses."

Burke frowned at the speaking glances Hunter and Gideon exchanged. Then, by silent accord, Burke and his companions urged their horses to a steady canter, making further conversation impossible.

Hauling out his thoughts and having his friends laugh at them did nothing to lighten Burke's already grim mood. Nor did the knowledge Jayne soon would be moving into

Agnes Sawyer's boardinghouse. The schoolmistress ha
barely entered his life, and now she was leaving it. H
should have...

What? Spent less of his energies finding out who wa
behind the robberies? That was the kind of idiotic behavio
a lovesick dolt would exhibit. He'd worked long and har
to build a life for himself in the West, away from the in
fluence and prestige of the Youngblood banking empire hi
grandfather had begun in Boston.

Lately he'd considered linking his network of banks wit
those his brother owned. If that happened, Burke woul
know the bitterness existing between him and Logan wa
finally past. To bring something of worth to the partnership
the First National had to be saved. That meant he had t
prove Dilicar was behind the robberies.

While she'd lived with him, he'd told himself the wa
he waged to save his bank was keeping him from her. Th
truth was, he was afraid to be alone with her, afraid h
wouldn't keep his word to behave as a gentleman.

He thought of her sleeping in her bed, imagining the so
friction of her nightgown brushing against her naked ski
thought of her sunk to her shoulders in scented bathwate
and lost himself to remembering the way she tipped he
head to expose the feminine curve of her throat. Damn, hi
thoughts made him dangerous and unpredictable.

Why *this* woman? Why now, at this impossible time? H
wanted to believe that, after she was gone, his feeling
would settle down.

Abruptly, the question he'd asked in Jayne's bedchambe
returned.

What does a man do with a woman who refuses to con
sider marriage and won't conduct an affair?

Reconsider his reservations against the state of ho
wedlock...

At the monumentally wrong answer, Burke almost fe
off his horse.

Chapter Nine

A sense of dislocation struck Jayne as she stood in the building she'd once envisioned as her school. Instead of two weeks, it felt as if a lifetime had passed since Burke had stormed into the tavern and demanded she join him in an upstairs bedchamber. Her footsteps echoed as she moved among barrels and nailed shut crates.

She was at a loss to explain the alienness of her surroundings. Neither she nor the lumber-strewn great room had changed discernibly in fourteen short days. Living with Burke couldn't have altered her. Sharing his home was like taking up residence with a phantom. He was gone during the days, seeing to his business affairs. Most evenings he failed to appear during the evening meal. Now and then she caught a glimpse of him as they passed in the hall, or he'd left a room as she entered it.

She ran a fingertip across the scarred bar top. He'd kept his word in all areas. Through his assistant, Owen Gardner, she'd been able to oversee the details of relocating and remodeling. Burke had found a buyer for the tavern, receiving an extremely generous price. Her mood should be optimistic, not disheartened. Jayne gazed morosely into space.

He said he would pursue you.

Whenever her thoughts regressed to "he" or "him," it

was always Burke they centered upon. Recalling the afternoon he'd come charging into the tavern, demanding her services as a good-time gal, she frowned. He'd swept her into his embrace and carried her upstairs as if he were an invading conqueror, and she was his to do with as he pleased.

It should have felt horrible, being at his mercy. Strangely, though, horrible didn't accurately describe the feeling of being held in his powerful arms. Nor did it describe the unforgettable sensation of his mouth moving possessively over hers.

At the conclusion of that shattering encounter—after he'd regained consciousness, of course—he'd informed her that he would return and forcibly escort her to a hotel. Hours had then passed with him failing to show up. She'd been primed for a major confrontation, and it had appeared there wouldn't be one. She'd felt restless, charged for a battle that had been canceled at the last moment. That was how she felt now, prepared to put the man in his place and make it clear that she was immune to his sneaky male charm. Only her phantom benefactor was nowhere to be seen.

How could one tell a puff of smoke to behave itself, er, himself? She shook her head in consternation. The man was confounding her ordinarily logical thought processes. He didn't know it yet, but tonight was her last evening in his home. Owen Gardner had secured her a room at Agnes Sawyer's Boarding Domicile for Single Females. Hopefully, placing distance between herself and Burke would render her the intelligent woman she'd been before he'd invaded her life. So, why wasn't the prospect of leaving his home shooting off firecrackers of enthusiasm?

Considering the new building Burke had found was speedily being transformed into the school of her dreams, it was ridiculous to feel anything less than euphoric.

A new consideration slithered into her reflections. The last time she'd written off Burke as all talk and no action, he'd scaled the tavern's outside wall and showed up in her bedchamber, oozing arrogance and a daunting kind of masculine appeal that had set her pulse aflutter and succeeded in making her his business partner and houseguest. Not only was he unpredictable, but so was she when in his persuasive company for any length of time. She'd best stay on her guard.

Burke might be a member of the brutish sex her aunt had warned her against, but doing battle with the rogue was invigorating. She thought it wouldn't be an altogether appalling experience for him to kiss her again. She would resist—eventually. But in the interest of conducting a scientific experiment, she could postpone that resistance for a few breathless seconds. This time she would explore the mysterious sensations he sparked within her.

How precisely had his solid chest felt beneath her fingertips? What was the nature of the heat he ignited beneath her fevered skin? And what would have happened if she'd opened her lips more fully to his tongue's trespass? When his hardened lower body pressed intimately against the sensitive cradle of her parted thighs, something elusive but powerful had stirred within her.

"Here, kitty, kitty, kitty..."

The call splintered Jayne's reverie. Flushing, she glanced around the empty room. Outside the glass-paneled door, a figure stood.

"Here, kitty, kitty, kitty..."

Light tapping sounded against the glass. Jayne went to the door and opened it. Immediately a cloud of heavy cologne washed over her.

"Excuse me." A tall, generously curved woman with red curls poking from beneath the wide, purple brim of a peacock-feathered hat greeted Jayne. "I'm sorry to bother you, but I'm looking for my cat."

Despite her painted face, the "cat seeker" modestly lowered her eyes and stared down at the threshold. The woman's shyness was at odds with her flashy appearance.

"Is it long-haired and gray?"

"That's Rascal. Have you seen him?" Her eyes remained downcast.

Jayne realized that she was carrying on a conversation with a person who earned her livelihood working in one of Denver's taverns. She tried not to stare, but it was hard to curb her curiosity.

"There was a large gray cat wandering around here two weeks ago."

"That sounds like Rascal." The woman glanced up, then quickly down. "He thinks he can come and go whenever he wants."

"Most cats like to roam," Jayne said conversationally.

"I have a dickens of a time keeping track of him. He hasn't been home for a while. Since this is where we used to live, I thought I'd check here."

Jayne blinked. According to Burke, the woman before her didn't just serve drinks to cowpokes, miners and farmers. If she'd lived at the Wet Beaver, then surely she was a prostitute. Despite the flamboyant clothing and improbable shade of red hair, though, she didn't fit Jayne's conception of a fallen woman. Instead of projecting a demeanor of wicked lasciviousness, there was an earnest quality about Rascal's owner.

"Your instincts were right," Jayne said. "Your cat has been back."

"I guess I'll keep looking then." She turned to leave.

"Wait a minute," Jayne called out. "Tell me where you live, so if Rascal shows up, I'll know where to deliver him."

The woman stepped back in astonishment. For the first time, her gaze was direct. Jayne stared into beautiful, but disapproving blue eyes.

"Don't you dare!"

"But I thought you wanted your cat."

"Of course I do, but I don't expect a lady such as yourself to come to the Fancy Pony on some foolish errand."

"You live at a place called the Fancy Pony?" Jayne asked, fascinated.

"Live and work there," the woman said, her earlier shyness retreating. "It's the last place on earth for a proper person like yourself."

"How do you know I'm proper? I'm in a saloon that used to be called the Wet Beaver."

"I know you're a lady because the girls have been talking about how you got skunked into buying this saloon, 'cause you didn't know it was a brothel."

It was daunting to learn she'd been the topic of conversation among a group of fancy women. "If I find Rascal, I'll have someone else drop him off at the Fancy Pony."

"You do that, Miss Stoneworthy."

"You know my name?"

"We all do. When we're not working, gossiping is about the only recreation we have."

A horrible thought struck Jayne. Had the fact that she'd lived with Burke for the past fourteen days become fodder for that gossip? Unfortunately, she couldn't inquire into the matter without revealing the unorthodox living arrangements she'd shared with the banker. Thank goodness she would be settled in a respectable situation by tomorrow evening.

"We think it's a fine idea for you to start a school for young ladies."

"You do?" Jayne asked in surprise.

The woman nodded. "Girls need to know stuff, too. You're going to teach reading and writing, aren't you?"

"Most assuredly."

"And manners?" A wistful quality coated the question.

"And manners."

Rascal's owner sighed. "I wish you the very best, Miss Stoneworthy."

"Thank you…" Jayne broke off. "I don't know your name."

"There's no reason why you should. I'll be on my way now."

"Hey! What's going on here? What are you doing pestering Miss Stoneworthy?"

Jayne recognized Newton White's booming voice.

Red-faced, the woman jerked around. "I ain't doing nothing."

"There's no reason for the likes of you to be talking to a lady. If y'er looking for work, this here's a proper establishment now, so clear out."

"Newton Timothy White," Jayne cut in, "stop that."

His bushy eyebrows converged in consternation. "What'd I do?"

"You're being rude to my visitor."

Two pairs of eyes widened in amazement.

"Beggin' your pardon, ma'am, but in case you haven't noticed, your visitor is a…uh…well…" Clearly reluctant to state the woman's line of work, the miner broke off.

Jayne extended her hand to Rascal's clearly stunned owner. "It was a pleasure meeting you, Miss… I really would like to know your name."

"Sally." She gulped. "Sally Haskell."

Jayne pumped the woman's hand. "Well, Miss Haskell, if I see your cat, I'll have someone bring him to the Fancy Pony."

"Th-thank you."

"You're welcome," Jayne said warmly. She might not know much about the nefarious doings that occurred inside of a brothel, and she certainly didn't approve of such immoral behavior, but she instinctively liked the lovely, diffident woman who'd reluctantly made her acquaintance.

"Umm, I guess I'll be on my way."

"'Bout time," Newt muttered.

"There's no call to be so ornery." Sally Haskell's blue eyes flashed fire. The change in her demeanor caught Jayne by surprise. Besides shyness, there were evidently other facets to the woman's personality. "I know my place." Her chin came up proudly. "Maybe better than you, so just keep your trap shut."

Newt's face reddened. His lips remained sealed shut, though. Evidently, he'd decided to follow Sally's advice and keep his thoughts to himself.

The woman glared at him. Apparently satisfied that she'd had the last word, she turned and sashayed down the boardwalk. As he looked after her, Newt's expression was a comical blend of anger and grudging respect.

"You were extremely rude," Jayne pointed out, stepping from the door to permit the miner to enter.

He didn't look particularly chastised. "Ain't respectable for her to be talking to you."

An unexpected spurt of righteous indignation uncoiled within Jayne. "But it is respectable for *you* to speak to me?"

"Nothing wrong with being a miner. It's honest hard work."

"And being a prostitute isn't?"

"Of course, it ain't," Newt said, clearly bewildered by her anger.

Jayne raised a forefinger and pointed it at his broad chest. "Two weeks ago you walked into this very room and tried to engage my services for Sally's line of work. I agree it's wrong for a woman to sell herself, but it's just as wrong for the man to use her. Maybe more so. The woman becomes trapped in her illicit occupation, virtually cut off from society. The man waltzes away, clothed in respectability, often with an unsuspecting wife at home."

"What you're saying is the honest truth, but it ain't easy being a man, you know. It's mighty hard living without the...uh...comforts a woman provides."

"Then you should get married."

Blank astonishment swept his features. "M-married?"

"That's right. You're a respectable miner with wheelbarrows of gold dust. If you want the comfort a woman provides, then you better stand up with her in front of a preacher.''

Newt took a step back. ''I ain't the kind of man to marry.''

''Nonsense, all men should wed. Think of the benefits. Your wife would cook, clean and keep house. You're rich. There's no reason to keep rattling around those mines. Find yourself a wife who will pamper you.''

''But...''

''And what about children?''

''Ch-children?'' he sputtered.

''Certainly. The world needs several little Newts and Newteenas.''

''I never heard the name Newteena,'' he protested.

''You're missing the point. It's wrong for a man to pay for a woman—wrong for her *and* for him.''

''I ain't arguing, but sometimes a man's hankerings get the best of him, and he—''

''You must fight those hankerings. I wish you could have met my late aunt Euphemia. She was an expert on men's weaknesses.''

He looked around as if fearing her arrival. ''She's dead, though. Right?''

If she hadn't known better, Jayne might have thought the miner was relieved her aunt was in the grave, so he didn't have to deal with her. ''She was well aware of men's fallibilities. It was her belief that marriage benefited men far more than women.''

''Oh.''

''I agree with her assessment. Get yourself a wife, and you'll never miss another hot meal, sleep in an unclean bed or worry about darning your socks. You'll have a twenty-four-hour-a-day personal slave.''

''I wouldn't expect her to work all day and all night,'' he said, obviously offended.

''Good for you.''

"But a man doesn't jump into anything as permanent as marriage without thinking about it first."

"You're right." She patted his arm. "But there's no time like the present to begin those considerations."

He took another step back. "I just dropped by to say howdy. Hadn't seen you in a while. Heard you were moving the school. Thought maybe you might want some help."

He looked as if he regretted the kindly impulse.

"That was sweet of you. Mr. Youngblood found another building. It's being fixed up now. We're supposed to move the rest of the furniture tomorrow."

"I'll stop by."

"Thank you."

"I'll be leaving now."

"Goodbye."

He turned, walking away as if pursued by a herd of snapping alligators. Good, she'd intended to dust him liberally with a dose of moral turpitude. It was inexcusable for a man to pay a woman to be intimate with him and then condemn her for the very act he'd instigated. If desperate women weren't forced to survive by selling themselves, there would be no prostitutes.

Jayne consulted the timepiece pinned to her bodice. She'd learned in dealing with Owen Gardner that he was extremely punctual. It was half past three. He should be arriving soon. He wanted to see the items needing to be transferred to the new building, so he could gauge the size of wagon needed.

A brisk knock at the door had her nodding in satisfaction. It was nice to deal with someone who appreciated being on time as much as she did.

It seemed fitting to spend her last evening at Burke's home in his art gallery. It was because of the beautiful paintings gracing the dark paneled walls that she had first made his acquaintance. On that not-so-long-ago afternoon, he'd seemed coldly remote. His brooding male presence had been a stark contrast to the Hempshire Academy's high-spirited students.

Little had she known the fiercely masculine Burke Youngblood would thunder into her life. She could scarcely believe she'd been living in his home. A few months from now, when her memory of him faded, she was certain this bizarre interlude would take on the elements of a disturbing dream. A dream, she decided, that had been interrupted before its completion. That was how she felt this evening, strangely incomplete. It was as if an unfinished act lay between herself and Burke. Of course, there was the business of reimbursing him for the funds he'd advanced. But the nagging sense of unfulfillment she experienced had nothing to do with monetary matters.

A grandfather clock chimed sonorously in the hall. She counted the deep bongs. Six o'clock. Dinner would soon be served. Her unsettled feelings stole her appetite. She had no desire to endure another evening meal alone.

Would he miss her after she was gone? It was a foolish question, spawned by her leaden mood. For no reason at all, her eyes burned with the pressure of impending moisture. Startled, she touched a fingertip to her cheek and was stunned to discover a teardrop. What foolishness was this, that she would weep for a man who had promised, no, *threatened,* to court, no, *pursue,* her and had then clearly repented of his rash declaration?

"Ah, there you are."

The deep voice made her jump. She spun around from the oil paintings that, while unarguably beautiful, weren't compelling enough to divert her thoughts from Burke Youngblood. And there he stood—not dressed like a banker at all. A heavy layer of dust liberally covered his dark jacket, denim trousers and Western boots. His black hair lay pressed to his scalp, testifying to the hat he'd obviously removed before entering the room. The patch of skin at his forehead was paler than the rest of his tanned face. A heavy growth of new beard stubbled his hard jaw. Her quick survey took in the well-worn gun belt visible beneath his opened jacket.

If she hadn't known better, she'd have thought she'd been joined by a wild "desperado," on the order of those dangerously unscrupulous characters found between the pages of popular Western novels that sold for a dime.

"My butler mentioned you haven't eaten. I'll scrub off some of this trail dust and join you for dinner."

"Take your time. I'm not particularly hungry."

Burke remained in the doorway, as if reluctant to track dirt into the gallery. "Aren't you feeling well?"

"Well enough," she answered, knowing there was no physical cause for her loss of appetite.

He moved into the room, his observant gaze traveling over her. "How are things going at the new building? Are the carpenters on schedule?"

"Everything's fine." She bit her lip. He'd done so much for her. That must be why she was reluctant to say goodbye. "Actually, things are better than fine. The men you hired are marvelous craftsmen."

"Owen tells me you're planning on having your possessions transferred to the new place tomorrow."

"That's right."

She didn't know why the prosaic words they exchanged added to the sadness unraveling within her. What sort of extraordinary conversation did she expect? As she stared into his dirt-stained, fatigue-lined face, she was struck by the insane urge to cross the room and lay her cheek against his chest.

He said nothing. Was he waiting for her to elaborate? Her throat was oddly tight, though, and she didn't feel up to a prolonged discussion.

His inscrutable dark eyes seemed to bore into her for several moments before he glanced away, taking in the walls of his art gallery.

"From your own taste in art, I'm surprised you would find this room of interest."

Since beautiful oil paintings abounded, he was obviously suggesting she was incapable of appreciating good artwork. So bleak was her mood, she was unable to work up any righteous indignation at the unexpected insult.

"Where did you get the impression I don't value the work of talented artists?"

"Aside from your outmoded taste in clothing?"

Two insults in a row. Her ire stirred. "There's absolutely nothing wrong with my clothes. I happen to prefer garments of understated elegance."

"If that gray dress you're wearing were any more understated, it would be gracing a Puritan's petrified corpse."

"Are you trying to pick a quarrel?"

He tipped his head. "It seems so."

"Why?"

"Damned if I know." He shoved a hand through his hair. "Maybe it's because I'm tired of seeing you in either dark blue, gray or brown. Don't you have anything that's yellow or pink or…bright?"

She raised her chin defensively. "Bright shades lessen the chances of a woman being taken seriously."

"And, of course, you must be taken seriously." The observation was a low growl that rippled across her flesh, leaving a trail of goose bumps.

"A professional person such as myself gains a certain stamp of authority by eschewing frivolous garments."

"Who told you that?"

"Aunt Euphemia maintained that women who outfit themselves in the manner of Christmas trees—replete with baubles, flounces, fluttering fabrics, as well as ribbons and bows—render themselves of only ornamental value."

"Aunt Euphemia, again. I can't believe we conversed for all of five minutes without her name coming up sooner."

"My aunt was very wise. You can't deny that members

of my gender spend entirely too much time decorating their persons, instead of engaging in meaningful activities.''

''Do you plan to be teach those revolutionary ideas at your school?''

''I won't have to. The best instruction is by way of example. By opening my students' minds to original thought, they will be able to reach correct conclusions about their true worth.''

''Are the parents who'll be placing their daughters under your care aware of your radical ideas?''

''My ideas aren't radical. They were taught and practiced in ancient Greece, where women owned property, voted and took charge of their destinies.''

''So, just like your aunt, they didn't need a man for anything?''

Jayne knew her cheeks were flushed. ''Obviously the human race would not continue, save men and women joined in holy matrimony and procreated.''

Burke scratched his bristly jaw. ''It's nice to feel needed.''

''But not every woman is obliged to fulfill her destiny by way of marriage,'' Jayne pointed out. ''Some of us can manage quite well on our own.''

Abruptly, she realized she *hadn't* been doing very well on her own. It had only been after Burke had shown up that her circumstances had improved dramatically.

''It's amazing that, never having met your aunt, I feel as if I've become intimately acquainted with her. If your unorthodox ideas impress themselves upon your students, their fathers will definitely thank you.''

''For what?'' Jayne asked suspiciously.

''The savings to their finances. Just think of the expense that would be eliminated if their daughters refrained from adorning themselves in silks, costly jewelry and a steady parade of new bonnets.''

''Trust a banker to think of that.''

''So, you intend to create a generation of sober-minded

females," he mused, "by instructing them in original thinking and modest dress."

"Among other things," she returned frostily. "There will be strong emphasis upon mathematics, history, literature and grammar."

"And manners," he added with deceptive blandness.

"And manners. The young woman graduating from my academy will also be prepared for a future in the twentieth century."

"Since your typical student will marry, a more sensible curriculum would teach her how to please her husband."

"That's exactly the kind of instruction I certainly will *not* include."

"Pity."

"From a man's point of view."

"That's the only point of view of which I'm capable."

"Pity," she mimicked.

A half smile twisted his mouth. "As much as I'm enjoying this conversation, I need to clean up. I'll tell George we'll dine at seven."

Burke turned toward the doorway.

"I doubt I'll be joining you," she called after him.

He spun around to face her. A sizzling bolt of energy seemed to arc across the few feet that separated them. "Do you have other plans?"

Mystified by his sudden intensity, she shook her head. "I told you I'm not hungry."

"You have to eat."

"No, I don't, not tonight at any rate."

"If you intend to enlighten the upcoming generation with your revolutionary principles, you'll have to keep your strength up."

His unreasonable concern startled a laugh from her. "It's just one meal. No doubt, it's the excitement of moving into Agnes Sawyer's boardinghouse tomorrow that has me too keyed up to eat."

Instead of leaving the gallery so he could clean up for dinner, Burke startled her by reversing direction and striding toward her.

''What do you mean, you're moving out?''

Chapter Ten

Knowing he was making an ass of himself did nothing to pacify the frustration seething within Burke. It was a foregone conclusion she would leave. Her stay hadn't been personal or sexual in nature. Since her arrival, they hadn't spent an hour alone together. Instead of soothing his sense of outrage, that realization scraped deeper into his composure.

"I finalized the arrangements yesterday with Mrs. Sawyer." Jayne folded her arms across her chest. "It's time I left."

Back off. Cool down. Once she's out of your house, you'll start acting normal again. Hell, you might even go to bed with a real woman, instead of fantasizing each night about losing yourself in this one's softness.

"Why leave now?"

"My bruises have faded, and…"

She was staring at him with those damnably appealing green eyes of hers, "witchy" eyes, he decided. He wanted to see them simmering with the sudden need he felt throbbing to life within him. Did independent, free-thinking females *simmer?* He damned well wanted the chance to find out.

"And?" he prompted, fighting to keep his voice even.

"Well, what with the gossip already going around because I bought that…uh…tavern, I'm not willing to press my luck any further.''

''I'm not aware of any gossip being circulated about you.''

''I was talking to Sally Haskell this afternoon. She told me that she and her…friends have been talking about the building I bought and its past.''

''Who the dickens is Sally Haskell?''

''She's… That is to say, she used to work at the… tavern.''

Jayne's face was brightly flushed. She was such a contradiction. On the one hand, she bravely tackled delicate subjects, and on the other, a boldness of speech clearly shocked her sensibilities.

She reminded him of a fragile, blown-glass vessel fashioned to hold an exotic perfume, but instead containing nitroglycerin.

The full import of her stammered explanation penetratcd. ''You engaged in a conversation with a prostitute?''

''Technically speaking, I suppose. But you would never know it by the way she conducts herself. Miss Haskell appears quite respectable.''

''Where did you and *Miss* Haskell have your respectable conversation?''

''At the tavern. She was looking for her cat. From her description, it's the very animal you carried into my bedchamber.''

At the reminder of his idiotic behavior, Burke's irritation grew. ''I know you're an intelligent woman, Jayne.''

Obviously surprised by his compliment, she blinked. ''Thank you.''

''So I've got to know. What were you thinking, to carry on a discussion with a prostitute?''

''I could hardly slam the door in her face.''

''That's exactly what you should have done. On several occasions, you've expressed well-founded concerns about protecting your reputation. You know as well as I do that, in order for your school to be a success, your name has to be above reproach. Society has a long list of rules that respectable women are obliged to follow. In your case, any deviation could spell ruin.''

Since he burned to take Jayne into his arms and make love to her, he was nothing but a hypocrite.

''Some of society's rules are too harsh. I didn't wish to be unkind. Besides, it's as I told Newt. The men engaging her…uh…favors should suffer censure also. Yet those men are free to mingle with polite society. That's not fair.''

Jayne's sincerity was unmistakable. Unfortunately, so was her naiveté. The woman shouldn't be allowed loose without a keeper. He struggled to curb his impatience. ''Life's not fair, but a mature person accepts the world the way it is. You want your school? Then abide by society's rules.''

''That's even more reason for me to move out tomorrow.''

He hated it when his own words were used against him. ''Living with me hasn't hurt your reputation.''

''Why are you so insistent about me staying? It's not as if we've spent any time together.''

Her blush was back. He wanted to caress a rosy cheek to see if it would be warm to his touch. ''I like knowing you're safe.''

''I shall certainly be safe at Mrs. Sawyer's.''

I will miss you.… Words he'd never said to any woman. It shook him that the weakening sentiment lurked within him.

''From what Owen Gardner tells me, the new building will be ready in about ten days. It's impractical to rent a room for such a brief time. Think of the money you'll save by staying here.''

She'd reduced him to appealing to her frugal nature.

''It will be an inconvenience,'' she admitted, ''but I can't continue to accept your hospitality. You've already been too generous.''

Her expression was earnest enough to soften the most cynical heart. Luckily, that particular organ was secured behind an unbreachable wall. Otherwise, Jayne's wholesomeness would have had him practicing various ways to propose matrimony. What a hellish prospect that would be for a confirmed bachelor—a fate worse than death, as the saying went.

"Until you showed up, I didn't realize the untenable situation in which I'd placed myself. You helped me sell the tavern and find a building that's absolutely perfect for my needs. You've provided a place for me to live and loaned me funds to stay afloat until Uncle Clarence's draft arrives. I owe you a debt of more than dollars and cents. I know I can never repay you, but I'll be grateful to you for the rest of my life."

It was a pretty little speech, but he didn't want her damned gratitude. He wanted her. In bed, which in the face of her innocence made him more gross than pig manure.

"I recognize a good investment when I see one."

Right, sinking thousands of dollars into a venture barely capable of paying its own way was a honey of an investment.

Jayne's delicate eyebrows drew together. "You haven't presented me with an itemized listing of the sums you've advanced. Before I go, I'd like a tally of what I owe you."

He kept his expression neutral. She would have a fit if she saw the exorbitant amount he'd funneled into the remodeling project. He'd left strict instructions with Owen not to discuss any financial details with her. Moving the glass door panels to the new place would cost more than a hundred dollars, comparatively speaking, a minor sum in the quickly rising building expenses.

"I don't have the paperwork here," he said smoothly. "Besides, I want to discuss you remaining here."

He was postponing the inevitable. She *would* leave, and he would have to accept it.

Jayne's expression shifted from mild consternation to

one of dawning comprehension, and did she appear pleased
by the substance of her conclusions. Sensing a coming
storm, he braced himself. He had no idea what her fertile
imagination might come up with, but he was reasonably
certain her thoughts were too chaste for her to realize she
was conversing with a man crazed by desire and exercising
every fragment of his will not to salivate.

"You're not fooling me. I know why you want me to
stay."

A flush crawled up his neck. "Do you?"

"You don't trust me to pay my debt and want to use me
as some kind of collateral until Uncle Clarence's bank draft
arrives. I'm right, aren't I?"

Since he'd already spent more than the twenty-five hundred dollars promised by her mysterious uncle, her accu-
sation couldn't have been more offtrack.

"If you qualified, you'd make the most delectable collateral I've ever held. Fortunately for us both, you don't
qualify. Only property pledged by a borrower to protect a
lender's interests can be used as collateral. The borrower
herself, no matter how winsome, cannot be part of the
transaction."

More rosy-cheeked than ever, she brushed absently at the
folds of her gray skirts. "That's a relief."

Perhaps for her, but how it would feel to possess her as
totally as other properties the law declared irrevocably his?

"Well then, my mind's made up. I would very much
appreciate your help moving into Mrs. Sawyer's place tomorrow."

Short of keeping her hostage, he had no choice other than
to let her go. He knew he was in trouble when he allowed
himself the fantasy of her locked in his bedchamber. He
was reasonably confident he could restrain himself from
such a lawless act. Before the night ended, however, he
would find some relief from his grinding hunger.

After the torture she'd put him through, she owed him
more than repayment of the funds he'd advanced. And he

intended to collect. He wouldn't claim the full measure of his desire, but he *would* have her mouth yielding under his. He wanted to hear her sigh, just once. For him.

Would once be enough, or would it only whet his appetite for more? That he had no intention of ending his relationship with this complicated, maddening, irresistible woman, staggered him.

He rubbed his unshaven jaw. Their first real kiss, one he vowed would make her as wild for him as he was for her, wasn't going to be marred by his coming to her travel-stained, sweaty and smelling of horse.

He forced his mouth to curve into what he hoped was a nonthreatening smile. "You win. One of my men will load your things tomorrow morning. Your move will go without mishap."

"Thank you."

He kept his smile plastered to his face. "But I want to make our last evening together...memorable."

"How?" she asked innocently.

There was no reason to feel like a vile seducer of virgins. He was only contemplating a few heated kisses. "I want to take you out to dinner."

"But the table's already set for the meal your cook prepared."

"The staff can have it. You and I are dining at the Edgemont."

It was one of Denver's finest restaurants, touting not one, but two French chefs. After he plied her with fine cuisine, generously filled goblets of wine and the most charming nature he could fabricate, she would become as pliant as soft wax. He thought of their return ride from the restaurant. A carriage was hardly the place for a sophisticated seduction, but was suitable for the restricted lovemaking he had in mind.

Jayne looked around the dining room and tried not to gawk at the resplendent couples seated at linen-covered tables adorned with candles and fragrant roses floating in crystal bowls.

The women wore low-cut silk dresses of vivid hues. Bare shoulders, shockingly exposed bosoms and diamond necklaces seemed the prescribed order of feminine garb. Muted tones of gray, brown and black comprised the attire for the gentlemen present, along with starched white shirts with crisp round collars. Black Western ties with turquoise, gold and silver boleros, along with handsomely tooled leather boots completed the men's dress code.

Sitting across the candlelit table from Burke, Jayne felt like an imposter of the fairy-tale heroine, Cinderella. While not a royal ballroom, the Edgemont—with its interior columns, vaulted ceiling, tinkling teardrop chandeliers, discreetly playing musicians and linen-draped serving carts laden with dome-covered, silver platters, was as close to a palace as one could find in America.

Unlike the fabled Cinderella, though, Jayne didn't wear a shimmering gown waved into existence by her fairy godmother. Instead, she was garbed in the gray dress Burke had pronounced suitable for a dead-and-buried Puritan. She felt as out of place as a mule in a stable of Arabian steeds.

She glanced at her dinner companion. Dressed as elegantly as the other men present, Burke looked at home in their palatial surroundings. Unconcerned about the growing lateness of the hour, he'd taken time to wash and shave. His still-damp, black hair gleamed beneath the chandeliers. The hard jaw that formerly sported a black scrub of whiskers was now invitingly smooth. He smelled good, too—of soap and hair tonic, with faint traces of leather and pipe tobacco.

He'd already placed their order with a formally attired server. Pheasant, mushrooms stuffed with pork dressing, potatoes au gratin and steamed sweet peas would soon be delivered to their table. The pudgy wine steward presently claimed Burke's attention.

"We'll have the champagne now. Serve the white Burgundy with our meal."

The steward nodded. "As you wish, sir."

The man left. Jayne searched her mind for something intelligent to say. "Do you come here often?"

Okay, so it wasn't a brilliant icebreaker, but she'd never felt as out of her element as she did now. It was unnerving to discover a rarefied setting could rattle her, but she did feel as if she were trespassing. Burke's impeccably tailored suit emphasized the social gap between them. America might not be a country of royal bloodlines, but definite social barriers separated the rich from the poor. She and Burke were a mismatched pair.

"I eat here about once a week."

The dip her stomach took wasn't caused by his answer. It was the rawly handsome smile he directed at her that caused the sensual plunge. "If the food is as pleasant as the surroundings, I can see why."

"The food is excellent. I guarantee your appetite will stir the moment you take your first bite."

His husky voice made eating sound as erotic as...as a lover's caress.

The wine steward returned, carrying two bottles. Behind him followed a young man with a silver tray and four glasses. Evidently one couldn't drink champagne and wine from the same vessel. With a flourish of unscrewed and popped corks the bottles were opened, sniffed, sampled and poured.

Burke presented her with a tall fluted glass, containing a sparkling gold liquid. Above the rim, dozens of bubbles fizzed.

The beverage looked tempting enough, like something a princess might drink. "I don't approve of alcohol."

"You mean, your aunt didn't approve of alcohol."

"I agree with her. Many of the world's miseries come from men overimbibing spirits and failing in their husbandly and fatherly duties."

"That's true, but even a champion of the temperance movement must admit some people handle their liquor without problem."

"One can't know in advance whether he will develop a weakness to the evil concoction. Why flirt with danger?"

Burke's gaze deepened. "Excellent question. When I learn the answer, I'll let you know. Until then, I assure you, alcohol poses no hazard to me."

"What about me? I have no such assurance."

Burke chuckled. "That's easy. If you fall facefirst into your soup, or try hanging from a chandelier, we'll definitely know you need to avoid strong spirits."

"Your levity is hardly appropriate for the inherent risks involved."

"Suit yourself. I just wanted to make tonight special."

She eyed the festive-looking drink. "I suppose a little won't hurt. I'm not likely to have another opportunity to taste champagne." She attempted to take a small sip. "It's a challenge to get past the popping bubbles."

"Hold your breath as you swallow," he advised. "You'll be amazed at how smoothly it goes down."

She did as suggested and discovered a tart drink that reminded her of a fruit she couldn't put a name to. She licked her tingling lips. "It's odd to swallow something so lively."

His smile bordered on indulgent. "If it's to your liking, have more."

She took another sip. "I can't quite put my finger on what it reminds me of, but it is delicious."

"Speaking of delicious, you'll have to sample one of the French desserts the Edgemont features. They have a concoction of chocolate, cherries and brandy that is unforgettable."

"It sounds wonderful."

A shadow fell across their table. She looked up into the narrowed gaze of an imposing stranger. The fastidiously dressed man presented a cold smile.

"Youngblood, it's been a while."

Neither man extended his hand, nor did Burke stand. Instead a palpable cloud of ill will fell across his features. "Dilicar."

Glaringly terse, the one-word greeting was all Burke said.

"How are things at the First National?" their uninvited visitor inquired, ignoring the clear signal that Burke wanted nothing to do with him. "Any robberies yet this week?"

The gentleman Burke identified as Dilicar evidenced no obvious signs of idiocy. Yet in the light of the recent string of attempted robberies Burke had warded off, the man was either a fool or being deliberately unpleasant. From the shrewdness his eyes reflected, Jayne decided the interloper's insult were calculated.

"It's been pretty quiet."

Dilicar smiled the thinnest, nastiest smile Jayne had ever seen. "No gunshots fired, no exploding dynamite or nitroglycerin? After all the excitement you're used to, this must be boring."

"Not boring, just quiet."

Burke's tone of menace made the fine hairs at the nape of her neck rise.

"Let's hope things stay…quiet. It would be a shame to lose your charter." The peal of laughter that followed the observation lacked any warmth. "You haven't introduced me to your lovely companion."

Becoming the target of the man's condescending gaze made Jayne tense. Despite the even white teeth exposed by his curved lips, his smile held all the humanity of a rattlesnake coiled atop a silver platter. Without his uttering a disparaging remark, his obvious disdain made her feel exactly like the gauche peasant she'd earlier envisioned herself.

"Move along, Dilicar."

At Burke's blunt rejection, a look of pure hatred entered the man's eyes. Jayne sensed he wanted to return the insult he'd received. Instead he retained his parody of a smile and backed away then turned and went to an empty table only a few feet away.

"Bastard...." Burke spoke under his breath.

"Not a friend, I take it."

"Not a friend."

The first course arrived. She reached for one of the three forks that had been laid out, grateful for the etiquette classes she'd taught. This might be her first experience in an exclusive dining establishment, but her manners wouldn't embarrass either her or Burke.

"Just a minute, waiter, I want to say hello to Youngblood."

The words rumbled across their table. Jayne looked into the coarse features of a heavyset man, who, though dressed as formally as others present, accomplished only a crude imitation of sophistication.

Burke laid down his fork. "Damn."

"Youngblood, I want a word with you."

"Pick a better time and place, Sutton. I'm busy."

"Sorry to interrupt, miss."

The most noteworthy aspect of the barrel-chested man was the healed slit in his left nostril. It was difficult to keep her gaze from lingering on what obviously had been a painful wound. When she was finally able to draw her gaze to his eyes, she shuddered. Deeply sunk in the folds of his wind-coarsened flesh, their hard brown depths seemed flat, as if the man who possessed them neither sought or reflected the inner light found in humankind.

His protuberant lips, pocked jowls and sloping forehead gave him a look of unwholesome appetites. Jayne immediately chastised herself for judging a person by his unfortunate physical appearance. And yet, as rough-edged as Newton White was, the miner hadn't inspired the repugnance this man did.

"I've been thinking about your visit today, Youngblood."

"What of it?" Burke asked indifferently.

"You've got no business coming onto my place and demanding to know who I got working for me. If I want to put a hired gun on my payroll, I got the right to do it. There's not a damned thing you can do about it."

"Point taken. Now that you've gotten that off your chest, get lost."

The man's cruel eyes glinted angrily. "I'll go when I'm ready."

Showing none of Burke's self-mastery, Sutton spoke with loud-voiced displeasure. Burke laid down his linen napkin and pushed back his chair. His quiet air of self-contained fury was in marked contrast to the primitive rage emanating from Sutton. The elegance of their surroundings made the men's animosity seem all the more primal. Jayne was aware of the silence gripping the other tables as the confrontation claimed their rapt attention.

"I have no intention of letting you spoil my dinner, Sutton."

"I don't have anything more to say, except stay off my property. My men have orders to shoot all trespassers. The rest of the people around here can rely on those Guardsmen to protect them. I take care of what's mine."

He stalked away. Not far, Jayne noticed, as he joined Mr. Dilicar at his table. The two men made a startling contrast. One was tall and leanly fit, and exhibited a studied sophistication. The other, equally tall, but scaled along the massive lines of a longhorn bull, was unarguably crude.

Burke sat down, reached for his wineglass and sipped thoughtfully.

"Neither of them appear to like you."

"That's an understatement."

"They're an unlikely pair."

Burke returned his glass to the table. "Dilicar and Sutton have two things in common. They're both rich, and they're both power-hungry."

"Does it make you nervous that they associate with each other?"

"Why should it?"

"Because I have a strong impression they're plotting against you."

"You're a smart woman."

The compliment warmed her. Aunt Euphemia always said the most meaningful praise a man could offer a woman was for her intellect or character. Yet, surveying the array of sparkling women present, Jayne wondered if it might not be more satisfying to be praised for one's beauty. As long as Burke mingled with glamorous ladies bedecked in satins and jewels, however, he wasn't likely to view her as anything but a drab wren.

"Burke, darling, how are you? It's been ages!"

No glaring man greeted Burke. Too bad. Jayne would have preferred another hostile confrontation to the radiant brunette gushing over Burke. The woman wore a ruby-colored velvet gown with a plunging décolletage that revealed the creamy expanse of a generous-sized bosom. Matching the gown, a ruby pendant had wedged itself into her bounteous cleavage.

Burke got to his feet. "Mrs. Bacus..."

The woman tipped her perfectly coiffed head and laughed. The sound that emerged from her slender throat tinkled as musically as a perfectly tuned piano. "Mrs. Bacus is my mother's name. Surely after our...intimate acquaintance, you can call me Rita." She laughed again. "You always have."

A swath of red swept across Burke's sharply angled face. Obviously, he was discomfited by the lavish attention. Jayne would have preferred him mortified. So, this glittering, dulcet-voiced creature was indicative of his taste in female companionship. What a revolting discovery. The only thing making the evening bearable was the champagne she kept sipping. Aunt Euphemia had certainly been wrong to condemn all alcohol.

"Rita, it's been a while since we...uh...talked. You're looking...robust."

Any more robust, and she would pop out of her gown. Depressed, Jayne realized it probably wouldn't be the first time he'd seen the woman's bosom. That glum thought had Jayne taking the champagne bottle from its silver bucket. Beaded water splashed on the tablecloth. A server miraculously appeared and performed the honors. At least someone knew she was still there.

The woman laughed again. Uncharitably, Jayne decided only a fool was amused at the least provocation.

"I've missed our...talks, darling." She ran her perfectly shaped nails down his lapel. "If you're not careful, you'll grow into a stuffy banker."

Jayne pictured Rita "stuffed" and exhibited in Burke's art gallery. She would be at home among the full-figured females featured in a number of paintings. It was probably no accident that the woman presently draping herself over him reflected his obvious preference for top-heavy females.

"Thanks for your concern," Burke responded, his tone stiff.

What else had *fun*-loving Rita stiffened on him? At the uncouth thought, Jayne flushed. She'd better get hold of herself. Such crudity was not the hallmark of an admirable intellect.

She certainly wasn't jealous of the woman batting her eyelashes and emphasizing every other word she spoke with a circular motion of her bare, right shoulder. Between sips, Jayne surreptitiously experimented, making her own shoulder perform the maneuver. Unlike Rita, however, the action didn't precipitate any noticeable jiggling of Jayne's bosom. Disgruntled, she realized she didn't have enough raw material with which to work.

"Burke, dear, I'll be holding my breath until I hear from you."

Jayne pictured the woman bloated and turning blue.

"I'm busy at the bank. There's no telling when I'll break free."

An unbecoming frown marred Rita's flawless complexion. Her vision oddly blurred, Jayne squinted. Upon closer examination, she noticed the woman had resorted to powder and blush to enhance her features. Hah! She was nothing but a phony. Why, she probably stuffed handkerchiefs under her breasts to push them up so that they almost spilled over her low-cut gown.

How many handkerchiefs would it take to push up her own bosom like that? Probably more than she owned. As the silence spun out between Burke and Rita, Jayne considered her empty champagne glass. The wine had been nice, but she was in the mood for more bubbles.

"I suppose I should return to my table. My dinner companion will be wondering what happened to me."

Bon voyage... Though she was still "tethered" to their "dock," Jayne figured "Good Ship Rita" had made her original, maiden voyage long ago. How often had Burke set sea on the curvaceous vessel? The nautical metaphors seemed apropos. Rita looked as if she could pose for a ship's masthead, while Burke had the appearance of man who'd dropped anchor at innumerable ports, and Jayne's stomach was beginning to pitch like a storm-tossed sea.

"Good bye, Rita."

"'Bye, darling." She brushed her lips across Burke's cheek.

Jayne fumed. The painted hussy was as disreputable as any good-time gal.

"I'm shooting the next person who shows up at our table."

"Sure, *now* you say that."

Burke's eyebrows drew together. "What?"

Jayne hiccuped. "Now that 'Miss Big Bouncing Bosoms' has crawled all over you, you're willing to resort to bloodshed. I'm just pointing out that, if you'd been firmer earlier, our food wouldn't be stone-cold now."

Jayne smiled to let him know she wasn't upset that a osom-flaunting female had put her hands and lips all over im.

"How much have you had to drink, Jayne?"

"Glasses and glasses." She picked up an empty goblet. 'I'm trying to decide whether I like the wine or the champagne better. Have the waiter bring more so I can find out."

"You've had enough."

She wagged her finger. "I'm not swinging from a chanelier, nor am I facedown in a bowl of soup."

He raised his hand and gestured. "You left out brainless hatter."

A waiter magically appeared. Jayne blinked. How amazing. She raised her hand to see if she could perform the ame trick.

"Take the food away and bring us whatever you have nat's hot and ready to eat."

"Certainly, sir."

The dishes vanished.

"Who are you waving at?"

Jayne brought Burke's face into focus. My, he was handome. Dark and scary, too. But that was part of his charm. he liked the way he tickled her stomach without even ouching her. "I'm not waving. I'm practicing."

"Practicing what?"

"To see if I can make a waiter appear."

"Did you need something?"

"I don't think so."

"Then stop practicing."

"Okey-dokey." She handed him her empty goblet.

"What's this for?"

"I want more of the white stuff."

"The Chablis?"

"Yes siree, that's what I want. You're so smart, Burke. don't think you stuffy, either. 'Good Ship Rita' was rong about that."

"I think we'll hold off on the wine until you've eaten."

"On second thought, I liked the bubbly better." Sh
handed him the fluted glass.

He set it aside. "There'll be no more to drink unt
you've had food."

"You're the meanest man I've ever known."

"Now, Jayne—"

"Don't 'Jayne' me. I just realized you insulted m
'Brainless chatter,' indeed."

"Let's just say you've lost your inhibitions."

"I know exactly where my inhibitchens are!"

He laughed softly. "Honey, your aunt was right abou
one thing. Some people shouldn't drink, at least as muc
as you've had on an empty stomach."

"It's not my fault your past is littered with chesty f
males and enemies who want to rough you up."

He balanced his chin on his steepled fingertips. "W
have better things to talk about than Rita, Dilicar or Su
ton."

She refused to be sidetracked. "I've got shoulders, yo
know."

As it was prone to do, his right eyebrow rose. "I neve
doubted it."

"I can move them just like Rita. See, I can do both
the same time."

"Honey—"

"Of course, mine are covered so you don't get the fu
effect." She glanced from her immobile breasts. "Are yo
laughing at me?"

He pressed a napkin to his mouth. "I wouldn't dream
it."

She leaned forward and whispered conspiratorially. "I'
positive Rita stuffs her chemise with handkerchiefs." H
eyes narrowed. "You would know, wouldn't you? I b
you've seen her—"

"I don't give a damn what Mrs. Bacus has under h
chemise."

"Don't you think it's discourteous to have affairs with married women?"

He rudely took a swallow of wine without offering her any. "Rita's widowed. I've never been involved with a married woman, but they've got to be less trouble than virgins."

"Virgins aren't any trouble at all. If you want one, just snap your—" She tried to snap her fingers but was unable to master the complex feat. Inspiration struck. "It's as easy as tossing them into bed and kissing them senseless." She smiled dreamily. "You truly are a magnificent kisser. I don't how any woman, widow or virgin, could resist—"

"Burke, Jayne, this is a surprise."

At the sound of another woman's voice, Jayne scowled. There would be no more to drink until she ate. At the rate things were going, that would be never. She was about to insist their new visitor depart until she realized Emma Cade and her husband, Gideon, stood before them.

"Emma, how wonderful to see you!" Jayne didn't understand why she was so emotional, but having her friend show up seemed so remarkably special that she wanted to cry. "Please sit down and join us."

"We wouldn't want to intrude," Gideon said.

"You're not intruding," Jayne assured him, gesturing expansively. "We just ordered more food on account of what we had got cold because two icky men insisted on snarling at Burke, and then a woman built out to here—" she pantomimed mammoth-sized breasts "—sailed over and dropped anchor at our table. She kissed Burke. Not on the lips, but I could tell she wanted to. She paints her face, and stuffs her chemise."

No one took issue with Jayne's observations. She smiled widely.

Emma glared at Burke. "We definitely will be joining you, won't we, Gideon?"

"It appears so, love."

"Damn." The oath was Burke's.

"It's all right, really. You'll like Emma, even if she doesn't flaunt her bosoms. She's a very nice person, isn't that right, Mr. Cade?"

"Call me Gideon." He held out the chair for his wife. "And yes, Emma is very nice."

Burke made another gesture with his hand. Again a waiter materialized. "Bring coffee immediately."

"Yes, sir!"

Chapter Eleven

After she drank two cups of coffee, Jayne's surroundings lost some of their haziness. She noticed Emma's frown. Was her friend's pregnancy causing discomfort? Jayne's gaze went to the white lace shawl draped discreetly over the small, but noticeable bulge beneath the beige satin smock trimmed in gold braid. Emma soon would be delivered of a baby. Life moved in mysterious ways. Not too long ago her friend, an orphan, had been completely alone in the world.

"I would like to freshen up before our food arrives," Emma announced.

Gideon bolted to his feet to assist her from the chair. Burke uncurled to his full height at a more leisurely pace.

"Are you feeling all right, darling?" Gideon asked.

"I'm fine." She rose with only moderate awkwardness. "Jayne and I wish to stretch our legs."

Jayne was surprised at being included in her friend's plans. Considering the amounts of champagne, wine and coffee she'd drunk, though, it seemed advisable to join Emma. Burke pulled back her chair, and Jayne followed the pregnant woman. They passed Dilicar and Sutton's table. The men's combined hostility roiled toward them.

As she navigated the carpeted hallway, Jayne attributed her unsteadiness to the uneven floor. One would think a plush establishment such as the Edgemont would have made sure their floorboards were flat.

They entered a chamber with green brocade walls, marble sinks and gold faucets. Jayne availed herself of the modern water closet. Indoor plumbing was something she would miss when she left Burke's.

As Jayne washed her hands beneath a stream of water she became aware again of her friend's somber regard.

Jayne accepted a pink hand towel from the uniformed attendant. "Are you truly feeling well, Emma?"

Also drying her hands, Emma's features remained grave. "What are you doing with Burke Youngblood?"

"Having dinner."

"How did that happen?" Her friend's forehead puckered. "One minute he's a virtual stranger, lending you money for your school, and the next he's escorting you to the most expensive restaurant in Denver."

"I didn't realize you knew that he'd extended me a loan."

"Well, that is to say…. Gideon must have mentioned it."

"Your husband has the right of it. Burke advanced me funds against Clarence's promised bank draft." Jayne studied Emma. "Is there something wrong about accepting a dinner invitation from Burke?"

"I wouldn't have thought so. In fact, I rather hoped that if you and he got to know each other, something might come of it."

"Of a personal nature?"

"Of course, of a personal nature." Emma's expression clouded. "But that was before."

"Before what?"

"Before Gideon and I found you…uh…inebriated. I don't wish to be unkind, but it's plain Burke Youngblood has been plying you with spirits. You're not at all your usual self."

"I'm not?"

"No, and the only reason a man would attempt to get a lady tipsy is for…underhanded purposes."

"You think he has underhanded intentions toward me?" If Burke had resorted to such nefarious measures, he must not know her resistance toward him was at a very low ebb. Chagrined, she realized she was ripe for the picking. His picking. The thought of him kissing her made her fingers twitch. She wanted to weave them through his thick black hair.

She was wanton, all right. Nor, in clear conscience, could she blame her moral demise upon the spirits she'd consumed. Ever since she'd awakened in that bedchamber, wearing only her chemise and pantalettes, she'd entertained carnal fantasies about him. Knowing he'd seen her in such a state of undress had awakened a primal awareness that bathed her waking and slumbering reflections in heat. She thought about his strong hands moving across her flesh. The image unleashed tremors that licked her insides.

"You're being unfair, Emma. Burke's been a perfect gentleman." If one didn't count their first twenty-four hours together. "He's far too noble to try and intoxicate me."

"*You're* too naive and trusting."

"I assure you, I'm neither of those things. Burke would never act so despicably as to take advantage of me while I was in a drunken state."

"When we joined you at the table, you were talking about *breasts!*"

The vague memory of doing so made Jayne blush. "I suppose you're right. I don't know what got into me to make such a shocking observation."

"Several glasses of Chablis and champagne got into you. And the man who provided them was Burke. It's a good thing Gideon and I happened along when we did. We probably saved you from a terrible fate. It makes me furious that I believed Burke was a gentleman. He's shown his true colors tonight. Don't worry, Gideon and I will see you

safely home. We won't leave you alone in that man's com
pany again.''

When they left the ladies' room, Jayne was feeling glum
Not another moment alone with Burke? How depressing
As for Emma and Gideon escorting Jayne home... Consid
ering they would be delivering her to Burke's house, tha
was bound to be tricky. It was difficult to unscramble he
thoughts. Perhaps the alcohol she'd consumed was foggin
her ability to think straight. But *not* being alone with Burk
seemed the most terrible fate of all.

When they reached the table, Gideon and Burke rose an
assisted them to their chairs. Euphemia had preached n
woman should allow a man to do something for her tha
she was capable of accomplishing herself. Rememberin
her aunt elicited a feeling of nostalgia. How she misse
Euphemia.

"You ladies timed that right," Gideon said. "Her
comes our food.''

As they were served, conversation fell by the way. Gold
bordered plates heaped with succulently browned slices c
pheasant, wild rice, along with a mixture of peas, carrot
and corn were placed before them. The mouth-waterin
aroma had everyone reaching for their forks.

Chablis was poured. When she was bypassed, Jayne'
defiance grew. After tonight, she wouldn't be partaking c
imported beverages. That didn't vex her overmuch, but nc
being alone with Burke did. If he took her into his arm:
she planned on being an active participant.

She had two concerns—the first was that he would con
duct himself as a gentleman and settle for a few measl
pecks. The second was that, if he should take her into hi
arms, she might disgrace herself by being too aggressiv(
How embarrassing for him to have to restrain her.

Conversation gradually resumed. "How is the remode]
ing at your new building progressing?''

Jayne turned to Emma. "Thanks to the crew of carper

ters Burke engaged, the school is coming along splendidly.''

''I would love to see it,'' Emma said.

Jayne was grateful no one felt the need to point out the madness of her purchasing a former brothel for the site of a girls' school. Some subjects were best left closed. ''It's in a bit of an uproar, but by the end of next week, it should be fit to show.''

''Things should be looking better in your office, Burke,'' Gideon said.

Burke appeared puzzled. ''What do you mean?''

''Ripping Pappy Pickman's sour-faced Wanted poster off your wall is bound to lift your spirits,'' Gideon observed dryly.

Emma turned to her husband. ''Who's this 'Pappy' you're talking about?''

''Just your run-of-the-mill, humpbacked, dynamite-toting bank robber. Burke nabbed him outside the bank.''

''You confronted a criminal?'' Jayne asked, jolted by his recklessness.

Burke shrugged. ''I recognized him from his Wanted poster. I sure wasn't going to let him rob my bank.''

''But from what Gideon says, he had dynamite,'' Jayne said.

''That's Pappy's specialty,'' Burke responded with infuriating calm.

''But you're a banker, not an expert on pistols. In the future, please allow the sheriff and his deputies to handle such dangerous activities.''

Jayne was aware of the incredulous stares she received from her dinner companions. Clearly, they weren't used to someone taking Burke to task. From his cavalier manner of dealing with armed criminals, however, he needed a stern lecture.

''I realize you're concerned about protecting your bank,'' she continued. ''And it's true Sheriff Donner hasn't provided a safe place in which to do business. But dashing about waving a pistol you've probably never fired won't do much good. Goodness, carrying on like that will likely get you shot. Someone might mistakenly believe you're proficient with firearms and strike first." She blotted her lips with a linen napkin. "Accept that you're not a competent gunman and let the authorities take care of matters."

"Are you through?" Burke asked with suspicious softness.

Jayne looked into his glittering eyes and realized he was upset. That was just too bad. Euphemia had stated on occasions too numerous to count that men didn't accept criticism well, but they needed it on a regular basis, lest they sink into a morass of primitive behavior.

"No, I'm not finished. It occurs to me that you've completely overlooked a major source of assistance."

"Don't hold back now," he drawled. "I'm dying to know how to cure my bankrobbing troubles."

"There's no call to be sarcastic." Her glance shifted to Emma and Gideon. The couple's fascinated gazes darted back and forth between her and Burke. "You've overlooked the Guardsmen," she announced triumphantly.

Drinking from her water glass, Emma coughed. Gideon solicitously patted her back. "Are you all right, darling?"

"F-fine," she managed in a strangled voice.

Jayne was at a loss to understand the stunned silence that settled over the table, or the laughter brimming in Gideon's eyes. Everyone in Denver had heard of the Guardsmen's fight against the lawless element that periodically tore through the area.

"While the Guardsmen are remarkably proficient, you're an amateur at confronting criminals," Jayne pointed out determinedly. "All you have to do is place an ad in one of the town's newspapers outlining your dilemma, and they will come to your aid."

Burke leaned back in his chair. "Why didn't I think of that?"

"No doubt you're too close to the situation," Jayne answered.

"What makes you so sure I can't handle a firearm?"

Jayne sighed. Clearly, Euphemia had been right. A man's pride was a fragile thing. "Goodness, Burke, you're a banker. As such, you're expected to excel at keeping accurate ledgers and columns of figures, *not* discharging a pistol."

"Thanks for the vote of confidence."

While Burke didn't appear to appreciate advice from a friend, Jayne was feeling magnanimous and more than willing to share the wisdom floating around in her head. "If I've wounded your sensibilities by speaking forthrightly, I apologize. You do look splendidly lethal prancing about with a pistol strung around your hips. But it's dangerous to try and trick people into believing you can hit the broad side of a barn if you can't."

"*Prancing...*" Burke growled. "I've never pranced a day in my life."

"Be that as it may, continuing to have that holster strapped to you is an invitation to disaster. You must desist wearing it at once."

"Like hell, I will."

"Now, Burke," she said firmly. "Getting angry isn't going to help. I suspect your need to wear a firearm has something to do with male pride."

"I know how to shoot a damned gun."

"I'm sure you do," she said soothingly. "But there's more to discharging a pistol than pulling a trigger. Aunt Euphemia went through her marksmanship phase using a single-action, silver-handled Colt 44. She practiced for hours at a time before reaching any degree of accuracy."

"I thought you said she was an expert with the bow and arrow."

"My aunt was an expert in many areas."

"You mean she thought she was," Burke snapped.

Who would have thought Burke would be so touchy

about his inability to shoot a gun? A solution came to her. "If you insist upon carrying a weapon, then you must begin regular lessons." She turned to Gideon to enlist his aid. "I notice you also wear a holster. Is it for show, or do you have some expertise with the weapon?"

The man's expression darkened. Emma shocked Jayne by bursting into laughter.

"I'm sorry, but I can't help myself. Gideon, if you could see your face…" She pressed a napkin to her mouth, which didn't quell the laughter rippling through her. "Please, forgive me. I don't mean to be impolite…. I must be more tired than I realized."

"It's been a long day. Let's get you tucked into bed."

At her husband's husky statement, Emma gained a semblance of control. Heated awareness flickered in eyes that had moments before watered with tears. Jayne felt as if she'd intruded upon a private moment.

"Yes, I am feeling…tired," Emma said breathlessly. "I promised Jayne we would drop her off on our way."

"That's not necessary."

Both Burke and Jayne spoke in unison. She didn't dare look at him. He was thinking of protecting her reputation, while she was thinking about…uh…unraveling it around its tightly laced edges.

"I must insist," Emma said with gentle resoluteness. "A promise is a promise, after all."

"Thank you all the same," Jayne responded. "But I'm not ready to leave yet. Burke mentioned a French dessert of chocolate, cherries and ice cream."

"That's right," Burke agreed. "I'll see Jayne makes it safely home when we're finished here."

Emma sank back into her chair. "Maybe we ought to stay and—"

"Darling, I'm sure everything is fine. Come along."

Emma rose with obvious reluctance. "I don't know about this…"

The remark was probably meant to have been uttered

under her breath. Wanting to assure her friend everything was under control, or as much control as she wished, Jayne sought to allay Emma's apprehensions.

"I'm very grateful to Burke. All the talk we hear about hard-hearted bankers simply isn't true. He's been wonderful. Truly, a knight on a white charger couldn't have executed a more needed rescue. The way he appeared out of the blue was almost like a miracle."

Emma's features tightened. "Both miracles and plagues can descend from a clear sky. In the beginning, one rarely knows whether it's fortune or plague that's found them."

Gideon cleared his throat. "Say good-night, honey."

Jayne pretended not to see her friend's speaking glance.

"Good night," Emma finally said.

After the couple left, Burke returned to his chair. Jayne was aware of his reflective gaze. Now that they were alone, her mind had been wiped clean of anything to say.

"So, you're in the mood for something creamy and sugary?"

"There was talk about dessert when we arrived," she reminded him.

"Then, by all means, let's indulge."

His voice was as deep and as dark as the melting chocolate she later slid into her mouth. As full as she was from dinner, she had only a few spoonfuls of the cherry-topped vanilla ice cream before pushing the silver bowl away.

"Is that all you're going to have?"

"It was delicious, but I wanted just a taste. You didn't order any for yourself. Would you like to finish mine?"

His eyes smoldered with enough heat to reignite the liquor-based concoction. "My dessert was watching your lips close around that spoon."

Jayne's womb contracted. "I'm ready to leave now."

"Not quite." He dipped the corner of his napkin into his water glass and leaned forward. "You missed some chocolate."

She ran the tip of her tongue across her lips. "Where?"

He groaned. "You're going to make me explode."

She stared at him in confusion. "You're angry?"

He shook his head. "Hold still."

His strong fingers cupped her cheek while he touched the dampened fabric to the corner of her mouth. Jayne suddenly felt as if *she* were about to explode. Her heart hammered and slick heat pulsed deep within her.

Impossibly Burke's gaze grew hotter. "Let's go."

When he held out his arm to escort her from the room she accepted it and pressed close to him.

They took a couple of steps and found their path blocked by Winslow Dilicar. Their exit had taken them past his table. Frank Sutton remained seated.

"What is it, Dilicar?"

"I've been sitting here for the past hour or so trying to come up with the name of your dinner companion."

"Sutton's not much of a conversationalist, I take it."

"I think I've placed her. There's talk around town that you purchased the Wet Beaver. I don't put much stock in improbable rumors, but I got to thinking. There's also been gossip, something about a former teacher at the Hempshire Academy opening a local school for young women. It seems she bought the cathouse in the misguided belief she could turn it into a girls' school."

Dilicar's voice was too loud. He was attracting the attention of other diners. Evidently his spiteful hatred of Burke was vitriolic enough to attack anyone associated with him.

"That's one of the differences between us, Dilicar. You listen to gossip. I don't. I suppose that rag you call a newspaper wouldn't exist, though, if you didn't churn garbage into slander."

Dilicar's fine-boned features became rigid. "Bastard."

A half second passed. Shock filled the man's eyes. Clearly, the insult had escaped without forethought.

Jayne glanced at Burke. Satisfaction simmered in his gaze. She knew intuitively his had been a premeditated provocation to deflect Dilicar's verbal attack on her character. Awe and respect for Burke trembled within her. She hoped she never faced so calculated an opponent.

With no additional comment, Burke turned to leave. Dilicar's long-fingered hand snaked out and grabbed his coat sleeve. Stunned by the sophisticated man's physical aggression, Jayne gasped. Maybe there would be a brawl after all.

Burke shook off the unexpected contact. "You're in over your head, Dilicar. Remember, you don't own the only paper in town. Your competition would like nothing better than to print a story about the prominent Winslow Dilicar being used to mop the floor of the Edgemont. I don't think those bureaucrats in Washington would approve of you being involved in a brawl."

"Your days of making threats are over, Youngblood." The whispered words were a far cry from the man's earlier loudness. He looked toward Jayne. "Not only are you going to lose that charter, but you're going to be brought down. And anyone standing too close will be crushed in the falling rubble. That most certainly includes any female foolish enough to think she can be your paramour *and* a respectable member of the community."

Without warning Burke's fist connected with Dilicar's jaw. The man fell hard against the table he'd been dining at moments earlier. A crash of breaking china and colliding silver resounded in the silent room. Sutton jumped to his feet to avoid being splattered with gravy and other flying debris.

"When your friend comes to, tell him that, if he follows through on his threats, he's a dead man."

Chapter Twelve

In the dim light provided by the carriage's gently swaying lantern, Burke's countenance was one of deep thought.

"There's something I don't understand."

"What's that?" he asked, his attention clearly absorbed elsewhere. An invisible barrier surrounded him as he faced her on the opposite seat with his arms folded across his chest.

"You told Winslow Dilicar that Washington officials wouldn't approve of him becoming involved in a public disturbance."

Burke's gaze bored into her. "So?"

"Won't they object to you resorting to violence in a public place?"

"You pick the damnedest times to be logical."

"There's no reason to get angry."

"Excuse my mood. I don't like being reminded that I've made an idiot of myself. Again. *Over you.*"

Though evenly spaced, his last words rocked with explosive impact.

"You can't blame me for that ugly scene with Dilicar."

He lifted his right palm, fingers raised. "The first time I regressed to idiocy was when I tried to teach you a hare brained lesson about the dangers of residing in a former brothel, which backfired when you knocked me out with a two-by-four.''

She didn't know what to say to that. Even if she now regretted hitting him so hard, it *had* been a harebrained scheme, and he'd deserved the blow.

''No response is necessary,'' he said, bending one finger and continuing. ''My next act of foolhardiness was telling you I'd decided to take on the job of running your life.'' A second finger curved. ''My third act of lunacy was scaling the outside wall of the whorehouse with a damned cat stuck to my back so I could make good on an ultimatum I never should have issued.'' Another finger curved downward.

''Next I found myself caught up in a drunken street brawl trying to save both our hides.'' His pinkie curled. ''Then, with absolutely no regard for propriety, I transported your unconscious body to my house and stripped you down to your female underpinnings.''

His thumb snapped across his curved fingers, forming a fist. ''My next act was to proposition you. Do you know what that means?''

''You need to start counting on your other hand?'' She didn't know where the quip came from. But something about Burke's barely restrained ire prompted the death-defying urge to rattle him further.

His eyes blazed. ''That's it, use your smart little mouth to push me over the edge.''

Pushing him over the edge sounded eminently dangerous and at the same time quite thrilling. ''I didn't force you to do any of those things.''

Like undressing and propositioning me...

''Nor did you force me to invest in your school and loan you an exorbitant amount against your limited future earnings, which means I've been acting like a demented wild man all on my own, hardly a comforting thought.''

''Wait a minute,'' she protested. ''It wasn't demented of you to invest in my school. Advancing me funds against

Uncle Clarence's bank draft was a canny business decision. I'm going to repay you with interest. I daresay you'll make enough of a profit from my venture to...to..."

Drat, the man was so rich the puny profits from her school probably wouldn't amount to what he paid a year on pipe tobacco. "All right, so maybe you won't make a fortune on our bargain, but you'll get your money back and the knowledge that you've helped another business get its start."

An enigmatic expression flickered in his eyes. "I stand corrected. The Stoneworthy School is a sound business investment."

It would have hurt unspeakably if he'd said otherwise. She hated thinking his loan might have been motivated by pity, or something even more repugnant—something based upon a lewd intent to bed her. A few impassioned kisses didn't violate her personal code of ethics. Selling herself did.

"I'm glad you realize my school is a superior investment."

"I realize several things," he said morosely.

She smiled hesitantly. "Are you going to start counting on your fingers again?"

His lips twisted. "Relishing the saga of my recent asinine behavior isn't becoming."

He was right, but even as she carefully erased the smile from her face she was smiling inside. Burke's confession that she had the power to affect his reasoning ability restored a measure of courage.

The carriage came to a stop. Time had run out. There had been no embraces or kisses. Disappointment welled inside her.

"The ride is over," she said hollowly.

"That doesn't mean our conversation is finished."

"I'm afraid it does." To her, the evening's end signaled the conclusion of a relationship that had never begun. It was one thing to converse with Burke in the neutral confines of a moving conveyance. After all, what could happen in a coach, other than exchanging a kiss, or two? However, entering his home, shrouded in darkness with the servants retired for the night, represented a risk to her virtue she dared not take.

"You have an objection to continuing our discussion inside?" His tone was mildly amused.

"When we go in..." She swallowed, "Things will be different."

"That's ridiculous. I—"

Several thumps struck the carriage door. "Are you ready to step out, sir?"

They had reached their destination, and their driver wanted to call it a night.

"Not yet, Walcutt. Take us for a turn around the city. Use the smoothest roads you know."

There was a pause. "Aye, sir."

Less than a minute later, the sway of the lantern resumed.

"Now, where were we, Jayne?"

"You were saying what a shrewd decision it was to invest in my school."

"Was I?" He uncrossed his arms. "Why are you sitting so far away?"

Her stomach fluttered. "No reason."

"Then please join me."

"All right."

He leaned forward. She braced herself for a leap off a high cliff.

"Do you want to tell me why you picked that fight with Youngblood?" Sutton asked in disgust.

He and Dilcar stood in a shadowed corner on the boardwalk. The banker pressed a bloodstained handkerchief to his bleeding nose and cut lip. Sutton admired the damage Youngblood had inflicted in a single punch. On more than one occasion, Sutton had itched to take his own poke at

Dilicar. It was a natural temptation to want to take the
arrogant bastard down a peg or two.

"I didn't pick a fight. I was just trying to needle him by
saying that any woman keeping company with him might
get caught in the cross fire between us."

"So you made taking the federal charter from him a
personal issue?" Sutton looked over his shoulder to make
sure that at least one of the half dozen bodyguards he kept
on his payroll was doing his job.

"How the hell was I supposed to know the schoolmis
tress meant anything to him? She's hardly the sort of fe
male he usually escorts around town." Dilicar jerked the
handkerchief from his face. "Is my nose still bleeding?"

"A tad. So you know who she is?" The prim creature
wasn't the type of full-bodied female he enjoyed tumbling,
but her face was passable enough to compensate for lack
of generous curves.

"I don't remember her name, but I recall hearing some
thing about one of the teachers from the Hempshire Acad
emy opening her own school in Denver."

"What makes you think she's that teacher?"

"My informant at First National keeps me posted on
Youngblood's personal activities, as well as his business
endeavors. The schoolmistress in question stupidly pur
chased the Wet Beaver. Last week Burke became the
place's new owner. He's recently acquired another building
that's being remodeled for the purpose of becoming a girls
school."

"From that sketchy bit of information, you figure he's
squiring the schoolmistress around town?"

"No banker of Youngblood's caliber makes witless busi
ness decisions. He's got to be interested in the woman.
Since he'll be lucky if he breaks even, I assume he antic
ipates repayment between the sheets."

"She's attractive enough to make the deal worthwhile,"
Sutton agreed. "But that doesn't explain why he knocked
you on your ass."

Dilicar winced. "Must you be so crude?"

Sutton smiled. Dilicar was one of the prissiest men he knew. It always gave him pleasure to ruffle his dandified feathers. "I call things the way I see them. You know that."

"I know that Youngblood's gone too far. You're right, it is personal. I'm not only going to take his charter away, I'm going to destroy him."

Sutton's eyes narrowed. Once theirs had been a partnership of three. When Lyman Thornton had ceased being a productive member of that group, Dilicar had had him murdered. Now they were splitting the pie two ways. The way Sutton saw it, if Dilicar started making decisions based on his personal feelings, it was time to keep the pie for himself.

"What do you mean, *destroy* him?"

"I want him broken, no money, no friends, certainly no female companionship."

"How would you accomplish that?"

"When I say 'broken,' I mean it. His legs, his arms, his back. Let's see how long he can hold his damned empire together if he's a cripple."

The violence of Dilicar's brutal words hovered in the night air. Sutton marveled that someone as cultured as Dilicar was capable of such primitive rage.

"Do you understand what I'm saying?" the banker asked. "After I get the charter, I'm going to have Youngblood staked out in the dirt and drive a loaded wagon over him."

"He wouldn't be crippled, he'd be dead," Sutton pointed out.

"Eventually," Dilicar agreed grimly. "But before he dies, his bones will be splintered into so many pieces no doctor will be able to put him back together."

Sutton looked toward the quiet Denver street. Getting the federal charter away from Youngblood was part and parcel of gaining enough wealth and power to take the Double H from Hunter Moran. Youngblood might have already helped him on his way, though. He'd publicly attacked and threatened Dilicar's life.

If anything of a fatal nature should happen to the newspaper publisher and banker... Those bureaucrats in Washington might be slow, but there was no way they would honor an agreement with a murderer.

"We'll see how Youngblood handles Corbett Baldwin," Dilicar said coldly. "Have the arrangements been made?"

"It makes me nervous that Youngblood's connected Baldwin to me."

"Someone saying they saw a man who looked like Corbett Baldwin on your ranch isn't evidence. Baldwin will make sure there's no witnesses to identify him. When does he plan to rob the bank?"

"Monday, maybe Tuesday. He hasn't said for sure."

Dilicar laughed, then flinched. "Any way you cut it, the First National isn't going to be a safe place to conduct business this week. Did you tell him it didn't matter if a few patrons caught some bullets?"

"I told him."

"Washington won't like dead customers littering First National's floor." Dilicar gingerly blotted the handkerchief to his nose as he lowered his head. "I think the bleeding's stopped."

"Do you need help getting home?"

"I can manage."

The two men stepped from the darkened boardwalk into the lit area and headed in different directions. Sutton made sure that a shadow detached itself from the darkness and covered his back as he walked to the livery stable where he'd left his horse.

Sitting so close to Burke was probably a mistake. Somehow in the cozy confines of his carriage, however, the familiarity wasn't all that alarming. The wheels turned steadily toward an unknown destination. Eventually, they would return to his home, and all she would have was the memory of tonight.

"Burke…"

"Hmm…"

"Uh, what are you doing?"

"Smelling your hair."

"Oh."

"I never knew lilacs could smell so sweet."

One of his arms rested casually along the back of the seat. There was nothing casual about the tremors uncoiling within her.

You smell good, too, masculine and…sexy. She couldn't tell him that. "About your quarrel with Mr. Dilicar, do you often resort to violence to resolve your differences?"

The topic seemed safer than inquiring if she could unfasten Burke's top shirt button and perhaps touch a couple of his springy chest hairs.

"Until you entered my life, I had a reputation for self-control, even when dealing with pain-in-the-necks like Dilicar."

"From the horrible things he said, it's obvious he hates you. He looked as if he wanted to…kill you."

"And you're probably wondering what I've done to make an enemy of him?"

"No, it's clear from the way he spoke that he's the kind of man who puts his own interests above others. Your federal charter is something he wants for himself, isn't it?"

"No question about it."

"Even though he's wealthy and dresses the part of a gentleman, I think he's one of those people who hasn't any scruples against furthering his own cause, even at the cost of hurting others."

"That's Dilicar."

"This Frank Sutton person who was with him…" Jayne shuddered. "He seems even more uncivilized."

Burke's hand drifted to her hair. She felt the sensation

of a hairpin being carefully withdrawn. Her shudder of revulsion quickly changed to a tingle of pleasure.

"Sutton's trouble, all right."

"They're such a contrast. One has the attributes of a devious, deadly snake, and the other is like a poisonous toad."

"That's a perfect description."

"They appear to have formed an alliance against you."

Burke chuckled softly. Another hairpin was eased from its mooring. "The thing about snakes and toads is they're natural enemies. Eventually they'll turn on each other."

"It's not fair that you have to contend against bank robbers *and* people taking advantage of your misfortune."

Burke adjusted his position. He placed the hairpins he'd gathered in his coat pocket.

"Don't worry about me. Despite your low opinion of my skill with a gun, I can take care of myself."

"Aunt Euphemia was right."

"Of course, she was. From what you say, the woman knew everything."

"Don't be snide. You never had the privilege of meeting her."

"Thank heaven for small favors."

Jayne poked an elbow in his side. "Don't say unkind things about her. What she was right about is, men don't appreciate being criticized."

"And women eat up every bit of criticism that comes their way?"

"I was trying to be helpful. It's sensible to call upon the Guardsmen."

"The Guardsmen help those who are too weak to help themselves. I've got enough armed guards at the bank to protect it against a small army. Any time you want to spend an afternoon with me, I'll be happy to perform some target practice to show you I damned well know how to hit what I'm aiming at."

Another hairpin skidded free. After tucking it into his

pocket, he turned so that both his hands moved lightly through her loosened hair. The liberty he was taking was shocking indeed. His caressing fingertips moved in a leisurely sweep from her scalp outward.

"Uh, what are you doing now?" The time had come to inquire. "With my hair, I mean."

"Playing with it."

"Oh."

"Have you ever sat on a man's lap before?"

"No."

With a firm tug, he pulled her onto his lap. She'd thought sitting alongside him had been an intimate experience. She'd been wrong. Now, with just the slightest inclination of her head, his smoothly shaven jaw and lean lips were a scant inch away. His rock-hard thighs cradled her as she sat sideways so that her legs were stretched out on the seat.

She folded her hands neatly on her lap. And waited. Surely now he would kiss her. Her heart thudded in her chest, and her stomach rolled over. She sneaked glances at him from her lowered eyelashes. Any second now he would make his move.

He continued to fool with her hair. Patiently, as if he had all evening to accomplish the simple task, he threaded his fingers through the unbound strands. His lingering caress stroked the sensitive area at the nape of her neck, making her tremble.

"One of the first things I noticed about you was your blond hair."

His husky voice was a caress in its own right.

"It's light brown."

"It almost reaches your waist." He lowered his face and gathered her hair into his hands. She felt him inhale. "It smells sweeter than sunshine, and it feels as silky as a mountain rain shower against my skin, every honey-colored, golden strand of it."

Being alone with an amorous Burke was a far more intoxicating experience than she had imagined. Hearing the deep timbre of his voice as he praised her, feeling the subtle stroke of his fingertips threading through her hair, and having his solid frame against her affected her senses more potently than the Chablis and champagne she'd drunk.

He rubbed his thumb along the side of her cheek. ''Your skin is so soft.''

The path of his touch moved slowly, deliberately from her cheek to her mouth. Again, moving with excruciating slowness, he ran his callused thumb along her upper and lower lip. Inexorably her mouth opened slightly.

She felt so vulnerable, aching with a need so intense she didn't know how she kept from reaching for him. It took every bit of willpower she possessed not to turn her head and seek the kiss she trembled to experience.

Abruptly he used his thumb and forefinger to grip her chin, tilting her face so that their moist breaths mingled. Determination burned in his gaze. She melted against him.

At last his mouth came. There was no hesitation. Firmly he claimed what she offered. The friction of his demanding possession sent currents of desire chasing through her. His tongue masterfully sought and conquered the territory she surrendered without a fight.

There was no fight in her. She wanted to yield, wanted to experience his fierce ardor. One strong hand cupped the back of her head. His other palm rested beneath the curve of her breasts.

Unprepared for the urgency of the passion she'd yearned to experience, Jayne felt as if she'd been swept into a silent storm. By some mysterious magic, the storm raged both around and within her.

A kiss. It was only a kiss, but somehow it loosened waves of endless need. It was as if, without knowing it, she'd been dead, empty of all feeling. Now, life was surging into every particle of her being. One winter in Philadelphia she'd had a mild case of frostbite. When the sensation of flowing blood had returned to her toes, she'd been racked by pain.

How could the pleasure Burke awoke within her incite that same kind of hurt? But she did hurt, with the piercing realization that life was surging into the barren shell of a woman's body who had never loved. She clung to him, wound her fingers through his thick hair and drew him closer.

A hunger had been freed within her. Squirming against him, moaning into his open, demanding mouth... None of it was real, none of it was enough.

He broke the primitive contact of their mating mouths, stringing hot kisses along her jaw and throat.

"Sweet mercy, I want you."

His low growl permeated through clothing, through skin, into her soul.

"I want you, too."

"Oh, honey, if only you meant that..." He turned her so that she straddled his lap, hiking up her skirts. "Can you feel how much I want to be inside you?"

She did feel him. Rigid, unyielding against the most private part of her. Only her pantalettes and the fabric of his trousers separated them from the ultimate caress. A wave of dizziness crashed over her. And something else, something deliciously arousing at the juncture of her thighs. She moved against him and felt tingling spasms of sensation.

"Oh, my goodness..."

His hands were on her bodice. He stroked her breasts through the material of her dress. Twin prickles of tightening pleasure leaped through her. His tongue probed her mouth.

The carriage bucked suddenly as it rolled over an uneven patch of roadway. She came down on the hardened bulge that seemed designed for the sole purpose of driving her insane with pleasure.

Burke's palms clamped her derriere, holding her to him. He squeezed the tender flesh possessively.

"Oh...my..."

White lights exploded behind her eyelids. Waves and

waves of hot, slick ecstasy shot through her. As Burke squeezed her buttocks, it seemed that every cell in her body clenched to savor the splendid eruption.

"Oh my, is right," Burke groaned into her mouth.

He moved abruptly so that she was sitting sideways across his lap. His hand slid beneath her skirts and up her leg, heading in a direct path for the pulsating chaos rippling through her.

"What are you doing?" she gasped. Having his hand at the apex of her thighs at any time, let alone when a whirlwind had convened there, shattered the sensual spell.

"I'm going to make it better."

Better? Obviously he had no idea how good it already was.

"I don't think—"

His fingers inched forward, gently stroking her through the wet fabric of her pantalettes, which because of their design, he was able to part and then he was.... He was touching her tingling flesh. Jayne buried her face against his chest.

"I love touching you this way. I can tell you love it, too, don't you?"

With her face pressed into his shirt, she could say nothing. But, he had to know. There was no way she could keep from moving against him, savoring, no, reveling in his masterful embrace. She'd never imagined one human being could make another feel this way, special, cherished and on fire.

"Talk to me, honey. I want to know if I'm pleasing you."

"I... Oh!"

It was happening again. A choked scream sprang free. His hot, wet mouth swallowed it. And she was there. Again. In that dark, rapturous place where fire and pleasure reigned. Spasm upon spasm of ecstasy rippled through her.

Finally, the storm quieted and she lay acquiescent in his

embrace. Mortified and sated. It was a disorienting combination.

His tender caress continued. Inexpressibly gentle, inexpressibly intimate. Her face grew hot. How did a woman ask a man to…er…desist with a liberty she'd brazenly allowed him?

"You're so soft, so responsive."

She tried to shut out his seductive words, trying unobtrusively to pull free.

"Am I being too rough?"

Did he honestly expect her to answer? Things had escalated far beyond the few kisses she'd envisioned them exchanging.

"Talk to me, honey."

"Uh, well… That is to say… Could you…uh…stop that?"

Immediately the stroking ceased.

"Having regrets, are you?"

His tone was amazingly cool, considering that she felt like a hot glob of melted chocolate, cherries and cream.

She looked away. "Everything happened so suddenly."

"Yeah, you pretty much went up in flames the second I touched you."

"Could you…uh…stop touching me? Now."

"You weren't complaining a few minutes ago."

Was there some kind of proper etiquette for situations such as this, which Euphemia had failed to teach her?

"I'm not actually complaining," she said carefully. "I admit that it was…well…quite frankly the most astonishingly pleasant thing that's ever happened to me. And, something of a shock," she couldn't resist adding. Goodness, who would have guessed that being touched by a man could spark such intense pleasure?

He kissed the tender skin beneath her ear. "There are a few more surprises."

Surely, he was making that up. "Burke, I think it's time we stop this."

"It's not over yet."

She bit her lower lip, silently reciting her ABC's backward to curb her runaway passions.

"Yes, it is."

Slowly, maddeningly, his fingers retreated.

"Thank you," she whispered.

"Thank you," he returned, his voice raw and gritty. "I'm still hurting, but I guess that's to be expected."

"I'll slip off your lap, and you'll be fine."

He laughed hoarsely, but helped her slide to the seat. "Oh yeah, this fixes everything."

Tears came to her eyes. She'd acted shamelessly, and now Burke wanted for himself the same pleasure he had given her.

He had every right to be furious. How could she possibly explain that all she'd wanted was his splendid kisses, not his earthy caress? But he had given her both, and she'd enjoyed both. Perhaps she did owe him the full measure of the desire he wished to satisfy.

She recoiled at the thought. The only thing she *owed* him was an explanation. She'd never dreaded anything more than offering it.

"I know I've behaved abominably, and the shameless liberties I allowed give you every right to expect to have carnal relations with me."

"Hell…"

"I'm sorry if my bluntness offends you, but we need to settle this."

"Obviously not in the way I'd prefer."

"Don't be vulgar."

He slanted her a quelling glance. "The way I'm feeling right now, you should be grateful we're talking and not… Oh hell, this whole night has been a fiasco."

"I keep telling you that you don't have to mince words with me," she admonished him. "You were going to say that I should be grateful that we're talking and not coupling."

He cleared his throat. "Right, that's what I was going to say."

"Then you should have said it. I am a free-thinking female, you know."

"So you are."

"And I'm mature enough to accept the blame for what happened. I wanted you to kiss me, you see."

An indecipherable expression claimed his shadowed features. "Did you?"

"It was all I could think about. It's why I accepted your dinner invitation. Even when you were talking to that painted woman who came to our table, I was thinking about it."

"You ended up doing more than thinking about it."

"I know," she said morosely. "I practically threw myself into your arms. And then when I was on your lap, I was afraid I was going to…uh…attack you, before you got around to kissing me."

"That would have been…interesting."

"After the suspense of waiting all night for you to finally embrace me, I think I snapped. And then, when I felt your fingers down there…" She swallowed, "something happened."

"It sure as hell did."

She winced. "It caught me by surprise."

She waited for him to say something. He remained obstinately silent. She gathered more courage. "That something took over. I didn't care about anything but letting those feelings envelop me."

"Is there a point to this apology? Because it sure as hell isn't helping."

"The point is, only an immoral woman would allow a man to…uh…have his way with her without the benefit of marriage. I don't wish to become that kind of woman."

"You said pretty much the same thing a couple of weeks ago," he pointed out.

''But I didn't know then how marvelous you could make me feel. At least now I understand one thing.''

''What's that?''

''Why women marry. It occurs to me that when Emma and Gideon went home tonight, it was with the intention of making love.''

''I imagine about now Gideon is feeling a whole lot better than I am.''

''He has a wife,'' Jayne said through gritted teeth.

''At least I understand something that's always eluded me.''

''What's that?''

''The unexpected interest a confirmed bachelor suddenly might have in matrimony, that is after he's come up against a moral woman.''

Chapter Thirteen

Agnes Sawyer's boardinghouse was a major step down from Burke's palatial residence. Jayne especially missed the water closet. She tied her bonnet's ribbons, concentrating on the advantages of her hasty move.

Had she remained at his house, she would have been in constant danger of hurling herself into his arms and begging him to make hot, steamy love to her. No doubt he would have obliged, in places more conducive to lovemaking than a jostling carriage. Though she had to admit the vehicle hadn't drastically impeded his success at making her body sizzle.

She swept her reticule from a chair and opened the bedchamber door. Besides protecting Burke from the wayward passions he'd awakened within her, there were other benefits to living at the boardinghouse. Her reputation would be safe. Also, the amount she was paying for her room and board was far less than what she would have spent at the hotel Burke had recommended.

He'd done more than recommend a hotel, she recalled. The night they'd returned from the scandalous carriage ride, he'd insisted she remain in his home as his guest until the school was finished. She'd declined, of course. A brief but heated quarrel had ensued.

Forever scalded into her consciousness was the torrid

passion he'd rained upon her. Even now, three days later, she was unable to pry her thoughts from Burke's electrifying effect. Just thinking about his intimate caress sent errant tremors skating through her.

As she descended the stairs to the parlor, she took comfort from the fact that she wasn't the kind of shallow woman who would sacrifice her personal ethics for unspeakably shattering ecstasy, or indoor plumbing.

The parlor's most noticeable feature was the four windows that faced Driscoll Avenue. Blindingly white eyelet curtains spilled from ceiling height to polished hardwood floors. Mrs. Sawyer was a zealous housekeeper. Not one particle of dust was apparent on a single table, lamp or piece of bric-a-brac.

"There you are, Miss Stoneworthy."

At the sound of her landlady's greeting, Jayne turned. The blond woman with strong Scandinavian features wore a friendly smile. Her hair was secured in a circular braid on top of her head. A spotless white apron was fastened over a billowy blue cotton blouse tucked into a gray skirt.

"Was breakfast to your liking?"

Jayne had come down promptly at seven, when the morning meal was served. Dinner would be provided at six this evening.

"It was delicious," she replied. There had been fried eggs, potatoes, scones and honey, and thick slices of ham.

"I appreciate you being on time. Dawdlers miss out. I'm not running a restaurant." She folded her arms across her ample bosom. "Are you sure the food was to your liking? You didn't eat much."

Mrs. Sawyer came across as a businesswoman, yet there was an underlying softness to her manner that hinted at a maternal nature.

"What with moving in and trying to get my school established, I seem to have lost my appetite." Hadn't she said something like that to Burke the night he'd taken her to the

Edgemont? She flushed at the new, unappeasable appetites he'd awakened.

Approval filled Mrs. Sawyer's blue eyes. "I think the school you're starting will be a fine thing for the young women who'll go there."

Sally Haskell had said virtually the same thing. How amazing—very proper housekeepers and gaudily dressed prostitutes sharing the same opinions.

"Well, I'll bid good-day to you."

"Good day to you, Mrs. Sawyer."

When Jayne walked from the boardinghouse, she didn't head directly to the new school. Instead she directed her footsteps to the post office. Maybe today Uncle Clarence's bank draft would finally arrive.

Burke slammed a new slew of Wanted posters onto his desk.

She'd moved out. He couldn't believe it. After the soft, earnest passion she'd sweetly surrendered in his carriage, she'd announced in that firm, no-nonsense tone that made him want to kiss her into dazed submission, that she was moving to Agnes Sawyer's Boarding Domicile for Single Females.

Burke stalked to the window overlooking Larimer Street and scowled down at the congested thoroughfare. Short of tying her to a bedpost, there was no way he could compel her to stay. She was the damnedest, stubbornest woman he'd ever had the misfortune to encounter. She was also the most honest.

He thought about their dinner at the Edgemont. Guilt stirred. He had set out to get her a bit tipsy to lower some of her inhibitions. He'd only been after a few kisses. It had never occurred to him his self-control would desert him. The trouble was, with her inhibitions lowered and her speaking her thoughts openly as they tumbled through her creative brain, Jayne Stoneworthy was absolutely irresistible.

I have shoulders, you know, even if I don't go around brazenly flaunting them....

She'd said something to that effect, and for some reason, her innocent defiance had utterly disarmed him.

Damn, he hadn't been disarmed. He'd been unhinged. Only an out-and-out bounder would take advantage of a slightly inebriated woman. Burke turned from the window. He hadn't meant for things to go so far. A couple of kisses, a caress or two. A man couldn't be hung for such minor offenses.

He'd taken more, of course. Or, to be more accurate, he'd given more. When they'd stepped from his carriage, he'd been as sexually frustrated as a man could be while still able to walk.

Now she was gone. And, just as he'd feared, she'd taken all the light and color that had recently filled his life when she'd left. Idly, he flicked through the flyers on his desk. What was eating a hole the size of Texas in his gut was that he had no reason to be upset. She was behaving exactly as a proper, if somewhat unconventionally brought-up young woman should behave. He was the one whose actions were unacceptable. The only decent destiny for a naive female like Jayne Stoneworthy was marriage. But, because of her eccentric aunt, along with Jayne's distorted belief that women should be allowed to act and think independently, she erroneously believed matrimony was a fate worse than death.

He'd believed the same thing. But that was different. Any fool could see marriage benefited women more than men. A woman needed to be cared for, sheltered and protected. Just because Jayne was oblivious to the fact, though, didn't mean she eventually couldn't be guided to the proper conclusion. She required a strong hand, and a man unintimidated by her free-thinking ways to manage her.

She was a passionate creature. It was asinine to think she could go her entire life without experiencing the full measure of her womanly desires. And, damn it, it didn't matter how stubborn she chose to be. He bloody well was going to be the man who shared those passions.

He was going to marry her.

Burke froze. The heresy came from nowhere. And yet, as it seeped into his consciousness, he realized its inescapable correctness. He would marry the independent, unpredictable, stubborn...

The adjectives trailed off. Maybe he'd feel better if he concentrated on her soft lips, sleek curves and the incredible responsiveness she'd demonstrated to his touch.

That line of reasoning didn't work. It wasn't just her body that drew him. It was her defiant brain, her courageous spirit and simple desire to stand on her own two feet that made her impossible to walk away from.

He wanted her, all right. All of her. For a lifetime. What made marriage acceptable was the knowledge he *didn't* love her. That insight made all the difference. Marrying her and loving her were two different things. As long as he kept his wits about him and a sense of perspective, he needn't worry about making the stupid mistakes of judgment other men did when they duped themselves into believing all that nonsense about romantic love.

It would be a sound match. He would offer security, loyalty, not to mention his skills in the bedchamber. She would bring honor, intelligence and unbridled passions to their marriage bed. There would be children. All things considered, it wasn't a bad arrangement. More than fair, in fact. Theirs would be a flawless partnership. And she could keep her school.

Because he was a man who counted costs in advance, even in his personal actions, it should have been easy to lay out the practical aspects of such a union. If *he* found it challenging to consider things pragmatically, Jayne would probably become paralyzed by indecisiveness. She'd want to know the answers to questions he couldn't begin to fathom. She was, after all, a woman and prone to emotional rather than coolheaded considerations.

He had no choice but to seduce her. It didn't matter how he got her to become his wife. Once she was committed before a judge or preacher, she would honor her vows. He knew that without question.

Feeling in control of his private universe, Burke sat behind his desk and began riffling through the Wanted posters. He paused when he reached a particularly nasty-faced desperado.

"Well, what have we here?"

Printed neatly beneath the sketch was the name, Corbet Baldwin. He'd last been sighted in the Wyoming Territory which, considering modern rail travel, wasn't too great a distance from Colorado.

A knock sounded on Burke's door. "Come in."

Looking more harried than usual, Owen Gardner stepped into the room.

"I thought you were overseeing Miss Stoneworthy's move to the new building." Burke frowned. There had been a couple of recent incidents when Gardner had failed to follow through on instructions.

"I am, sir. I mean I was. She's just come from the post office, though, and wishes to speak with you."

"She's here?" A flash fire of excitement swept through Burke. There was no time like the present to initiate his plan. Not, of course, that he would seduce her in his office. He glanced around the room. Actually, though, it was tastefully decorated, and there was a couch. The door could be locked—

He noticed the Wanted posters with their ugly faces leering at him. What was he thinking? He shoved a hand through his hair. He wasn't thinking. He was reacting like an untried boy trying to lure a girl into a barn for a round of juvenile pawing. If he wasn't careful, it wouldn't matter that he didn't *love* Jayne. His crazy behavior would prove just as debilitating as if he were trapped in the throes of the self-destructive emotion.

"Did you wish to see her without an appointment?" Gardner asked.

Burke looked at his assistant in consternation. "Jayne never needs an appointment to see me. Notify everyone here that any time she shows up, I want her ushered into my office without delay."

"Yes, sir."

When Jayne stepped into the room, an unpleasant feeling of insecurity plagued Burke. It might not be smooth sailing to get her to accept his conclusions about marriage. He squared his shoulders. There was no way this petite woman dressed in a gray jacket and plaid skirt could hold out against a relentless assault.

"Jayne, what a pleasant surprise."

She waved an open envelope. "It's finally come, Uncle Clarence's bank draft. And it's more than he said he would send."

Her cheeks were flushed, her green eyes bright with excitement. Burke's groin tightened. He wanted to see the same animation in her lively features for an altogether different reason than picking up correspondence at the United States Post Office.

His gaze fixed on her gray bonnet. Its stark simplicity was relieved by green, yellow and pink satin ribbons fashioned in a bow attached at a jaunty angle above its brim. The colorful bits of ribbon matched the plaid in her skirt and mirrored the wellspring of hidden fires he knew burned within her. The world might not realize it, but he did. Jayne Stoneworthy marched through life with banners flying. Her directness, idealism and innate honesty in no way dulled her femininity.

Free-thinking females could be sweetly passionate. The discovery stunned him. Where had society gotten the idea that feminine intelligence was at odds with womanliness?

Jayne swept into Burke's office, her feelings a jumble of warring emotions. Being in a position to discharge her debt was immensely satisfying. Yet mingled with that satisfac-

tion was the unwelcome realization that settling her obli
gation would cut the final thread connecting them. Did she
really want to sever all association with him?

Added to her turbulent feelings was the keen self
consciousness she felt. There was, after all, another kind of
business between them—the liberties she'd permitted. It
was one thing, she learned, to cozy up to a man in a dimly
lit carriage and quite another to confront him in broad day
light. A person could forget oneself in a darkly seductive
setting, forget about proprieties and limits, and stringent
warnings from maiden aunts.

Part of Jayne hoped he'd put the unfortunate incident
from his thoughts. She wouldn't want him to form the
wrong idea about her virtue or lack thereof. Yet another
part of her wanted him to remember everything and hold
it close to his heart. Did men have that capacity? To cherish
stolen moments and liberties granted, and to esteem them
as precious? Perhaps only women possessed that unique
ability.

One thing was certain. When she settled her debt, he
would no longer hold any momentary power over her. The
one-sided nature of their relationship would irrevocably
shift. As she stared into his steady gaze, however, a shiver
teased her spine. Canceling her financial obligation would
not eradicate another, deeper, darker power he exercised
over her. The daunting realization swept through her that
Burke Youngblood had done more than enter her life. He'd
entered her soul. Whatever transpired between them in the
future, he held a very real power over her. Did she hold
that same kind of power over him?

Could she make him ache? For her?

Jayne shook her head. What was she thinking? The last
thing she wanted was to arouse a storm of uncontrollable
lust in the male creature staring down at her with such
ferocious intensity. To be guilty of such a singularly witless
act would thrust her into the category of foolish female

Euphemia had repeatedly reproached for their biological weakness in submitting to men.

What a revolting discovery, to find that, after all these years, she was the very sort of biological weakling her aunt had held in such benign contempt.

"I've come to settle my account," she announced starkly. Surely, the way to gain control of her rioting thoughts was through intelligent conversation. Perhaps feigning an attitude of confidence would steady her.

Burke had risen to his feet the moment she entered the room. She couldn't sustain his penetrating gaze for more than a few seconds. Her attention darted around his office's opulent trappings. Without knowing anything about Burke, and judging him solely from this lushly appointed chamber, she would have concluded it belonged to a man of means and power.

Her investigation came to an abrupt halt when she encountered the paneled wall behind his massive desk. Dozens of brutally evil faces stared back at her with malevolent intensity. The purpose for her visit receded briefly in her thoughts.

"Why on earth do you have all those men hanging on your wall?"

"Because the law hasn't been able to hang them from the gallows." It was a weak attempt at humor, he knew. But, as Gardner hastily excused himself, Burke had to do something to relieve the sudden tension gripping him.

Having Jayne in his office awoke a barrage of startlingly violent yearnings within him. In the two nights she'd been gone from his home, a searing hunger had grown within him to reclaim her, or more accurately to truly claim her once and for all.

"I assume their display has something to do with the robberies."

"Since their ugly pusses don't reflect my taste in art, that's a safe assumption."

"Uh, I don't wish to be critical, but there don't appear

to be that many guards posted out front. Do you thin now's a good time to relax your security precautions?''

''Things aren't always as they appear. Not all the guard I've hired are dressed in uniforms.''

She looked at a loss for words. Her gaze kept sliding t various corners of the room. Her obvious nervousnes smoothed the ragged edge of his composure. She was re membering, he thought with savage satisfaction. She wa remembering how he'd made her feel in his arms. Unfor tunately, his easing tension was bittersweet. He was caugh in those same sweetly tormenting memories. The soft, slee texture of her trembling flesh, her strangled sob of release her female scent... All of it was branded into his brain wit a feral power that made his heart pound and his groir tighten.

Her pink cheeks put him in mind of how her soft breast would look, hard-peaked and flushed. He wanted desper ately to see and touch them without the impediment o clothing. How had he let things progress as far as he ha the other evening without unbuttoning her bodice?

He'd gone at things backward, with a total lack of fi nesse, driven only by a primal need to touch her. Her un inhibited response had driven him to show her the awesom splendor her body could deliver.

The silence in his office pulsated with tremors of un voiced need. ''Maybe you'd better show me the ban draft.''

Could she hear the rawness in his voice?

''Uh... Well, yes, I suppose I should.''

Standing on the other side of his desk, she extended he hand. He looked at both it and the letter. Sweat broke ou on his brow. Only a madman would believe he could gras the hand rather than take the letter. It staggered him ho much control it required to choose the sturdy envelope Fanning out in his mind was the incredibly sexy image o Jayne sprawled across his desk, her eyelids closed in sen sual surrender while he caressed her.

"Please," he said, his voice as gritty as if it had passed through a pile of sand. "Sit down."

Sit down, before I throw you down—on my desk, or the sofa or... Good grief, the floor would do.

He rubbed his eyes and claimed the chair behind his desk, forcing himself to concentrate on the amount of the draft. "Uncle Clarence must have been feeling generous when he sent this."

"I was astonished when I saw it. Frankly, because of the delay, I'd begun to fear he'd changed his mind."

"And you wish to apply all of it against the debt you've incurred?"

"Goodness, Burke, the size of that draft should be more than enough to totally clear my financial obligation."

He glanced up, carefully keeping his expression neutral. He'd already decided she would never discover the amount he'd funneled into the school of her dreams. She was a proud woman and would insist upon complete repayment, even if the burden caused her financial hardship.

"You're right. This more than cancels your debt."

"Naturally, I'll expect a complete tally of the costs I've incurred."

Her crisp tone scraped his patience. "Don't you trust me, Jayne?"

The unnatural flush returned. "It isn't a matter of trust. As a banker, you must understand the importance of keeping careful records."

"Then you do trust me." He needed to wring that admission from her.

She licked her lips. "It goes without saying that you're extremely scrupulous in matters relating to business."

"And in other areas?"

She damned well was going to say she would trust him with her life, as well as her virtue. In the light of his planned seduction, his desire for such a declaration was absurd. His intentions were honorable, though, he reminded himself fiercely. He was going to marry her. That kind of sacrifice warranted a pledge of trust. His gaze narrowed. Hell, after putting him through the recent torture he'd experienced, he wouldn't be satisfied until she told him she loved him.

Again, her gaze avoided his. Her feminine advance and retreat put him in mind of how she might make love to him. Would her gentle caress draw close to the hot, pulsing part of him that burned for her touch, only to slide away before he felt her fingers touch his skin?

"In other areas," she said softly, "I suppose I'm not quite so sure of your...dependability."

"What the hell does that mean?" he demanded, incensed by the slur to his character.

"Well, there is the matter of what happened in your...carriage."

He had to strain to hear the last softly uttered word. "And you hold me completely responsible for that?"

"It was *your* hand beneath my skirts." Her face was beet-red.

"You didn't exactly fight me off," he pointed out, hanging on to his temper by the frailest thread.

"I know I should have, but I wasn't prepared for...well..."

"How good it felt," he ground out.

She ran her forefinger around the high collar of her white blouse and encountered the tied bonnet strings. When she reached up with her other hand to loosen the restraining ties, the unconsciously seductive nature of the feminine gesture made him grit his teeth.

"Emma suggested that you had an ulterior motive for taking me to dinner and providing a veritable fountain of alcoholic beverages to imbibe. At the time, I defended you. But, after careful reflection upon the matter, it occurs to me that you...well...that you *did* have an ulterior motive for engineering our evening together."

Burke felt a wave of heat creep above his shirt collar. It galled him that his actions had been that callow *or* that transparent. Adding to his discomfort was the knowledge that his present behavior could not withstand the harsh light of close examination. He doubted either Emma or Jayne would condone his current goal to bind Jayne to him under the full measure of God's and man's laws by the expedient means of anticipating the wedding vows he expected to exchange with her.

"If it had been my intention to compromise you, I would have done it." He leaned forward, planting his palms on the desktop. "And you wouldn't have offered a single protest. Because, as I recall, you were fully satisfied. I, on the other hand, most certainly was *not*."

Her eyes glistened with emotion. "I'm painfully aware of what happened. I know that I acted with shameless abandon, just as I know you didn't find...uh...the same release I did."

Her obvious distress smote Burke. It wasn't his intention to embarrass her or to make her think less of herself. "Jayne—"

"But, if you're telling me," she interrupted, her voice trembling, "that there still remains an outstanding debt between us because of that night, I can only say that I will not barter myself to repay it."

The quiet dignity in both her words and bearing made him feel like the vilest of vermin. "Damn it, Jayne, that's not what I meant."

"Isn't it?"

The direct question and the hard honesty she imposed upon both herself and him tunneled through the carefully layered walls of self-deception he'd erected to justify simply reaching out and taking what he wanted.

In one sweeping moment as he stared across his desk at her, he accepted the fact that a deliberate seduction of this woman went against something deeper within him than his rigid rules never to be governed by his heart. The revelation swept through him that Jayne Stoneworthy was a woman of honest emotions, and, as such, deserved to be treated with uncompromising honesty.

When that thought struck the bedrock of what had once been the single unifying theme of his reality, another truth surfaced. If he let go of his cold-blooded, analytical approach to capturing and securing Jayne, he would be at her mercy. No, that wasn't exactly right. Because being at Jayne's mercy shouldn't have loosened the primal storm of resistance surging through him.

He knew with an absolute conviction transcending logic that Jayne posed no threat. Why then did he feel as if he were standing before a bottomless black hole? What was he afraid of? Hell, face it, he was terrified.

His chest was so tight he couldn't breathe. He looked into Jayne's vulnerable gaze. The answer hit him with ice-cold clarity. What he resisted was the very vulnerability she unconsciously exposed. He damn well didn't want to be vulnerable. He wanted the armor-plated walls of his logic and his reason encircling him. He wanted the security of distancing himself from the real, debilitating pain that had invaded him when his younger brother had turned his back on him because he'd chosen to believe the lying evidence of his eyes instead of the older brother he'd once hero-worshiped.

Burke never wanted to experience that kind of pain again.

He stood at a crossroads. Jayne *was* his for the taking, whether she knew it or not, whether she admitted it or not. He had the ability to make her want him in the most fundamental way a woman could want a man. All he had to do was reach out and take her. A few kisses, a few husky words of adoration, a few intimate caresses...

He could keep his own feelings under lock and key. Hell, he was a master at that. She would eventually marry him because she would have no recourse. He would have everything necessary to make his life complete. He was pretty sure he could even get her to love him. Despite her aunt's teachings, Jayne had a lot of love to give.

Just take it, take her....

"Emma Cade was right, to an extent," he said quietly, carefully choosing his words. Total honesty equaled a total loss of control. He would sooner cut his throat than lower the shield that had protected him most of his adult life . "I wasn't thinking of seducing you, though." *Not then, but I sure as hell am now.* "I was thinking more along the lines of a few kisses."

The truth mocked him. Had he really thought a few paltry kisses would satisfy him?

A tentative half smile curved Jayne's mouth. "I was…uh…thinking the same thing."

Even though he'd heard her soft confession before, it seriously weakened his resolve to court her honorably.

She glanced down at her lap. "At least things didn't get *completely* out of control."

Because I didn't get completely inside you.

But, he could. Now. Here. Her awakening desire was clearly evident in the shallow breaths lifting her breasts. Just talking about that night had her hot and bothered. He shifted his position. He was experiencing the same problem. It was a problem with a simple solution, one he would have seized with another woman. But he'd already accepted the fact that Jayne wasn't just another woman passing through his sterile existence.

"Things didn't get out of control because you ran away."

"That's unfair," she protested swiftly. "You had no right to expect further liberties."

"I had no right…." He tasted the words and found them bitter. Pushing back his chair, he rose slowly to his feet.

Evidently his action startled her, because she immediately stood. "What are you doing?"

Hell if I know… He circled the desk.

She backed up. "Burke, I don't like that look in your eyes."

"What look is that?"

"Th-that look of decisiveness."

Wishing he knew what in blazes he had decided, he cupped her shoulders, drawing her to him.

"Kiss me."

Not knowing how she would react to his blunt command, he brought his mouth down. Her lips trembled before parting, slowly. He took his time exploring the moist territory she so sweetly yielded. The taste of her was a bewitching combination of sultry flavors that spoke of woman, innocence and...eagerness.

Two opposing desires slammed into him. He wanted this moment to continue forever, to draw out his leisurely possession until each of them was fully satiated by joining their mouths. Another, more primal, need clawed for release.

He tried to lessen the intensity of the kiss that threatened to incinerate them. Jayne would have none of it. Each time he retreated, she pressed forward, the dainty tip of her tongue demanding a response. He shuddered against her.

How could any man resist such temptation? And why should he? Why not take what she was so obviously fired up to give? She'd had a sampling of physical pleasure and clearly wanted more. What could be simpler?

The word shimmied through his raging need to possess. Hadn't he already decided that things weren't meant to be simple between them? In an effort to clear his thoughts and gain a measure of control over his hunger, he tore his lips from hers.

"Jayne..."

She stood on tiptoe, her upturned face raised to him. Her eyelids were lowered, her wet, pinkened lips parted, her warm breath teased his skin. *Not* leaning forward and surrendering to the madness ripping at the steel restraints he'd clamped on the desire ricocheting through him almost brought him to his knees.

Take her.... Now....

He couldn't. A great wave of—the closest thing he could equate it to was tenderness—washed over him. He could do nothing to hurt this woman. Oh, he wanted her and would have her, but not on his desk, on his office settee or on the floor. He would have her in their marriage bed.

"Jayne..." He shook her shoulders.

Slowly her lashes rose. The naked, unmasked feminine passion staring at him threatened to shatter the strength of will he'd momentarily summoned.

"Yes?"

"I need your help."

"I thought I was...helping."

"I need your help to stop." Confessing his weakness took as much grit as keeping his trousers fastened. Now, there was a humbling admission.

She ran the tip of her tongue across her kiss-swollen lips. "Uh, is there a particular reason you want to stop?"

He groaned. She was killing him by inches. "Jayne, we're not children. There's only one way things will end if we continue."

"Tell me how it's going to end."

Tell her? He wanted to *show* her. "You're playing with fire."

"I know. I can feel the heat."

Caught in a dark spell of his own making, he became fixated with the top black button fastening her jacket. He imagined sliding it free from its closure. "I don't want to seduce you."

Had that hoarse whimper crawled from his throat?

She rested her cheek against his jacket. "I'm being horribly brazen again, aren't I?"

He had to strain to hear the soft-voiced utterance. His hands clenched around her shoulders as he held her close. He wanted to protect her at all costs. Her security suddenly meant more to him than guarding his own pride.

He removed her bonnet and laid it on his desk before

resting his jaw on the crown of her head. Carefully, he framed his next words. There were some he wasn't capable of saying, like *love* and *cherish*.

"I want you...."

The bald emptiness of his declaration mocked him. He felt her stiffen. In a minute she would be struggling to break free from the embrace she'd instigated. He couldn't let that happen.

"I can be gentle, Jayne." Again the word "cherish" drifted through his thoughts. *I want to cherish you....* And again, he couldn't speak it. *I want to woo you—mind, body and soul.... I would offer my heart, but it's a shriveled organ that's barely keeping me alive.* "I've missed you," he finally said. "The house hasn't been the same since you left."

This time when she tried to squirm free, he released her. He wasn't sure, though, that if she attempted to leave his office, he was capable of letting her go.

"How could you miss me?" she asked, obviously skeptical. "You hardly saw me when I was there."

With her bonnet gone, her shiny blond hair was mildly disheveled. He longed to extract the remaining pins and see it hanging free around her shoulders, her bare shoulders, the ones she'd assured him she had at the Edgemont. Again, a wave of unspeakable tenderness rolled through him.

"Just knowing you were there made things different. Now that you're gone..."

"Yes?"

"Everything seems flat. There's no color." He jammed his fists into his pockets. This business of speaking honestly was worse than suffering a gunshot wound. In his thoughts, chaotic though they were, things seemed reasonably clear. It was when he tried to share them that confusion spiraled. He hated confusion.

Maybe he should share his rules about love and marriage. Would that clarify the situation or get it more jumbled?

"I rather miss you, too."

It took a moment for her confession to register. When it did, a roaring surge of energy swept through him. He didn't feel any more in charge of his feelings, but he was more optimistic about their future.

"Maybe you should move back in."

"Oh, Burke, you know that's impossible."

"Not if you're my wife."

Her eyes became huge. "You want to marry me?"

This was it. Once the words left his mouth, he wouldn't be able to recall them. But what earlier had loomed as a bottomless black hole, now seemed less fatal, as if he were staring down into a forty-foot mining shaft. A man could conceivably survive such a fall. If the ground were soft, and he got lucky.

"Yeah, I want to marry you."

Seeing the radiant flash of excitement sweep her features was almost his undoing. He knew without her saying anything that she was investing his proposal with all sorts of romantic trappings. If the word "love" came up, he was in deep trouble. He wouldn't lie. She deserved the truth, no matter how cold.

And, the truth, he discovered, made him uneasy. Wanting to protect and possess her was as close to loving as he could get. Would that be enough for a passionate, independent woman like Jayne?

"Kiss me." This time it wasn't a harsh command but a gentle plea.

He cupped her flushed cheeks and drew her close.

And the kiss? It was unspeakably tender, transmitting, he hoped, all his pent-up longings. The joining of their parted lips, the thrust of their tongues and sultry heat sank deeply into his being. The sense of urgency prodding him earlier became a steady throb that pulsed deeply within him.

He wanted her. He would have her. Any moment now, she would admit her love and accept his proposal. Everything would work out. She would be…content. The word's

relative weakness kindled dissatisfaction. He would deal
with that later.

Now he was picturing the row of black buttons running
up the front of her jacket, beneath which was a white blouse
with another row of buttons, beneath which was…

He reached between them and fumbled with the first button.

Several bursts of gunfire outside his office had him leaping from Jayne and reaching for the pistol strapped to his
hip. The office door's wooden casings splintered as five
men charged through it. Burke raised his Colt, but it was
too late. One of the gunmen aimed his weapon at Jayne.

"If you don't want anything to happen to the lady, drop
your gun, mister."

Burke stared into the cold, dark eyes of the masked man
who'd cocked his pistol and pointed it at Jayne. Wordlessly
Burke laid his Colt next to her bonnet on the desk.

"That's a good boy. Now step back."

Chapter Fourteen

The armed intruders propped the bullet-riddled door against its frame. Their guns raised, two of them flattened their backs against the wall on either side of the entry. Next to the settee, another man crouched, while a fourth dropped to one knee beside the desk, his pistol aimed at Burke. The remaining villain found shelter in a corner partially protected by a bookcase.

Jayne looked at Burke. Was he feeling as exposed as she was, standing in the middle of the chamber? His posture, straight and unyielding, evidenced no fear. The tender lover was gone, replaced by a cold-eyed stranger.

"Tell your guards not to shoot, or she's dead," the masked gunman next to the bookcase ordered.

A full second passed before Burke called out. "Hold your fire!"

"Yes, sir, Mr. Youngblood!" He recognized Harry Lansing's voice. Steady man, Harry, which was why he was in charge of security.

"Keep behaving, and you'll make it out of this alive," the scoundrel in the alcove said approvingly. "Burly, grab that gun off the desk. We don't want our banker friend getting any ideas."

"Sure thing, boss."

"Things didn't work out like we expected," the gang's

obvious spokesman continued, "but that's all right. I've got a plan."

"Forget whatever scheme you've concocted. There's no way you're leaving here alive. You'll be cut down before you make it to the street."

"Not with you helping us."

"If you think I'm going to cooperate, you're crazy."

"There's different kinds of craziness. Take, for example, you *not* telling your guards to drop their guns."

"Your only way out is feetfirst."

"We're walking out of here with our saddlebags filled with gold and cash," he said nastily. "You'll be our shield."

"I'm not going anywhere."

"How about you, pretty lady?" Jayne found herself the sudden focus of his evil gaze. "You feeling more sociable than Youngblood?"

Jayne's heart pounded. "It was your choice to rob his bank, and now you must pay the consequences."

"What are you, a Sunday school teacher?" He moved from the protective shelter of the books and, using his pistol's barrel, stroked her cheek.

"Get the hell away from her." Burke's roar increased the intolerable tension.

"Now, why would I do that, seeing how she's our ticket out of here? From the tender scene we interrupted coming in, I'm betting if we take her, you'll come along as peaceably as a whipped pup."

"You're wrong. She means nothing to me. If you want a hostage, I'm the one who'll get you out of here."

Even though Jayne knew Burke was lying about his feelings, she flinched at his callous rejection.

"Amazing how fast you changed your mind about coming with us. I'm thinking she's our safe passage out of here."

"I told you, I don't give a damn about her."

The man trailed his fingers across her snug-fitting jacket.

Burke erupted, lunging toward the would-be robber with his bare hands. Three of the men tackled and wrestled him to the floor. Her tormenter shoved the gun's barrel between Burke's eyes and cocked the trigger.

"No, don't shoot," she cried. "I'm all right, Burke. He didn't hurt me. Please, don't do anything foolish."

"Listen to the lady," the gunman urged. "Besides if you're dead, how you gonna help her?"

She didn't know if it was her plea or the thief's threat that cleared the savageness from Burke's gaze.

The man raised his weapon abruptly and pointed it toward the ceiling, carefully releasing the cocked hammer. "Glad you've decided to be sensible. Nowadays, a dead hero ain't worth a bucket of spittle."

The men who'd pinned Burke to the floor cautiously released their hold. He uncoiled to his feet. "Leave the woman and take me. I won't give you any trouble. Take her, and you will pay with your life."

"Feisty bugger, ain't you? But I always follow my gut, and it's telling me the only way we're gonna make it out of here *alive* is if the little lady comes along."

He jerked Jayne to his side and clamped a sweat-soaked arm around her neck. He placed the gun's barrel to the side of her head. Numbed by his casual violence, she stumbled forward.

"Call off your men, Youngblood."

Burke went to the door. "Hold your fire," he ordered tersely. "They're taking me and Miss Stoneworthy hostage."

The next few minutes passed in a series of stark images that Jayne knew she would remember for the rest of her life. She was dragged forward. Armed bank guards surrounded them. The gang's leader had Burke order his men to put their weapons on the floor. They obeyed with obvious reluctance. The descent down the stairs progressed in oppressive silence.

When they reached the ground floor, the tellers were instructed to fill saddlebags dropped in the gun battle that had reigned earlier. Three bodies lay on the floor.

The next event to register on her dazed senses was being tossed to a man on horseback. He shoved her on the saddle in front of him. As they galloped through town, she braced herself for a hail of bullets. No shots rang out. Her world shrank to clinging to the saddle horn and trying to stay on the thundering mount. The man behind her held the reins with one hand and grasped her waist in a viselike grip with the other. She strained to draw enough air into her lungs to keep from fainting.

She had no idea how long they rode at breakneck speed before stopping. Despite how fast they'd traveled, they weren't that many miles from Denver. Surely rescue parties had been formed and were close behind.

When she was lifted from the saddle and allowed to stand, her knees buckled. Unprepared for the weakness pervading her legs, she crumpled. From the corner of her eye, she saw men scuffling. Burke struggled to get to her.

"She needs my help."

The man acting as the gang's spokesman laughed. It took a moment to realize what was different about him. Then it hit her. He'd lowered the bandanna he'd used to shield his features, as had the other thieves. Fear spiraled. After revealing their faces, would they let either her or Burke live, to later identify them?

"For someone who don't care, you're sure in a hurry to get to her."

"I'm unarmed. There's no reason not to let me help her."

"Sure there is. We're here for as long as it takes to get fresh horses. Don't worry, you can start playing hero when we reach camp." He guffawed at his own joke. "Come on, let's mount up. Burly, the lady rides with you."

"Sure thing, Baldwin."

Rough hands gripped Jayne and threw her up to Burly. He yelled giddap, and they were off again. This time the pace wasn't as swift, but as hours passed and the sun began to lower, a crushing wave of fatigue washed over her. She'd been pushed to the breaking point.

Mile after mile passed. They no longer followed a road, traveling instead across open country, heading toward a nearby range of mountains. The air turned cooler. Sagebrush gave way to open meadows and fields of blue and purple wildflowers. Three times the horses waded through narrow streams.

Darkness was almost upon them when the man addressed as Baldwin directed them to stop. Almost in a stupor, Jayne looked around. They were in a small clearing surrounded by a dense circle of pines. This time when she was lowered to the ground, she didn't try to stand. Her goal was to collapse in a somewhat seemly fashion.

A groan escaped her. In an attempt to forestall the tears burning to be released, she closed her eyes. Her thighs felt hot and quivery, her bottom numb.

"Go ahead, Youngblood. You got ten minutes."

"Ten minutes?" Burke snarled, hunkering down beside her.

"That's right. It wouldn't be proper to let you and *Miss* Stoneworthy share the same bedroll, now, would it? I consider it my duty to protect her reputation." He spat a rivulet of slimy chewing tobacco at her skirts, then wiped his mouth with his sleeve. "Don't fret. I'll keep her warm for you."

The men broke into laughter. Crude comments were hurled, striking her like the disgusting stream of tobacco spittle. Things were definitely going from bad to worse. But she hurt so much that Baldwin's threats scarcely penetrated the trancelike cloud hanging over her.

Burke wasted no time joining her and helping her sit up. She couldn't suppress a second groan. "I'm sorry."

"For what?" he asked gruffly.

"For being a weakling. I've only been on a horse a couple of times. I'm not very good at it."

"You're doing great. I'm the one who should be horse-whipped for not keeping you safe."

He was probably blaming himself for not having enough guards. Now was hardly the time to point out she'd been right.

"Honey?"

"Hmm?"

"How sore are you?"

His fingers slid beneath her skirts. "It's too dark for me to see if you've blistered."

"Burke," she whispered, shocked by his actions, "what do you think you're doing?"

"If your muscles aren't loosened, you're going to be in a world of pain."

"I'm already in a world of pain, but I have no intention of putting on a show for Baldwin and his men."

"We're in the shadows. With me in front of you, no one can see what I'm doing."

With whisper-light softness, he began to massage her skin.

She sucked in her breath.

"I know it hurts, honey, but it's got to be done."

Her muscles cried out in painful protest of his well-intentioned ministrations. She turned her face into his shoulder.

"They're going to kill us, aren't they?"

"They're probably planning to, but it won't happen. We'll be out of this mess before morning."

"How?"

"I'll find a way. They'll keep us breathing for a while. To collect the ransom Baldwin's hoping for, he might need to prove I'm alive."

"I didn't hear him mention a ransom."

Burke's fingers continued their rubbing motion. The pain receded. "He hasn't, but I can tell he's trying to figure out a way to get one. Men like him are always looking for extra cash."

"Oh."

"This is going to be hard, but you've got to go along with whatever Baldwin wants."

Icy premonition uncoiled within her. "What do you mean?"

"Evidently Baldwin fancies himself a lady's man."

She recoiled. "I'd rather die than have him touch me."

"Damn it, Jayne. You dying isn't an option."

"But—"

"I'm not telling you to give yourself to him. It won't come to that. Stall him, any way you can. Use the God-given talent you have for verbally castrating anyone in pants."

"What?"

"Be the shrew you were born to be. He thrives on crushing those weaker than himself. Show him that a shrewish woman with Euphemia Stoneworthy's blood flowing in her veins is more disagreeable than bedding a she-bear in heat with two broken legs. In other words, just be yourself."

"Really, Burke—"

"I'll get us out of here," he cut in. "Trust me."

"I do trust you. But—"

"If things start looking grim, hold that thought."

How could a man be in love with a woman, want to marry her and have such a low opinion of her disposition?

"Time's up, Youngblood," Baldwin called out.

"Wait," Jayne cried softly as Burke drew away. She'd clear up his misunderstanding about her temperament later. "When those men broke into your office, you were in the middle of proposing."

"That's right." The words were hardly more than a thread of air. "You never officially accepted, did you?"

"That's not important."

"It isn't?"

"*You* never got around to saying that you loved me."

"And hearing that is important to you?"

"Of course. After all—"

"I said time's up."

Burke moved away. Jayne drew herself to a sitting position and watched as one of the thieves took a knife to several cans and dumped their contents into a pot suspended on metal stakes above the fire.

The minutes slid by, and she began to hope Baldwin had forgotten her. As she looked around, she realized no one appeared to be watching her. It seemed possible to slip into the deeper shadows that lurked at the clearing's perimeter and simply disappear into the night. Had she been alone, she would have tried it. But she couldn't abandon Burke. They were in this together.

"So, how you doing, little lady?"

With a start, Jayne realized Baldwin had crossed to where she sat. Burke's advice drifted back. She was to use, what had he called it? Oh yes, her God-given talent to verbally castrate anything in pants to keep Baldwin from touching her. For a man in love, Burke certainly had an unflattering assessment of her nature.

"I detest being called 'little lady.' Cease doing so at once."

Baldwin moved closer, squatting on his haunches to meet her at eye level. Fortunately, the semidarkness engulfing them made it difficult to see his bestial features.

"I'm just being friendly, cutey-pie."

"I have standards about choosing friends. You fail to meet them." Disliking intensely his closeness, she struggled to get to her feet. Thanks to Burke's massage, she was able to stand. "I don't associate with bank robbers."

"Before now, you mean. It's time you got something to eat."

She remembered Burke's instruction not to directly oppose the man and allowed herself to be guided to the campfire. In short order, a spoon and battered tin cup of beans were thrust into her hands. Almost twelve hours had passed since breakfast. She ought to have been famished. She wasn't.

Burke told her to stall. Eating would delay whatever Baldwin had in mind. She took the cup to an edge of the clearing and sat down on a large rock. Her bottom and thighs immediately protested with flashes of searing pain. She tried to ignore the burning spasms and concentrated on slowly dipping her spoon into the beans. She blew the steam away and held the utensil for several minutes before putting it in her mouth. If she ate the mixture one bean at a time, she could drag the meal out for hours.

She tracked Burke from the corner of her eye. He was also eating. Gradually, she became aware of bedrolls being spread out. Several men checked their guns and called out guard locations. Burly pointed to the ground, and Burke stretched out on a blanket.

"Ain't you done?"

"I'm a slow eater." Baldwin's arrival turned her stomach. "It's going to be a while before I'm finished."

"Don't have time to cater to finicky femalcs." He grabbed the cup and stalked to the fire, dumping the thickening mixture over the flames. The acrid smell of scorched beans filled the air. "Come on, it's time for bed."

"I'm not tired."

"Good, we'll get acquainted."

"I don't choose to know you any better."

"You ain't got no choice, little lady."

Steeling herself against the anticipated pain, she shot to her feet. "I told you not to call me that."

"What do you want me to call you?"

"Nothing. I prefer we remain strangers."

He laughed. "Too late for that. We're gonna get real cozy, if you get my drift."

"Believe me, your 'drift' is impossible to miss. The rank odor you're emitting smells like a pig who's been rolling in manure."

This time he didn't laugh. "If I don't smell as fresh as one of them...what do you call 'em? Oh, yeah, daisies, it's because I've been working."

"Robbing banks can't be classified as honest labor."

"I didn't say it was honest..." He gripped her arm again. "Ah hell, let's go to bed."

"I would rather lie down with a flea-bitten mongrel."

He shoved her to the blankets he'd spread out some distance from the campfire. "I ain't got fleas!"

"Are you sure?" She sprang back up. "Some kind of crawly vermin is biting me."

"Those are mosquitoes, Miss High and Mighty." Sounding aggrieved, he joined her on the bedding. "What did your ma nurse you on, rattlesnake piss?"

"I'm under no obligation to be gracious to a bank-robbing, kidnapping, tobacco-spitting, belching weasel."

"You never heard me belch!"

"I'm sure it's only a matter of time."

"A man's gotta do what a man's gotta do," he said defensively.

"The next thing I know, you'll be passing gas."

"We ate beans! Both of us. Before morning you'll be doing the same."

"Accompanying you in a gaseous duet is the last thing I plan on doing."

"Come on, sugar, show me your sweet side." He reached out and urged her to lie down.

"Get your hand off me. I can't abide dirty fingernails."

"It's too dark for you to know if they're dirty."

She scooted away. "From the primitive level of personal hygiene you practice, it's safe to assume your nails aren't any cleaner than any other part of your loathsome anatomy."

"Hell, you sure know how to spoil the mood." He let her go and flopped onto his back. "I'm as soft and shriveled as a boiled prune."

Thank heavens. Jayne racked her brain for more spiteful observations that would keep him permanently "shriveled." What sharp pricks would Euphemia have employed to annihilate his amorous urges? Abruptly, Jayne realized she was already responding as her aunt would have in a similar situation. That the role came so naturally made her uneasy. Was Burke right about her...uh...castrating tendencies?

"I would just as soon keep company with a...a dusty old buffalo," she continued. "At least he wouldn't smell as bad."

Baldwin rolled to his side and leaned on an elbow. "I'll wash in the river. You, too."

"It would take a month of baths to rid you of your foul odor. Besides, I doubt you have a sliver of soap with you."

"We only got room in our saddlebags for necessities."

"Like extra bullets and someone else's hard-earned money and gold," she observed contemptuously.

"Like I said, necessities."

"Most people regard soap as essential."

"That's their problem. Yours is you talk too much. Come on, pucker up. Some smooching will soften that cruel tongue of yours."

"Don't complain when I throw up on you. But then, mixed with the other noxious odors wafting from your sorry hide, what's a little vomit?"

"You're too refined to throw up on anybody. Come here."

"Be warned, those beans are at the top of my throat. You'll be wearing them any second."

"Why are you so ornery? I don't get complaints about my kissing from my wife."

Despite Burke's caution about openly resisting Baldwin, Jayne twisted free. "You're *married?*"

He nodded. "I got me a little gal down Mexico way, too, and she purrs when I kiss her."

"Two testimonials, from a wife *and* a girlfriend, no less."

"Keep your voice down. I don't want it getting back to Edna that I've got me other female companionship."

''You're absolutely despicable. Do you have children by either women?''

'''Course, I do. It's a man's duty to pass his name on.''

''It's a man's duty to set a good example for his children by working to support them. What are their names? How old are they?''

''I'm not about to talk about my kids!''

''Why, are you ashamed of them?''

''Hell no, it's just that—''

''I consider it my duty to instruct you about the responsibilities of being a father.''

She took a deep breath and began speaking again before he could collect his thoughts. It was a one-sided conversation. He answered in monosyllabic grunts while she proceeded to lecture him most sternly. Despite its being a summer night, the air turned cool. She wrapped her arms around herself, scarcely pausing between breaths as she stridently reprimanded him.

At some point during her diatribe, he lay down again, his back turned. She kept talking for what must have been another hour after that. Her voice went hoarse, and her words were probably unintelligible. It was only when she was convinced that Baldwin had fallen asleep that she ceased the lecture.

She felt like a malevolent Scheherazade, weaving a perverse version of *A Thousand and One Nights*.

Since he was an inherently immoral man with no conscience or moral code, she didn't dare lie down beside Baldwin. As time passed, she found herself dozing. It wasn't the most comfortable position to fall asleep in, but she felt herself surrendering to the pull of her fatigue with her cheek resting against her upraised knees.

''Come on, honey, it's over. Let's get out of here.''

Disoriented by the wispy layers of her restless sleep, she glanced immediately toward where Baldwin had lain. Burke shifted, using his broad chest to block her view.

''We've got to leave. I've taken care of two of the men standing watch, but there's more.''

He urged her to her feet. She sagged against him.

''That's a girl, I saddled two horses. We have a couple of hours before dawn to get as far away from here as we can.''

Chapter Fifteen

Jayne was aware of Burke's horse behind her. It probably frustrated both man and beast to be restricted to her slower pace. She regretted holding Burke back. As it was, though, she didn't know how much longer she could continue hanging on to the reins. Hours had passed since they'd escaped the outlaw encampment. Along with the rest of her, the muscles in her arms and neck now throbbed.

The rays of the rising sun drenched the passing landscape in light and heat. Her face stung from what she suspected was a sunburn she'd received yesterday, riding without her bonnet beneath the strong Colorado sun.

Unexpectedly, Burke came alongside her. "Let's stop."

Fearing he thought she'd exhausted her strength, she lowered her chin and urged her horse onward. The beast's gait seemed to become irregular.

"I can keep going!" she called back.

He had no difficulty catching up again. His arm snaked out. Startled, Jayne watched his fingers close around the reins.

"Whoa!"

In less than a minute, both horses slowed, then halted. They tossed their heads restlessly. Burke was probably stopping out of consideration for the animals, not her.

He stepped from his mount and turned to her. "I'll help you down."

She rested her palms on his shoulders, and he lowered her. This time when her knees buckled, he was there to support her. Gratefully, she leaned against his solid frame. His arm curved around her waist, and he half lifted her across the rocky terrain, through a stand of aspen trees, into a secluded mountain meadow.

A backdrop of boulders jutted skyward, lending the clearing an air of isolation. They walked alongside a crooked stream of clear water that gently splashed over partially submerged rocks.

"How beautiful," she breathed, absorbing their surroundings.

"A regular paradise." The comment reeked with sarcasm. "It will ease the cramping in your legs if you walk around. I'll get the horses."

"I can help you unsaddle them," she protested.

"You ever unsaddle a horse before?"

"No, but how hard can it be?"

"Harder than you think. I don't have the patience to watch you fumbling with thirty pounds of tack leather."

Her cheeks burned with more than the heat from the sun. "There's no call to be rude."

"I'm not being rude. I'm being practical." His gaze dropped. "Why don't you decide whether you're going to button your jacket and blouse or take them off."

She glanced down and was stunned to discover her bosom, modest-sized though it was, practically spilled over the top of her corset, which was fully exposed. "I had no idea—"

He turned away. "Your horse looks like it's picked up a rock."

Jayne stared after him, mystified by his terseness. She began refastening her blouse and discovered several buttons were missing, as well as three from her jacket. Clearly, the thread securing them wasn't strong enough to withstand bank robbery, kidnapping and escape by horseback.

After trying to walk the stiffness from her legs, she approached an inviting expanse of lush grass and lay down. Cradling her hot cheek against her hands, she became aware of a new source of discomfort. She examined her palms and found several raw calluses.

From throbbing feet, to hurting hands, thighs and bottom, to her sunburned face—she was falling apart. Too bad she couldn't will herself, dressed in a soft, fresh nightgown, back to her bed at the boardinghouse. She yawned. As long as she was wishing herself in bed, it should be Burke's. Lying next to him was a fantasy worth weaving—after he apologized for his snarly behavior. With that thought, she surrendered to sleep's embrace.

"Wake up, honey."

The words pitched her back to the outlaws' encampment and Baldwin's pallet. Then her mind cleared, and she gazed up into Burke's grim visage.

"I am awake."

He hunkered down beside her. "Good, let's get your shoes off."

She marshaled her dream-scattered wits. He was already suiting his action to his words.

"Do you think that's wise? Shouldn't we be on our way?"

Easing a shoe from her swollen foot, his head came up. "Your horse is lame. The only direct way to Denver is across that valley. Baldwin's men have the high ground. If we leave, they'll spot us."

"Won't they find us if we stay?"

"Not as easily as you might think. There's hundreds of secluded clearings like this. They can't search them all. With the trees and boulders surrounding us, we'll be safe enough."

"How long do you think we'll be here?"

He glanced skyward, shading his eyes against the sun

"A couple of days." His gaze returned to her. "I managed to steal some canned foods, along with a pistol and a knife. We won't have trouble surviving."

"What did you do to Baldwin?"

Burke's eyes went cold. "You don't want to know."

"Is he…is he still alive?"

"No."

It was preposterous to feel a pang of grief at his death, yet she did.

"After what he did to you, you didn't expect me to let him live?"

"He didn't do anything to me," she said quickly. Did Burke believe the outlaw had forced himself upon her? Was that why he'd reacted so sharply at seeing her blouse unfastened—because he thought she'd been molested?

"Other than kidnapping you at gunpoint, dragging you halfway across Colorado and—"

"And nothing. I followed your advice and nagged him into leaving me alone."

"I knew you would." Burke's stare was unrelenting. "I warned him, if he took you from the bank, he would pay with his life."

So hard, so cold… With what manner of being had she fallen in love? "I still hate the thought that you…killed him."

"It was the law or me. Either way, he was a dead man." Burke sat down, stretching out his long legs. "He was a murderer who left a lot of widows and orphans in his wake."

"And now that he's dead, another widow with children has been left behind to try and survive."

"Likely, they'll be grateful to have him gone."

"What will they live on?"

"That's their business."

So harsh, so stern… "I don't think I will be able to forget about them that easily."

"Why not? You've never met them."

"I know Edna exists and so do her children. After surviving the horror of being forced to live with an animal like Baldwin, it doesn't seem fair that things will get even worse for them."

"You don't know that she was forced to become his wife."

Jayne turned toward him, rising to her knees. "I can't imagine any woman giving herself freely to him."

"I guess I can't, either."

"It really wouldn't be that difficult to track her down."

"Why would I do that?"

"To offer her assistance, of course."

"You expect me to give money to Corbett Baldwin's widow?" he asked incredulously.

"It probably wouldn't take much to make a big difference in her life. Who knows, your help might alter the direction of her future and that of her children. Besides, as rich as you are, you'd hardly miss the funds."

"I can't believe this. You want me to track down Baldwin's widow and *support* her?"

"And her children," she reminded him.

"I must be losing my mind."

Sensing victory, Jayne smiled. "Does that mean you're going to it?"

"Why not? After all, I'm so rich, it would be a shame not to give some of my money to strangers. As my future wife, though, you should know this robbery probably cost me the charter."

"I have complete faith in your ability to triumph over any setback," she said with the utmost confidence. "You can accomplish anything you set your mind to. You're an amazing man, Burke."

"Sure I am." His tone definitely bordered on skeptical.

"Baldwin's family will think you're wonderful."

"Yeah, right."

Jayne touched his sleeve. "I'm glad you decided to be reasonable."

He eyed her as if she were insane. *"Reasonable!"*

"I can't think of a better word."

"Then you're not trying." He rose to his knees to face her. "Choose stupid, asinine, moronic or witless."

"You're acting in the true tradition of a gallant hero."

"I'm no hero."

She leaned forward and brushed her lips against his stubbled jaw. "Of course you are."

His palms closed around her shoulders. "Give me a real kiss."

Her hands rested against his shirtfront. "There's one more thing."

He groaned. "Do you need to talk about it now?"

"Well, it is important." She hesitated. He wasn't especially eager to help Baldwin's wife and children. How would Burke react to her next request?

He traced the outline of her lips with the tip of his tongue. "Tell me what's so important."

Despite the rising temperature, she shivered. "Baldwin said he had a...uh...girlfriend down Mexico way."

"What does that have to do with us?"

"Well, she'll need financial support, too. Don't you think?"

"I *think* that you're more softhearted than I realized.

She removed her hands from his. "When men say softhearted, they generally mean softheaded."

"You told me that before. I don't like being lumped with every man who's ever lived."

"You're not like other men. In my eyes, your concern for Baldwin's family makes you a gallant knight."

"I'm not *concerned*, and you know it. You just want me to dig deeper and come up with a little something for his...what did you call her? His *girlfriend?* My question is, will it make you happy if I do?"

"I'm happy just being with you." Tears stung her eyes. He had to know that. "If you can't see your way to helping the woman, I'll understand."

He shook her gently. "Assuming responsibilities that an outlaw like Baldwin probably shirked has to be the dumbest thing I've ever done, but I'll try to track down both women and make sure they have enough money to get by."

Jayne felt her tears give way. Still kneeling, she launched herself at him. "Thank you!"

"Don't mistake my reasons for doing this. Neither kindness nor nobility is involved." His arms closed around her and he lowered her to the lush carpet of grass. "My only goal is to make you happy."

"Oh, Burke."

He kissed her slowly, with toe-tingling thoroughness, before raising his head. "Let's make ourselves comfortable."

"All right."

He drew back. "Let me have a look at your feet."

She gazed up at the clear blue sky above the clearing. Her feet weren't what craved his touch. "And that would be because?"

"I want to make sure you don't have any blisters."

How...*romantic?*

Hardly...

"I don't know how you could have missed it, but I've been riding, not walking."

"Neither your tender skin, thin stockings or stiff shoes are designed for the wear and tear they've suffered." He pushed her skirts to her knees, slid down her garters and peeled away her stockings. "Since coming West, I've learned to pay attention to such small details."

The cool breeze circulating around her hot, bared flesh brought a sense of relief. The contrast, though, of seeing the pale skin of her foot gripped between his darkly tanned fingers while being raised for his inspection engendered a feeling of vulnerability.

Her breath hitched in her throat. "What kind of details?"

Those supple fingers of his began to rub her foot. She lowered her lashes against the brilliant sunlight and resisted an overwhelming inclination to purr.

"Details like broken skin becoming infected."

Nope, there was nothing at all romantic about his words. He touched a sensitive spot near her heel. She shivered.

"Did I hurt you?"

The husky concern she detected wrapped itself around her heart. She battled the impulse to explain that her reaction was one of melting enjoyment, not discomfort. "Actually, that…uh…feels pretty good."

"Glad you like it."

"I *love* it," she corrected, feeling her inhibitions slipping away. Still curbing her desire to purr, she allowed herself a sigh. "It feels heavenly. Your hands are…magical."

"I aim to please."

Minutes passed, with her enjoying the blissful sensations of Burke's gentle stroking.

"I checked the stream."

"Did you?"

"With the July sun bearing down on it, and as slow as it's running, the water's warm."

"That's nice."

His fingers stopped their bone-melting magic. "Dipping your bare feet into it should make you feel better."

Jayne opened her eyes. "Not so fast."

He tipped his head. "You've got a problem with soaking your feet?"

"Not at all, but first things first."

"What's on your mind?"

"The massage you gave me was nothing less than pure bliss. It's only fair I return the favor."

"Oh, honey, you don't want to rub my sorry-looking feet."

"Why not?"

"Because they're big and ugly, nothing like your soft, dainty ones."

"I should hope not. You're a big, strong man. It would be ridiculous to expect any part of your body to be less than thoroughly masculine."

His features reflected his reluctant pleasure at the compliment, just as they reflected his dismay at having her perform so common a task on his behalf.

"They probably don't smell very good. I've been wearing these boots for almost thirty-six hours."

"We're going to be husband and wife. I'm bound to become acquainted with every aspect of your person."

His eyes took on a gleam. "Believe me, I'm looking forward to the same adventure, but I hardly imagined starting with our feet."

She looked at his dusty boots, then raised her gaze. "Let me have my way with you, Burke."

He made a strangled sound deep in his throat. "All right, honey. But, uh...you can't say I didn't warn you." He pulled off one boot, then the other. "You're not going to see a very pretty sight."

She moved closer. "Every part of you is beautiful. To me."

"When you talk that way, I'm like soft clay in your hands."

She tugged off both socks and began to rub his feet.

He groaned with obvious pleasure. "You're right, that feels unbelievably good."

She smiled. The sun might be baking her back, and various muscles might be rebelling at the rough treatment they'd suffered, but knowing he was enjoying the humble act of service offered a strange contentment.

"So, this is love," she said quietly, "the desire to give without expecting anything in return."

"That's one definition."

She glanced into his shuttered features. "Do you have another?"

In one swift movement, he surged to a standing position, drawing her up with him. She winced at the sundry twinges sweeping through her.

"What I have is a better idea of how we can relieve our

body aches. Let's strip off our clothes and soak in that stream.''

Goose bumps leaped across her skin. "You mean... totally nude?''

His fingers went to the top button on his shirt. "Exactly.''

"Uh, I'm not sure I'm ready to do something quite so...bold.''

"Are you going to marry me, Jayne?''

She took a deep breath. "Yes.''

"The first chance we have?''

"I haven't considered the timing.''

He pulled his shirt from his waistband. "There's nothing to consider.''

The garment was casually discarded. His naked chest, covered by a lush carpet of black hair, filled her field of vision. There were sculpted muscles everywhere. Her fingertips itched to acquaint themselves with the masculine texture of his hard flesh.

"The minute we make it to town," he continued, "we'll be married. A ceremony performed by a judge is as binding as any preacher's.''

She stared at him in helpless fascination as he unbuckled his belt. "That's true.''

He slid the strip of narrow leather from its loops and dropped it to the ground. "I have your promise, then. We'll be married at the first opportunity.''

He unfastened the top button of his trousers. Seeing Burke Youngblood, barefoot and shirtless was a singularly inspiring experience. Beyond that... There was no beyond that! She wasn't ready to see any more of him than she already was.

"Burke, stop! You can't remove your trousers in broad daylight.''

His heated gaze burned into her. "I'm willing to bet I can.''

She trembled. "I'm having trouble breathing as it is. I don't know if I can survive seeing...all of you."

His lips curved. "You already survived seeing the worst."

She glanced down. He'd sunk his toes deep into the grass. Foolishly, the boyish gesture further endeared him to her.

"It so happens, you have another part of which I've become aware."

His eyes flashed with wicked enjoyment. "Don't stop now. I'm dying to hear what you're going to say next."

"I'll just bet you are. The point is, I've led a very circumspect life."

"Being raised and guarded by your late aunt who despised all men?"

"Not all men, and despise isn't the right word. She recognized their shortcomings."

"Both genders have shortcomings. It's easy enough to watch life as it passes by, picking out other people's failings, of which there's no shortage. But it takes courage to jump into the fray, into *real* living."

"I am living," she protested. "As for jumping into life—I've been mistaken for a wanton woman, involved in a brawl, seduced in a carriage, proposed to, kidnapped by bank robbers—barely escaping with my life and with my virtue. Besides those spectacular events, I've begun my own girls' school and—"

"You've barely dipped your toes into the sea of life."

"Forget the sea." She turned and stalked to the nearby stream. A spindly twig stabbed the tender spot of her foot. "Ow." A rock bruised her heel. "Ow." Several sharp pebbles dug into her skin. "Ow."

"Wait a minute. I'll carry you."

"I don't need your help. I've already arrived at my destination."

She scooted down the low embankment. Several more "ows" escaped her clenched teeth.

"Damn it, I said I would carry you."

Sitting on the grassy bank with her skirts hiked to her knees, she lowered her feet into the water. She sucked in her breath. Burke's interpretation of a warm stream and hers were vastly different.

"I thought you said the water was warm."

He sat down next to her and rolled up his pant legs. Two well-muscled and surprisingly hairy calves dangled beside her. She was grateful he'd left his trousers on. She just wasn't prepared to see all of what was surely a magnificent frame exposed in total naked glory, not in broad daylight, anyway. In a darkened bedchamber, things might be different.

"The water *is* warm, once you get used to it."

Gradually, she discovered the truth of his observation. The meandering stream gently swirling over her skin felt almost as good as Burke's touch.

"Why are you acting so prickly?" he asked after a lengthy pause.

She took umbrage but wasn't about to get into another debate about bathing nude together in the stream. There were other perfectly good topics they could bicker over, ones with less potential for embarrassment.

"Why did you snarl at me because my blouse was unbuttoned?"

"What's that got to do with anything?"

Nothing at all, which was the point. "I've decided that as your future wife, I need to understand your moods."

"*Moods?* I don't have moods. I'm as steady and even-tempered as they come."

She rolled her eyes. "You acted as if you were angry with me, and I want to know why."

"Damn, is this what marriage is like? Conversations that go nowhere?"

"Oh, they go somewhere. We'll learn to understand each other better."

"I'm not so sure I want you to understand me."

"Why not?" she asked, genuinely mystified.

"Look at me."

There was no way to ignore the command. When she turned, she found herself consumed by his intense gaze.

"I'm looking."

"I'm not as good or decent as you seem to think."

Her stomach tightened. "You underestimate yourself."

"No, you *over*estimate me. I hate to admit it, but your aunt was right about men's less sterling qualities. Do you have any idea what it did to me when I saw your blouse open?"

"I wasn't deliberately trying to—"

"Seeing you like that made me forget about everything you've been through. The only thing on my mind was feeling your skin next to mine."

His primitive declaration was fiercely exciting.

"Do you know how that made me feel?"

"Aroused?"

"Hell, yes, I was aroused, but that's not what I'm talking about."

"You aren't?"

"No. Only a scoundrel would think of taking his wife' virginity in an open meadow at high noon when she's a bruised and battered as you are. You can hardly walk. How do you think you would feel, rutting with me under such circumstances?"

Catapulted to paradise? "I'm...not sure."

"Like you'd been trampled by a bull," he ground out "Not only did I fail to protect you, but I can't think o anything except making love to you."

His blunt admission stirred the embers of her own smoldering need. She wanted to reexperience the same rioting sensations he'd produced before.

"I've been thinking the same thing," she confessed softly. "I know it's bold of me to say, but making love to you seems like a magical gift that I never knew existed Now that I'm aware of it, I must have it or perish."

"Now's not the time to encourage me. I need help resisting you."

She touched his cheek. "I fear you've come to the wrong person."

He shut his eyes. "Haven't you heard what I've been saying?"

"I've listened," she said absently. "I've always wanted to do this."

"What?" he growled hoarsely. "Drive me crazy?"

"Wanted to feel your bristles scrape my fingertips."

A shout of laughter rang out. "You *are* trying to make me insane. Believe me, I have a far more needy part that aches for your touch."

"Like this adorable dimple in your very manly chin?" She explored the indentation with her forefinger.

"What are you doing?"

"Playing," she replied, intrigued by the interesting contours of his whiskered jaw.

"It would be more fun to play in the water."

"Ahem, we've talked ourselves into a circle. I'm sure there will come a time in our marriage when I'll be quite comfortable with having you stroll about unencumbered by clothing. In our bedchamber," she added.

If I don't stop telling lies, I'm going straight to Hades. There would never be a time, not even after sixty years of marriage, when she would be blasé about Burke's body—with or without garments. He was just too gorgeously male. Goodness, being exposed to his bare chest was enough to mesmerize her.

"Honey, let me prove there's nothing to be afraid of. That way our wedding night won't come as such a shock."

"Uh, what is it precisely that you want to prove?"

"That you can trust me, and there's nothing about me or yourself that's the least bit shameful."

She shifted restlessly. "Could you be more specific?"

"I guess it's your nature to be suspicious. The first time

I tried to help with your school, you had unfounded doubts about my character.''

She thought back to his autocratic assumption that she needed him in order to begin her academy. In view of how events had transpired, he'd been right. He'd rescued her from certain financial ruin. Still, she didn't appreciate being reminded of it in such heavy-handed fashion.

''Any well-brought-up woman would have been suspicious under such circumstances. How many honorable men would make such a generous offer without expecting a reward?''

''A reward like your luscious body?''

She blushed. ''I have heard of such incidents occurring to women forced to make their way alone in the world.''

Burke grasped her hands and pressed them to his lips. Internal tremors frolicked. ''You fascinated me the first time I saw you. It was in my front hallway. You were a tranquil island in a sea of giggling schoolgirls.''

He remembered their first inauspicious meeting... Satisfaction simmered.

''I saw you again at Gideon's wedding. You flitted about the fringes of the room. I found my gaze drawn to you again and again.''

''You also made a memorable impression upon me,'' she confessed.

''Did I?''

''But you spoiled it when you tried to buy my favors.''

''You needed to be taught a lesson.''

''This isn't one of my favorite topics,'' she warned.

''Then let's talk about something else.'' He released her hands. ''Right now, we should take advantage of this stream.''

She wriggled her toes in the current. ''Take advantage how?''

''We could both undress and stretch out in it.''

''I can't possibly—''

With startling ease, he unfastened her top button.

"Burke!"

"Relax, this is where trusting comes in. I won't break my promise."

He'd already reached the third button. "What promise?"

"The first time we make love, we'll do it as man and wife."

"I don't think this is a good idea. I can testify that passion has a way of overcoming good intentions. Heavens, when we were in your carriage and you touched me, I lost every bit of good sense or control I'd ever possessed."

He slipped off her jacket. "You have no idea how much that pleases me."

"Leave my blouse alone." She slapped at his hands. "Not five minutes ago you wanted my help in resisting you, and now—"

The blouse disappeared. "I'm proving a point, honey."

"If this is another one of your infamous lessons, we're in big trouble."

"Have a little faith. Damn, I've never seen such a beautiful shade of pink."

"Using a religious term and profanity side by side proves you're not thinking clearly."

He leaned to brush his lips against the sensitive skin above her corset.

"Burke!"

"I'm in complete control. You were right, talking things out helped. I know exactly what I'm doing."

"I doubt that."

"First, I'll get you naked. Then I'll give you another massage, one that covers your whole body. After that, seeing me naked won't be all that disturbing."

"I'm already disturbed!" She writhed beneath his steamy kisses. "I can hardly think or breathe."

"That's because you've got your corset on. I'll fix that."

"I don't think—"

"Good, it's a waste of time."

She grabbed his head between her hands and yanked on his hair. Hard. "Burke Youngblood, listen to me."

He lifted his mouth from the swells of her breasts. "Yes, dear?"

"I agree to undress. To my chemise and pantalettes. But that's all."

"You drive a hard bargain. Have you ever thought about going into banking?"

"Oh, Burke…"

"I meant what I said about waiting until our wedding night to make love. But I want to…" His glittering eyes made her mouth go dry.

"To what?"

"The word is cherish," he said slowly. "I want to cherish you."

Chapter Sixteen

Several yards farther into the trees, Burke found an area of streambed with a sandy bottom. The water was deeper there, almost reaching their waists. With their backs turned to each other, amid blushes and reminders from her not to turn around while she peeled down to her undergarments, Burke had removed his trousers and slipped into the water.

He'd closed his eyes while she'd waded in after him. By bending her knees, she was submerged to her shoulders. There were complications she hadn't foreseen. First, the water was perfectly clear. Second, the thin material of her chemise and pantalettes became transparent when wet.

"Why are you so far away?"

"We're hardly more than a yard apart." Wasn't that what he'd asked in his carriage? Remembering what had happened in consequence to that question, she bobbed deeper in the water. He stood at his natural height, which meant she had to watch where her gaze chose to wander.

"Streams like this can be dangerous." He waded toward her. "You never know when a nasty current will pull you under."

"Really, Burke, I'm much too smart to believe such foolery. There's barely any current at all here."

He drew closer. "A storm could come up."

"There's nary a cloud in the sky."

He grinned. "A giant, killer fish could come along."

His humor was so unexpected, she couldn't help laughing. Where was the brooding man with whom she'd fallen in love? "For someone who doesn't have moods, you're certainly in a good one."

He lunged forward. "Come here, woman."

Shrieking and giggling, she allowed herself to be drawn into his arms.

"If you're my hero, who's going to rescue me from you?"

"No one. That's the beauty of my plan."

She squirmed against him, feigning resistance because it felt so good to rub against his hard, hairy body.

"Damn, you're slippery."

One minute they both were laughing, the next she was gazing silently into his eyes as he lowered his mouth. It felt strange to kiss him wet. His hands moved deliberately over her, stroking, squeezing, possessing.

His raised his head. "Come on. There's a shallow place where we can stretch out."

She stepped back. Brazenly, she let him look his fill, knowing that to her waist, at least, her wet garments allowed him to clearly make out the shape of her body. He took his time.

"You're more beautiful that I imagined any woman could be."

She accepted his hand and followed. They didn't walk far before the water hit them at the knees. She couldn't bring herself to look at…him. But she knew he suffered no such compunction in regards to her.

He lowered himself until he was kneeling in front of her, bringing him to eye level with…

She swallowed. "Burke?"

"Hmm?"

"Isn't this the place?"

"Oh yeah." He leaned forward and kissed her, there

Her hands went to his water-slickened shoulders to brace herself. "Burke!"

"Don't worry, it was only a quick visit. Wrap your hands around my waist."

She did. Very carefully, so as not to bump into anything out of the ordinary. Floating, they drifted downstream.

"We need to get out here."

"*What?*"

"Close your eyes and trust me. I'll be your guide."

"What will you be looking at?"

"Where we're going, of course. And any other interesting scenery I happen across."

Amused despite herself, she permitted Burke to lead her from the stream. He was her future husband, she kept reminding herself. Her school and lessons plans seemed a million miles away.

"Here we are. Step down."

She did. Into water that barely rippled over her feet!

"You can open your eyes now."

She glared into his laughing eyes. "What's going on?"

"Nothing. I keep telling you, you're safe with me." He pointed to a pile of sun-bleached limbs and branches. "That used to be an old beaver dam. We're standing on a sandbar below it."

And you're naked as the day you were born, Burke Youngblood. A breeze scented with pine and wildflowers, along with the trill of an unseen bird, reminded her this was no dream.

He grasped her wrist and pulled. "Stretch out and see what happens."

She told herself, she might as well go along with his bizarre suggestion. When they lay side by side, she appreciated the merits of his discovery. The sand was hard-packed, and the water sluicing over them was oddly invigorating. The only thing she had to remember was not to lower her gaze.

"Nice, isn't it?"

"Peachy," she answered. What would he do if she touched the wet hair matted to his chest?

"I was thinking more of a rose color," he said, not suffering the inhibitions that racked her. His forefinger circled the peak of her breast.

She trembled. "Now, who's playing with fire?"

"You're right, this was a dangerous idea."

Did that mean his control was in danger of snapping? She shivered.

"I wouldn't want to disappoint you, though. I promised you a massage."

"Aunt Euphemia was wrong. Some men have exceptional willpower."

"Honey, do me a favor. Whenever we're naked or almost naked, don't mention your aunt."

Jayne couldn't refrain from trailing her fingertips across his chest. "Spoils the mood, does it?"

He groaned. "Nothing, I repeat, *nothing,* can spoil the mood when I'm with you. Let's just say thoughts of your dearly-departed aunt aren't conducive to sensual pastimes."

She supposed he was right.

He bent his head and nuzzled her shoulder before trailing kisses along her throat and lower. She arched against him. His lips closed around one taut nipple outlined by the clinging fabric, and suckled lightly.

"Oh!"

"Sorry, I didn't mean to do that. Forget it ever happened."

She gnashed her teeth.

"I'm supposed to be helping you loosen those muscles. Better roll over. This will make you feel better."

He was a fiend. How dare he get her insides all riled up and then leave her hanging? Maybe he didn't realize how agitated she became when he touched her. It wasn't his fault she felt like a stick of dynamite about to explode. Grumbling inwardly at her feeble morals, she turned over.

"Here, lean up a bit." His fingers moved along her back.

"Don't stiffen up." He continued on a downward path, shifting their positions gradually so that they were at an angle to each other, an angle where one of his knees was lightly wedged against the part of her that ached for the friction of movement between them.

Wrenching away, she sat up. "Look, I don't know what you had in mind, but this isn't working. You've got me turned inside out." The shallow stream continued to flow around them. She grabbed a twig floating by and pointed it at him. "You said you wanted to loosen my muscles. Well, here we are, you naked and me practically so. If you're not going to make love to me until after we're married, then do me the favor of keeping your hands to yourself. I don't appreciate being set on fire and then left to burn myself out!"

She threw the twig at him. He snatched it from the air. "I'm trying to be the hero you've made me out to be. Heroes don't make love to saddle-sore virgins."

"I'm not just any virgin. I'm going to be your wife."

"That makes it all the more important that I show you some consideration. I refuse to make love to you for the first time to a litany of 'ows,' which is what I'll hear with your bruised and hurting thighs wrapped around me."

She tried to struggle to her feet, lost her balance and flopped into the water in an ungraceful splash. "Oh, let me go. Get your hands off me."

He pinned her wrists against the sandbar. Water skipped over her. Burke laid a heavy leg across her thighs.

"We're going to try this again."

"I don't want your massage. Let me up."

"Sure you do." He grasped both of her wrists in one hand. "Now where should I begin?"

"I'm warning you, Burke."

"I think I'd like to peel away just a little of your chemise. You don't mind, do you, honey?"

"Burke!"

"Yes, dear?" As if he were doing nothing more exceptional than brushing aside a newspaper page, he uncovered her.

She bit her lip. All right, so she was embarrassed at having betrayed how easily he could arouse her. Did she really want to order him to stop? What was this fight about, anyway? She wanted him to make love to her. He refused to do so, leaving her frustrated because...

"If you're not going to make love to me, what are you going to do?"

"This..." The tip of his forefinger journeyed lower. "I'm not heartless, you know."

"Oh!"

Delicately, he teased and cajoled. "I never want to hear that I got you hot and bothered and—" he probed deeper "—and failed to give you what you needed."

She couldn't speak. At first slowly, then with escalating speed and pressure, he brought her to the summit of her fervent need. He bent his head and lightly flicked his tongue against the tip of her exposed breast. Her entire body lurched upward, and she cried out.

Several shattering moments passed before anything like sanity tugged at the edges of her mind. She opened her eyes to Burke's nearly savage gaze.

"What about you?"

"I'll survive."

"But I'm willing to endure a little pain in order for you to find the satisfaction you gave me."

"Just what every man yearns to hear when he's contemplating making love for the first time to his bride."

She licked the beckoning patch of flesh at the base of his throat.

"I don't understand you." She stared pensively at him. "If you're feeling anything like I was a couple of minutes ago, you are in extreme agony. I'm still feeling hot and fluttery inside."

"Jayne!" He sat up, and water poured down his torso. "When you're my wife, I'm going to take you in every sense of the word. Until then, I'm going to atone for not protecting you by...by cherishing you, damn it.''

That word again. *Cherish....* It seemed of great import to him.

She also sat up, crossing her arms in front of her.

''You're the most stubborn man I've ever met, and the most decent,'' she couldn't help adding.

''I swear if you say the word 'noble' or 'heroic,' I'll throttle you.''

''Why can't you recognize those qualities within yourself?''

''Because you're the only one who mistakenly believes I possess them. I don't want you to be disillusioned after we're married and you realize I'm just an ordinary man.''

''It's going to take me a lifetime to show you how wonderful you are.''

''I'm willing to let you try.'' His tone lightened. ''Hell, I'm looking forward to it.''

''You're just not used to being in love, that's all.''

The light in his eyes dimmed. ''For someone who didn't believe in love *or* marriage a few weeks ago, you sure bring it up a lot.''

''You're right. Until I met you, I didn't believe in either the sentiment or the institution. Then my former opinions ceased to matter. Admit it, the same thing happened to you, or you wouldn't have proposed.''

A cloud passed overhead, casting a slow-moving shadow across the clearing. ''It's getting late. We'd better get dressed.''

Their discussion apparently at an end, he vaulted up. She rose at a more sedate pace and accepted his hand as he led her around the abandoned beaver dam.

Burke finished dressing first. ''I'll get us something to eat.''

She watched him head for the saddlebags he'd taken from the outlaws' camp. Why he was so uncomfortable discussing his love for her? He withdrew a long knife from one of the bags. Seeing the lethal weapon and the skillful way he used it to open the cans made her wonder if that was how he'd killed Baldwin. With skillful efficiency. Burke had done what he'd felt he had to do. She wouldn't judge him. Because of his actions, they now had a lifetime to work through their challenges.

Every couple probably started their married life with obstacles to overcome. Euphemia had conducted an endless search for the perfect mate. There were no perfect men, or women. It was only the miracle of love that enabled one to overlook another's faults.

Not perfect, but capable of great courage and sacrifice. The combination of manly traits was more than enough.

"Here you go." Burke held an open tin of peaches and a spoon. "This will take the edge off your hunger."

Not my true hunger. *Tell me you love me.* Her gaze lingered on the humble eating utensil. "How on earth did you think to pack spoons?"

"It seemed the logical thing to do."

"For some men, it would be logical to reclaim the stolen money bags."

"It came down to survival. Neither currency nor gold is worth much in this wild country. Food is the valuable commodity." He shrugged. "The gold packed in those bags would have weighed us down. We needed to move quickly."

"You made the right choice," she said loyally, accepting the food and walking to a felled log that had entered its season of slow decomposition.

"I know this is poor fare, but it's better than trying to bring down a deer and having the shots pinpoint our location."

She dipped into the tin and withdrew a plump slice of the golden fruit, which she poked into her mouth, chewed with exaggerated enthusiasm, then swallowed. "The peaches are delicious."

One corner of his lips tugged upward. "You're a good camper, Jayne."

"Thank you." She scooped up another peach and quickly dispatched it. "It infuriates me that those men get to keep their ill-gotten loot."

"They haven't gotten away yet. It won't be difficult to track them. There are probably fifty men on their trail right now."

"Really?" The large number surprised her. "Do you have that many employees skilled at hunting outlaws on your payroll?"

"Most of the posse will consist of deputized citizens experienced in tracking. Then there's the Guardsmen."

"I hadn't realized you'd contacted them for assistance."

Burke frowned. "Eat your peaches."

She stared after him thoughtfully as he picked up the knife and opened another tin. Whenever something came up he didn't wish to discuss, he was adept at ending the conversation. Her eyes narrowed. That attitude did not bode well for open communications between a husband and wife. Euphemia always said it was best to nip in the bud any form of unacceptable behavior.

Burke stood a few yards away from her, eating from the can. She pursed her lips and considered his indifferent stance. A prudent woman didn't tolerate being dismissed in so summary a fashion.

"Come eat beside me, Burke."

The spoon he held stopped midway to his mouth. A dripping peach slice slid dangerously close to its limited borders. "It feels good to stand."

"If you expect to marry me, a few points must be made clear."

His jaw tensed visibly. Without warning, the halved peach lost its chancy perch and plopped to the ground. "Damn."

She sighed. "I suppose your addiction to profanity is something to which I'll become accustomed."

"I'm working on it." His gaze shot back to her. "It would help if you didn't take every opportunity to incite my anger and my passions."

"Bah, there's no getting around it. You're of an excitable disposition when it comes to losing your temper or becoming physically aroused."

He threw the spoon to the ground. It landed three feet from where the peach had fallen. "I'm the most coolheaded man you'll ever meet."

"Why does talking about the Guardsmen upset you?"

"I'll be happy to discuss the Guardsmen, once we get something settled."

"What's that?"

"There is no 'if' you're going to marry me. You're already mine. I don't share, and I refuse to be blackmailed with sentiment."

"Well, I refuse to marry a man who walks away whenever the conversation turns unpleasant. I expect to be able to discuss our problems."

"That seems fair." He was silent for a full minute. "Are you going to keep your promise to marry me?"

The unexpected flash of vulnerability flickering in his eyes softened the last of her residual anger. "You have my word."

"No matter what?"

"No matter what."

"Then you'll never say 'if' I marry you again?"

"Never," she murmured tenderly.

"About the Guardsmen...." He joined her on the log. "The reason I know they're searching for us, as well as trying to find those thieving bandits, is because I'm one of them."

"A thieving bandit?" The jest was weak, but discovering Burke belonged to a group of modern warriors stirred awe and admiration along with excitement. She *was* marrying a true hero.

"You know what I'm saying."

"Oh, Burke, I'm so proud of you."

"You can lose that misty-eyed look. Being a Guardsman isn't glamorous like the newspapers make it out to be. It's the monotonous kind of work associated with running a ranch, or a bank. We keep track of suspicious characters and watch over likely targets."

"You mean people too vulnerable to protect themselves."

"Don't start painting me as a hero again. We fill in the gaps the law doesn't reach."

Jayne's thoughts leaped forward. "Gideon and Hunter are members, too, aren't they?"

Burke's expression became cautious. "What makes you think so?"

"Because they're so much like you." Her eyes widened. "That's why Gideon looked as if he was trying not to laugh the night we dined together. He must have thought me a ninny, when I said you couldn't handle the situation at the bank. And Emma knows, too. She was just as amused as Gideon."

"He told her about being a Guardsman after they were married."

"I suppose that's something. At least you trust me enough to reveal the truth before we exchange our vows."

"There shouldn't be secrets between us."

"I feel the same way. People in love should be honest with each other."

He took the tin of peaches from her and set it on the ground next to his. "You want complete honesty, right?"

She rested her head against his shoulder. "Absolutely."

"And, if my honesty doesn't please you, it will have no effect on your promise to marry me?"

Uneasiness stirred. "Truth is always the most important consideration."

The pat declaration was at odds with apprehension building within her.

"The truth is, I lost whatever capacity I had to love years

ago. That defect has nothing to do with my feelings about you, however.''

She raised her head from his shoulder. ''What *are* your feelings?''

''Don't pull away. What we have is better than illusions.''

She definitely didn't like the sound of that.

''Even as a boy, I wasn't prone to sentiment. My father is a cold-blooded banker. My mother is equally in control of what might be called female sensibilities.''

''What does that have to do with you loving me?''

''I'm explaining that. My younger brother and I managed to escape their demand that we function as passionless automatons.''

''You have a brother?''

''Keep interrupting, and it will take forever to tell this story. Logan is two years younger than I am. He became my shadow. I got used to the hero worship he innocently lavished. We were close, even for brothers.''

Jayne remained silent. The thought of two little boys growing up in such an unfeeling household tugged at her heart. At least, she'd had loving, well-intentioned parents until they'd both succumbed to a foreign flu that had swept through Philadelphia when she was twelve. Then, spirited, freethinking Euphemia had taken her in, openly relishing her role of substitute mother.

''That all changed,'' Burke continued, ''when the conniving Robeena Stockard slithered into our lives. Initially she set her snare for me. I never told Logan, at first because I didn't think it was serious between them, and later because... After they became engaged, I thought she'd forgotten about me and was in love with my brother.''

Burke withdrew his arm from Jayne's shoulder and rested his elbows on his knees. ''My parents were active in politics. They hosted a ball for the new governor. Robeena and a supposed chaperon spent the evening as our guests. I retired alone for the night and woke up with Robeena snuggled beside me. I scrambled out of bed, but not soon enough. Logan was standing in the doorway."

"Oh, Burke…"

"On cue, my parents arrived, courtesy of the chaperon, no doubt. Robeena had a convenient case of hysterics, demanding that I marry her. I informed all interested parties that would never happen, not in this lifetime or the next."

"What happened?"

"My parents knew me well enough to accept my word as final. They escorted a subdued Robeena back to her bedchamber. What I didn't realize was they expected Logan to continue with his wedding plans."

Jayne gasped. "But why?"

"To preserve the family name. Knowing I was immune to such pitiful logic, they directed their energies to convincing Logan it was his duty to protect us from gossip. We're talking about Boston, remember? In my parents' social circle nothing was more feared than the breath of scandal."

"That's terrible."

"It destroyed what little sense of family we had. Logan escaped their manipulations by going West and beginning his own network of banks. I left, too, and headed for Denver to do the same thing."

"It seems unusual for young men to have so much wealth."

"As the elder son, I'd received inheritances from my grandparents."

"And Logan?"

"He didn't know it at the time, but I became his silent partner, secretly funneling money to him so he could establish himself in the West."

"Oh, Burke, that's so like you."

He raised a palm. "Don't start."

"How do things stand between you and Logan now?"

"Eventually he found out I'd been helping him behind the scenes for some time. By then, he'd fallen in love and married a remarkable woman named Victoria. She's also from Boston. I saw him a short while ago and met her. They've taken on the responsibility for caring for an orphaned girl, named Madison, and have two young children of their own."

"Have you mended your differences?"

"As far as I know, there isn't any contention between me and their children."

She poked his side. "You know what I mean."

"Logan and I have…talked. There's no longer open hostility between us. I think he believes my explanation about what really happened that night. But it will never be the same between us. Victoria and their children are his world."

"Don't you think that would have happened eventually, even without that dreadful scene? Logan wouldn't have remained your tagalong brother forever."

"By the time he'd become engaged, we were pretty much equals." Burke's fists clenched. "But that night changed everything. I went from a beloved brother to a hated enemy."

"And that's when you decided you'd lost the capacity to love?"

He turned to her. "If there was any woman on this earth I could love, it would be you. But there's nothing there, not where my heart should be. I want you, Jayne. That's got to be enough, because that's all I've got."

Was it enough?

"Maybe I should tell you about my rules."

She assumed he referred to rules of conduct governing character. They were probably noble platitudes about honor, integrity and doing one's duty. How such sayings pertained to his gloomy disclosure was beyond her.

"Go ahead."

"There are three of them. Rule number one—only an imbecile gives his heart to a woman. Rule number two—

marriage is a lifelong prison sentence. Rule number three—always remember rules one and two.''

A low hum vibrated in her ears. She jumped to her feet. The entire clearing seemed bathed in a red haze.

''Jayne?''

''Aunt Euphemia was right!'' Jayne had to pace or blow up.

''Are you upset?''

She rounded on him. ''Those are the most juvenile, most self-centered, most cowardly rules I've ever heard. I bet this is what happened to Euphemia. She would let down her guard and start thinking she'd met an intelligent, clear-thinking man, and then he would say something so...so stupid that she would have no recourse but to call off the engagement.''

Burke grabbed her arm. ''We're past that point. The engagement stands.''

She tried to jerk free. Naturally, the effort was wasted. ''How can I refuse you? The thought of being bound to a man who looks at marriage as a prison sentence has inflamed me with an uncontrollable desire to learn how to knit. Your touching words have inspired me to fix Sunday dinner every day of the week and...and darn your socks every night. I've been called to the mountaintop of wifely servitude and yearn, no *burn,* to wash tubs of laundry, beat rugs and...and pluck chickens!''

''I live in a mansion with a dozen servants.''

She swiped a tear. ''Hah! You'll probably fire them the moment I cross the threshold.''

''It's because of scenes like this that men resist marriage in the first place.''

She didn't appreciate the droll tenderness she perceived in his voice.

''I don't know why you're so upset, honey. Not too long ago you didn't believe in love, either.''

''I grew up,'' she said loftily.

''So I see.'' He dragged her into his arms. ''It's hard for

me to put my feelings into words. If you'll settle down, I'll do my best to explain what you mean to me."

Somewhat mollified, she relaxed the tiniest bit against him.

"I do want you. Maybe that's not what you would like to hear, but it's the truth. You've got a... For lack of a better word, a light that shines within you."

"Just last night you called me a shrew when you advised me how to handle Baldwin."

"Well, there's that. But you're also brave, honest as a messenger straight from God and...sweet."

"I don't see how I can be sweet and—"

"Shh, let me finish." He squeezed her. "As I was saying, I crave your body, but I also crave what's inside you. I don't know what to call it, some kind of spiritual core that shatters my cynicism. I know you're beautiful. It isn't only that which draws me to you."

She pressed her forefinger against his lips. "Enough, you don't have to exaggerate. What you said just now, about your feelings toward me... It's enough. I don't want you to tell me you love me, not if you don't feel it. I'll be honored to become your wife."

During the next three days and nights, Jayne's simple words weighed heavily on Burke's thoughts. The declaration of her love and acceptance of his own limited capacity to return it should have soothed him. It didn't.

As each day passed with him seeing to their survival, he grew more restless, more unsettled with the state of affairs between them. When darkness fell and he held her in his arms, he had to remind himself of his vow that he wouldn't make love to her before they were married. He didn't lie to himself, though. The only thing preventing him from claiming her was the knowledge that he couldn't possess her without hurting her. Her steadily improving condition, however, made that consideration growingly precarious.

Burke looked toward Jayne. She was shaking out one of

the blankets. During the past few days, it had become clear that he was marrying an industrious woman. His glance fell on the discarded peach tins she'd pressed into service as vases for the colorful wildflowers she picked. An industrious woman with nesting instincts that utterly beguiled him.

He rubbed the back of his neck. He was a banker. The idea of coming out ahead in a deal should have pleased him. A nagging sense, however, that, in marrying him, Jayne was receiving the short end of the bargain, diminished a portion of his pleasure.

The sound of hooves thundering toward the secluded clearing slammed Burke to the present. ''Damn, where'd I put that gun?''

How could he have been so careless? Jayne's survival depended on him. If nothing else, this would prove to her he was no hero.

''Mr. Youngblood, is that you?'' Newton White's booming voice resounded across the meadow.

Burke shaded his eyes against the sun's glare. Relief rolled through him. They'd been found. He squinted at the sight of the miner atop a horse big enough to pull a fully loaded hay wagon. He'd never seen a four-legged animal of such monumental proportions, save a buffalo or elk.

Jayne waved at Newt as he barreled toward them. Burke hoped the monstrous horse obeyed the miner's forceful pull on its reins.

''Whoa, I said whoa, you infernal beast.''

Burke prepared to leap toward Jayne to push her from the careening mammoth's path. Amazingly, Newt brought the rambunctious creature to a halt.

The miner jumped from the saddle, and Burke swore the ground trembled. ''After we caught up with them robbers, and they told us you'd escaped, we split up and went in different directions looking for you. I remembered this pretty spot from a little mining expedition I was on a couple of summers back. It seemed a likely place for a man to hide from a bunch of murdering rascals.''

A huge grin shone on the man's sweating red face. Burke thrust out his hand. "When we get back to Denver, you can expect a substantial reward for your shrewd reasoning."

"Aw, shucks, I don't want no reward. Finding you and—" He broke off and swept the mauled hat from his shaggy-haired head. "How do, Miss Stoneworthy. It's good to see you."

"It's wonderful to see you! You've saved us."

It was immature to let Jayne's effusive gratitude to the homely miner disturb him. But, as many times as he'd told her he wasn't a hero, he preferred she reserve her admiration for him alone.

"Thank you, Miss Stoneworthy." Newton plopped his hat back on. "Hearing such kind words makes me feel like a Guardsman—you know, sort of a hero."

Burke smothered a groan. Evidently no man could resist being thought of as noble, even if he damned well knew he didn't have a noble bone in his body.

Jayne hoped Newt was right and that the family whom he said lived in a nearby cabin would allow them to stay the night. She shared the miner's horse, sitting sidesaddle because she couldn't straddle the huge beast. Burke's mount was one of the two they'd used to escape. He hadn't appeared enthusiastic about the riding arrangements, but agreed Newt's animal was better suited to carry two riders.

"You said they caught the men who kidnapped us?" She asked, repeating the thrilling news.

"Sure did. First thing this morning. They're headed for jail."

"And the saddlebags with the loot were recovered?" Jayne asked.

"Yep, every gold coin and bill they stole," came Newt's sunny reply.

"That's wonderful, isn't it, Burke?"

"Yeah. How much farther is the cabin, Newt?"

"Just beyond that hill over there."

"I don't think Jayne's up to riding back to Denver. Do they have a buggy? I'll pay for its use."

"The Dobsens are good Christian folk. They won't take your money."

The cabin came into view. Jayne had never seen so beautiful a sight.

Newt proved to be right about the Dobsens' generosity. They didn't have a buggy but were willing to lend their wagon. If she and Burke started out early the next morning, they would reach Denver by nightfall.

The couple's hospitality was such that another guest was in residence—Erastus Lowder, a traveling preacher. At her and Burke's introduction to the wiry man dressed in a black coat and baggy brown trousers, Burke's demeanor became almost garrulous, if one could imagine such a thing. Jayne recalled her impetuous promise to marry Burke at the first opportunity that presented itself. She sensed he would hold her to that promise.

They finished dinner. As she looked around the cabin, Jayne was impressed by how cleverly it had been designed. A table and cooking area occupied most of the ground floor. An open loft had been built along one wall. The pine dresser and bed she glimpsed left no doubt about the room's function.

"Reverend Lowder," Burke said without preamble. "I assume you're always ready to conduct a wedding ceremony."

The little man pulled the pipe from his mouth and straightened in his chair. "Can't do a wedding. Don't have my Bible. Wouldn't be official." He jammed his pipe between his teeth.

"For goodness' sake, *I've* got a Bible." Mrs. Dobsen went to a small shelf and withdrew a battered leather volume. She turned to the preacher. "Here you go."

The reverend eyed the book as if she were handing him a snake. Laying aside his pipe, he got to his feet. "It's been

a while since I've done one of these. Not sure I remember
the words.''

''I know them,'' Mrs. Dobsen announced. ''You can repeat them after me.'' She turned to Jayne. ''Well, time's
awasting, come along.''

''Yes, Jayne, come along.''

Burke's commanding voice beckoned, but her feet
seemed frozen to the wood-planked floor. Three days ago
in the meadow when she'd given her rash promise, she
hadn't thought she would have to honor it quite so soon.

''Go ahead, Miss Stoneworthy. I know it's scary, but it
ain't so bad. I got hitched yesterday. It didn't hurt nearly
as much as I thought it would,'' Newt said.

''But when I talked to you last week, you were dead-set
against marriage.'' She frowned. ''If you had a sweetheart
what were you doing at the tavern, trying to—''

''Miss Stoneworthy, there's no call to go into that.''
Newt glanced around self-consciously. ''There's a reverend
in the room.''

''And a *Christian* woman,'' Mrs. Dobsen added.

''I don't care who's here,'' Jayne snapped. ''You have
some explaining to do.''

''I wasn't cheating on no sweetheart, if that's what
you're thinking. I found Rascal.''

''Sally Haskell's cat?''

''That's right. It turns out she's a right nice person. I
'membered what you said about getting married and all.
It's kinda lonely at camp. Anyway, Sally and I got to drinking, begging your pardon, Reverend. One thing led to another, begging your pardon, Mrs. Dobsen. The fact is Sally
and I woke up the next morning hitched.''

Jayne shook her head. ''That's the most astonishing story
I've ever heard.''

''It's original, anyway,'' Burke drawled. ''Shall we begin?''

The preacher drummed his fingers against the Bible

"I've been ready for five minutes. Let's get this over with. Miss Stoneworthy?"

Dazed, she moved forward. "Yes, of course."

The bizarre ceremony, that of having Mrs. Dobsen say the time-honored phrases with the reverend parroting them seemed to end before it even began.

"You can kiss the bride," the woman said, daubing her eyes.

"Right." Lowder mopped his forehead with his sleeve. "Kiss the bride."

Burke took her into his arms and brushed his lips across hers. "I was holding my breath when they got to the part about obeying," his whispered.

"I'm sure that portion of the ceremony is there for the poetic flow," she whispered back. "It isn't meant to be taken literally."

He threw back his head and laughed. "Oh, my beloved Jayne, I was born to be your slave."

A short time later they retired to the Dobsens' loft. Being overheard by the cabin's other occupants was reason enough to stifle any utterances of a personal nature. She and Burke undressed with their backs to each other. A faint stream of moonlight came through the small window above them. Totally nude, at least she assumed he was, they climbed into the narrow bed. A distressingly loud creak sounded. She was certain the Dobsens, Newt and the Reverend heard the embarrassing noise.

Burke rolled toward her. Another fiendish creak rattled the cabin walls. "This is never going to work."

"I know." She responded in the same low voice he'd used. "I'm so embarrassed. If we…do anything, the bed will announce it to the world."

"Just to the people downstairs," he corrected. "But that's enough to dampen thoughts of making love. I want to hear all the sweet sounds you make. As for me…"

"Yes?"

"I intend to roar."

"Under the circumstances, do you want to...wait?"

"I can't." Burke left the bed, causing the strident groan of straining wood. "Don't move."

He padded, naked, as she'd supposed, to her side of the bed. Making no sound he scooped her and the quilt from the tick mattress. He placed her on her feet and unwound her from the bedding.

Burke spread the thick quilt over the floor, took her hand and pulled her downward to join him. "This isn't how I pictured things."

He lowered his mouth to hers for a torrid kiss. His touch was...everywhere. She bit her lip to keep from crying out when he stroked her intimately. There was something to be said for the seclusion provided by a mountain meadow.

"I've never made love to a virgin," he said, his deep voice a husky murmur against her ear.

She rubbed against him. "I'll die if you don't do something."

Above her, his visage seemed carved in damp stone. He put his hand over her lips, while his mouth ranged lower. She practically leaped from the floor at the incredibly intense waves of liquid pleasure that surged through her.

The torment continued until she knew she was at the edge. As the golden tremors began to overtake her, he eased himself into her. At first, she wanted him, *needed* him there. Then pain cut through the shimmering waves of release. She cried out. He pressed his palm more tightly against her mouth, withdrew with agonizing slowness, then filled her again, deeper than before. Pleasure returned, then eluded her. He paused for a moment. She ran her hands along his back, awed by the powerful muscles he'd locked into submission.

Then he thrust forward. Completely. She subdued the instinct to fight him. This was Burke, her husband. This was what men and women did. He wasn't deliberately hurting her....

"I love your womanly scent. I love being this close to you. I love—"

He continued thrusting. The pain was gone. All she felt was the tantalizing sensation of being stretched to fit his fullness. She relaxed, discovering she could better accommodate him when her muscles weren't tight. Hot, steamy minutes passed. When she thought she couldn't endure another second of the heavy passion building within her, he removed his hand from her lips and replaced it with his mouth.

A half second later she felt the pressure of his touch against her throbbing center. Something snapped, uncorked or... There was a sudden moment of change. Everything that had been gathering inward, convulsed, then surged outward.

She surrendered to the avalanche of unbearable joy. Burke surged into her once more. Perceiving that this stubborn, arrogant, heroic man was more vulnerable, more out of control than she'd thought him capable of being, moved her to tears. His triumphant shout flowed silently into her mouth.

He shuddered, then went lax. The memory of the afternoon she'd knocked him unconscious rose in her thoughts. So similar and so earth-shatteringly different. A full circle to paradise...

He touched her cheek. "I made you cry."

"Being well loved made me cry." Would he ever understand the wrenching emotional and physical dimensions his lovemaking had on her?

He buried his lips in her hair. "Jayne, you totally unhinge me."

It was quite an admission for a proud man like Burke to make. Yet she yearned for other words.

Chapter Seventeen

It was almost dusk of the following day when Jayne, Newt, Mr. Dobsen and Burke reached town. News of their arrival must have preceded them. Dozens of people had gathered. Shouts of welcome heralded the wagon as it rolled to a halt in front of the sheriff's office. Jayne wondered if the excited murmurs were on behalf of their safe return or the recovery of the stolen gold and money.

Sheriff Donner, a lean man whose darkly tanned skin appeared as taut as stretched leather, stepped onto the street. "Glad to see you made it back, Mr. Youngblood."

Burke's jaw was clamped tight. *No thanks to you...* He didn't say it, but Jayne was certain that was what Burke was thinking. He jumped from the wagon and assisted her down. "Are you doing okay?"

"I'm fine," she answered.

Owen Gardner pushed his way forward. "I never doubted you would make it back, sir."

Burke's expression was enigmatic. "How are things at the bank?"

Gardner ran his finger around the inside of his starched collar. "Pretty much as you left them. There is...uh...one problem that's come up."

"I'll be in tomorrow to take care of it."

"All right, sir." His assistant faded into the thinning crowd.

Burke scanned the clusters of lingering people. A scowl crossed his face. He turned to Newt, who'd joined him and the sheriff. "Please see that my wife gets home safely. I don't want her waiting here while Sheriff Donner and I conduct our business."

"Sure thing, Mr. Youngblood."

"I appreciate it, Newt."

"Your wife?" a familiar, distinctly unwelcome voice inquired.

Jayne turned. Winslow Dilicar stepped forward from the small knot of people who remained on the street.

"That's what I said." His stance altering subtly, Burke slid his arm from her waist.

The sound of Dilicar's laughter grated on Jayne's nerves. "You must have been born under a lucky star. You're the only man I know who can be kidnapped at gunpoint, escape and return a few days later married."

Every line of Burke's tensed muscles transmitted a warrior's readiness to do battle as he stalked toward his antagonist. Dilicar's posture also emanated an intent to strike. They were like two growling dogs, teeth bared, circling each other.

"I'm going to prove you're behind the robberies. When I do, you're finished, Dilicar."

Hatred filled the man's eyes. "I don't know what you're talking about."

"When you caught Jayne in your net, you crossed the line. Better make sure your affairs are in order, including your will."

The enraged banker turned to the sheriff. "Did you hear that? He's threatening me. And this isn't the first time. I want him arrested. Now."

"Calm down, Mr. Dilicar." Donner looked at Burke. "You, too, Mr. Youngblood. We don't need any hotheads taking the law into their own hands."

"Does he have to kill me before you take action?" Dilicar demanded.

"I'm sure it won't come to that." The lawman spoke reassuringly.

"Don't bet on it." Burke's words were softly voiced, but Jayne was sure both the sheriff and Dilicar heard them.

"If you'll come with me, Mr. Youngblood, I'd like to hear your account of the robbery and your escape."

Jayne followed Newt to the wagon as Burke and Donner headed toward the sheriff's office.

The rest of the onlookers drifted away. Frank Sutton joined Dilicar. "You're not really worried about Youngblood making good on his threats, are you?"

"The man's so caught up in protecting that woman, he's become deranged. What was Baldwin thinking when he took her?"

"That the best way to control someone as dangerous as Youngblood would be to use his woman as an ace in the hole to keep him in line."

"Why didn't Baldwin put a bullet through Youngblood?"

"He was probably thinking that First National would pay to get him back."

Dilicar nodded. "Greedy bastard."

"Aren't we all?"

"We've got to do something about Youngblood and his damned threats. If I'm connected to that robbery, he's going to hunt me down like a dog."

"Don't worry. The man would be crazy to come after you."

Dilicar's haunted expression eased. "That's right. No matter how much he wants me dead, he'd be a fool to try anything. He'd be the first person Donner arrested."

Sutton was smiling as he and Dilicar went their separate ways.

An hour after Newt had delivered her to Burke's home, Jayne paced the library. In theory, she knew it was her home, too. It didn't feel that way. Instead, she felt as if she were a visitor in the grand residence. She still wore the dusty, stained outfit in which she'd been kidnapped. Ordering one of the servants to prepare a bath was an awkwardness with which she wasn't prepared to deal.

Second thoughts... How could she *not* have them? An entire lifetime of prudent and logical behavior leading in a particular direction, and she'd discarded it for all the wrong reasons—love and passion for a virtual stranger who'd managed to coerce her into an impetuous marriage. After telling her he was incapable of loving her or any woman! And, what about the plans for her school?

Oh, Aunt Euphemia, I fear I've taken a path I'm ill-equipped to follow. Heaven only knows where I shall end up.

"Jayne, what are you doing in here?"

At Burke's question, she pivoted. The black stubble carpeting his jaw had grown to beardlike thickness. His hair was tousled, his expression speculative. She wanted nothing more than to fling herself into his arms, but a constraint she was at a loss to understand held her back.

"I didn't know where else to wait." The only way to vanquish the queasy doubts shredding her peace of mind was through honesty. "I know we're...married, but this house..." Her sweeping gesture included the rooms beyond the book-lined library walls. "It's all too much."

His expression remained thoughtful. "You lived here two weeks."

"As a visitor," she reminded him. "Everything's changed."

"That's right, you're my wife." Possessive satisfaction rippled from the words. "This is your home now. *Our* servants are paid to accommodate your needs. You should have ordered supper, along with a hot bath."

"The people working for you don't know we're married."

"A minor point," he muttered, moving into the chamber. "If it's that important, I'll wake the entire staff and make a formal announcement."

"Don't you dare," she protested, nonplussed by the vision of dozens of bleary-eyed servants—from parlor maids, to the cook, housekeeper and butler, lined up in their sleeping apparel to officially welcome the new Mrs. Burke Youngblood. "What kind of impression would I make, looking as if I crawled here all the way from the outlaws' camp?"

"You're not obliged to make a favorable impression upon my employees," he said, as if struggling for patience. "They damned well better please you."

"I want to begin on the right foot."

"I suppose I can understand that." He studied her with shuttered eyes. "I thought perhaps you were regretting the haste in which we married."

And that hurt me....

Again, she felt as if she had the uncanny ability to know his feelings without his expressing them. If she were wrong, a dangerous self-deception... Right or wrong, she could no longer withstand his pull.

"Pay no attention to my insecurities." She bridged the distance between them. "Even if I'd ordered a bath, I had nothing to change into afterward."

"Lying between my sheets would have solved that dilemma."

She pictured herself naked, waiting for him in his bed. "I didn't think of that."

"If you ever find yourself in the same situation, I trust you'll remember that solution."

"I'll keep it in mind." She wrapped her arms around his waist.

"Don't...doubt me, Jayne." His broad palms moved along her back as he held her close. "I know I'm not the kind of man whom women dream will enter their lives. I can't say the words you want to hear. But you come first."

She blinked back tears. What he had to give *was* enough, she told herself again, more fiercely than before. "You come first with me, too."

His chin rested on the crown of her head. "Have you noticed how well we fit?"

She rubbed her cheek against his shirt. "It's rather strange, isn't it, considering how much taller and bigger you are."

"I'd call it fate." He stepped back. "Come on."

"Where?" *To your bedchamber, to demonstrate how well we do fit?* Tonight there would be no creaking bed. They would be free to make as much noise as they wished. Burke could roar, and she could...moan.

"Since we need to eat, we'd better head for the kitchen."

"Oh."

"Then we'll retire to our bedchamber for a bath."

Her stomach dipped. "That sounds...practical."

"In a tub big enough to accommodate us both. I hope you're not too tired. We're bound to be there a while."

"Why's that?" She recalled the last time they were in water together.

"You have a lot of intriguing curves that demand my attention, as well as a couple of secret spots requiring a delicate touch."

Doubting he referred to the area between her toes, her insides became hot and slippery with desire. "I will be equally diligent."

The following morning Burke was in his office later than his usual custom. As it once would have, though, being behind schedule didn't bother him. The hours he'd spent making love to Jayne... No single word described what having her in his arms did to him. But bringing her to one dizzying peak after another satisfied a need he'd never re-alized existed within him. It was more than satisfaction, more than release, more than sexual gratification or possession. It was an intangible submission to a force beyond his comprehension.

As he sat behind his desk, three things became unmistakably clear. Nothing would ever induce him to give up Jayne or the primitive feelings she stirred. He would do everything within his power to protect her. And he was damned well going to pump some life into his barren heart. She deserved to be loved.

There was a knock at the door. Having a strong idea who was there, Burke forced himself to focus on the unpleasant business at hand.

"Come in, Owen."

As his assistant entered the room, Burke appraised the man's furtive expression and trembling hands. Though anxious, Owen obviously was clinging to the vain hope his perfidy hadn't been discovered. That false notion was about to be shattered. Without rising, Burke gestured to one of the chairs that faced his desk.

His assistant stumbled forward, virtually collapsing into his chair. "Allow me to tell you how well you look, sir. I'm thrilled you were able to escape those thieves."

"I appreciate the sentiment." Burke knew very well that the man would have been more "thrilled" had the escape failed.

Owen quickly raced on. "About that small problem I mentioned last night— Considering your recent nuptials, this is bound to be…sticky."

Burke temporarily shelved his plan to confront his assistant. "What does my marriage have to do with the bank?"

"Uh…well, since you're both owner and president, I'm sure you won't want to bring formal charges against your wife. If you cover the amount of the bogus bank draft from your personal account, we can keep everything quiet. There's certainly no need to involve the law."

"What in blazes are you talking about?"

"The bank draft Miss Stone— I mean Mrs. Youngblood presented was…" A nervous tic seized the man's right eye.

"It's an utterly worthless piece of paper. There are no funds to cover it."

A chilling numbness invaded Burke's extremities before moving relentlessly toward his heart. Since it would be a simple matter to disprove a lie about the matter, his assistant must be telling the truth.

"You're correct. I will cover the amount of the draft."

"I thought as much." Owen continued to sit tensely in his chair.

Burke steepled his fingertips. "Let's move to another subject."

Perspiration gleamed on the man's pale skin. His gaze reflected the trapped defeat of one who'd hoped against hope he could bypass judgment.

When Jayne awoke in Burke's bed, she was alone. Her eyelids drifted closed. Recalling the intimacies she'd experienced at her husband's skillful hands, thorough mouth and sensual mind, she burrowed deeper into the bedding that carried his masculine scent.

Tender, passionate, shockingly inventive, he was the kind of lover every woman secretly yearned would enter her life, and her person. It was difficult to comprehend that such a magnificent male creature was her husband. A rueful smile tugged at her lips. She never thought she'd live to see the day she considered any man magnificent.

A light knock sounded, and the bedchamber door was pushed open several inches. "Miss, I mean, Mrs. Youngblood," a feminine voice called out. "Your husband sent word from the bank. He'd like you to join him there."

Jayne glanced in dismay at the ruined clothes Burke had peeled from her last night. "But I haven't anything to wear."

"Begging your pardon, but Mr. Youngblood sent two men to Agnes Sawyer's boardinghouse and had them fetch your things. There's a trunk and valise next to the wardrobe."

"You may close the door. I shall get dressed at once."

Jayne scrambled from the sheets. Standing nude in his bedchamber, she remembered the possessive manner with which her new husband had familiarized himself with every bare inch of her. It astounded her that one inflamed, emboldened man could generate such fevered excitement and pleasure. A new sense of competitiveness stirred. She fully intended to inspire that same thundering ecstasy within him. Flushing, she went to the trunk.

Burke's office door stood ajar. She noticed that in the short time they'd been gone, it had been replaced. Obviously, her husband surrounded himself with efficient associates. She attributed her breathless anticipation as she stepped into his office to having to face in daylight the daring lover of last night.

She was greeted instead by a cold-faced stranger who, while bearing a startling resemblance to her new husband, evidenced none of his warmth. "What took you so long?"

The antagonistic question pricked the romantic bubble she'd cultivated since waking. She sighed. The lecture she'd meant to issue regarding his shifting moods had been interrupted. There was no time like the present, however, to inform him that he couldn't change from fiercely passionate to gloomily hostile without a good reason. Bah, even if he had a good reason, he would have to curb his brooding tendencies.

She seated herself, aware that her brown dress was wrinkled from its recent unpacking. Nor had she been able to locate the bonnet she usually wore with the gown. She folded her ungloved hands and dismissed those items as inconsequential. "As soon as I was told you wished to see me, I came."

"I sent word over an hour ago."

She rolled her eyes. "I thought it prudent to dress before leaving the house."

"I don't believe I've ever seen a gown as ugly as the one you have on."

Jayne jumped to her feet. "That's it! I've struggled to be patient with your erratic disposition, but this is too much. I forbid you to engage in foul displays of temper or gloomy moods."

He also stood. "You *forbid* me?"

She squared her shoulders. "I did not seek marriage and a husband. But now that I am legally bound in wedlock, I have every intention of requiring my mate to adhere to certain standards.

"Standards?" he all but hissed.

"Absolutely. There will be no bouts of brooding melancholy. Just as I insist upon a husband willing to engage in unpleasant discussions when they arise, I also insist upon a companion who doesn't sulk."

He leaned forward and flattened his hands on the desk. "Then by all means, let's discuss an unpleasant topic. For starters, whether or not I should have you arrested."

A sense of unreality gripped Jayne. "What are you talking about?"

He straightened and circled the desk. "I'm talking about the little matter of you palming off a fraudulent bank draft."

"B-but that's preposterous."

He grabbed her shoulders. She braced herself to withstand the impending violence his furious gaze promised. "I suppose my desire for you made me an irresistible target. You assumed that even after I discovered I'd been duped, I would cover the loss. Hell, a man crazy with lust will do just about anything to get what he wants."

"It wasn't lust," she whispered. "You can't tell me that your only feelings toward me are carnal."

"Would hearing that make you happy?" He smiled grimly. "Sorry to disappoint you. There was only one thing I wanted from you."

Don't say it, she cried silently. The pain she knew he could unleash within her loomed black and deadly.

"We both know what that was," he continued relentlessly. "Of course, the price was steeper than I wanted to pay. From the moment I laid eyes on you, though, I recognized what having you would cost. Marriage."

"I offered myself to you at that stream, *without* marriage."

"You knew me well enough to realize I'd feel obligated to pay for your virginity with my name."

"You're twisting everything," she protested, unwilling to let him trample what was beautiful and real between them.

"At least I got what I paid for." His gaze burned. "I feel more than amply compensated. Getting a hot-blooded virgin is every man's fantasy."

As she knew he meant them to, his cruel words struck the center of her heart. She wanted to pull away and run as far from him as she could get, just as she instinctively sought to hide her pain. But even in that awful moment of despair, she wanted to throw herself into his arms and beg him to take back every hurtful thing he'd said.

"Rest assured, you guessed right. I'll cover the loss, and I won't turn you over to the sheriff." A terrible sound masquerading as laughter tore free from him. "He wouldn't know what do with you, but I sure as hell do."

Strong hands pulled her to him. "Open up, dear wife. I mean to collect everything I'm due."

Without warning, his office door burst open. A feeling of déjà vu swept over Jayne. In a blink, she was transported back to those first horrendous moments of the bank robbery.

This time, though, Sheriff Donner stood in the entry, his gun drawn and pointed at Burke. Several other men, also with drawn pistols, were positioned behind the lawman.

"Burke Youngblood, you're under arrest. Step back from your wife and raise your hands."

"What's the charge?" Burke asked, doing as ordered. "Having too loud an argument with my bride?"

"Save your smart-ass remarks for Judge Pinegar. Put your hands behind your back." Handcuffs snapped shut. "As for the charge, you're being arrested for the murder of Winslow Dilicar."

Betraying no emotion, Burke allowed himself to be turned around. "When did that happen?"

"Last night, as you well know. Now move along."

Burke remained immobile, his stare centered upon her. "When this misunderstanding is settled, Jayne, I expect to find you waiting at home."

Burke's fingers curled around the cell's iron bars. She hadn't come. More than a month had passed, and she hadn't sent so much as a note to him. Fortunately, Gideon and Hunter's friendship had proved more reliable. They'd engaged the services of one of Denver's most skilled attorneys to handle his defense. The only thing connecting him to Dilicar's murder was the rashly uttered threats to the banker's life.

Knowing he was in this mess because of those recklessly spoken words gnawed at Burke day and night. Even more galling was the knowledge that that same lack of control had cost him his chance of happiness with Jayne.

His grip tightened on the bars. He'd sent her several letters. Not that he'd been able to put the apology she deserved on paper, but he'd been clear about wanting to see her. Had she given up on him? If only he could take back the ridiculous accusations he'd hurled. Jayne Stoneworthy, no, damn it, Jayne *Youngblood* was as inherently decent and honorable as any being the Almighty had placed on earth. It had been Robeena's ghost and the haunting legacy of Logan's desertion that had made him lash out as he had.

The thing about the past was that it sank invisible tentacles into the present, tentacles that had one reacting to events that no longer mattered. At some point, a person had to let go, accept what couldn't be changed and move on. How ironic that he should make that discovery while locked in a jail cell. No amount of wishing would erase the pain he'd seen in Jayne's eyes. He didn't delude himself that he could seek her forgiveness without groveling. And in order for groveling to be truly effective, one had to do it in person.

All right. He would bury the past once and for all and concentrate on the present and future, if he had one. There was always the possibility he would be found guilty of Dilicar's murder and hanged. His frustration grew, and he shook the immovable bars. Surely Jayne was capable of forgiving his twisted accusations, just this once. She was special that way, soft and compassionate, even when she was taking him to task for the male shortcomings her late aunt was so skilled at listing.

Despite his dismal surroundings, Burke smiled. Jayne prissily informing him of what behavior she would or wouldn't tolerate... He had no idea why her cultured chastisements so disarmed him, but sensed the answer hovered close by.

Five weeks to the day he had been arrested, Burke found himself inside a packed courtroom. He felt oddly indifferent to the unfolding drama as Judge Pinegar entered and everyone stood. There had still been no word from Jayne. Clearly, when it came to forgiving him, her seemingly limitless compassion had reached its breaking point.

He supposed he deserved no better. In comparison to Jayne's abandonment, whether or not he would be hanged for a murder he hadn't committed shrank in consequence. Did he really find death preferable to living without Jayne? Actually, being banished to the bleak confines of his existence before she'd entered it was in its own way a death sentence.

After the judge was seated, the gavel sounded. Conversation diminished to subdued whispers as the people in the gallery sat down. Another series of thumps produced the total silence requested. After returning to his chair, Burke raised his eyes and looked around. He expected to see a room of strangers.

He wasn't surprised to see Gideon and Emma. Hunter was there, along with many of the men who worked undercover with the Guardsmen. His emotional response to his friends' loyalty caught him off guard. His throat muscles tightened, and an odd pressure built behind his eyes. No longer did he feel totally alone. Scanning the crowd, he was unprepared for the sight of all his bank employees jamming most of the gallery. Good grief, who'd authorized them to close the bank on a weekday?

Newton White was also present. Sitting next to him was a large-boned woman wearing a gold dress and an enormous hat decorated with purple plumes and papier-mâché strawberries. The miner and flamboyant woman made an…interesting couple. Burke's gaze moved on.

The stunning sight of his brother sitting in the front row of spectators struck Burke with the impact of a physical blow. The burning in his eyes increased. Returning his stare, Logan grinned and gave a little nod, signifying his support. The gesture threatened to undo Burke's composure. Overwhelmed by his reaction, Burke forced his glance to continue on. He nearly fell off his chair. Beside Logan sat their parents, and next to them was…Jayne.

It was too much. Knowing the moisture in his eyes was that of impending tears, he hurriedly fished in his coat pocket for a handkerchief. Crying was for women. He refused to disgrace himself by publicly succumbing to the female weakness.

Judge Pinegar pounded the gavel once more. Burke swung around to face the black-robed justice. Standing as instructed, he heard the charges rattled off in a stony, neutral tone.

"…how do you plead?"
The question brought instant reality to the dire situation into which his own intemperate words had thrust him. "Not guilty, Your Honor."

Chapter Eighteen

"Your Honor, I know this is unusual, but may I approach the bench?"

Burke and his attorney, Jared Larimer, had discussed the case at length. Nothing had been said about Larimer attempting to speak out of turn.

The opposing lawyer, George Wilcox, jumped to his feet. "Your Honor, I protest. Mr. Larimer knows he can't interrupt the proceedings."

Judge Pinegar coldly contemplated Wilcox. "Return to your chair."

Red-faced, Wilcox did as instructed.

The judge's harsh glance fell upon Larimer. "Though rashly expressed, Mr. Wilcox is correct. Be advised, these proceedings will not corrupted by dramatic shenanigans."

Burke buried his face in his hands. Great, within one second of the trial, his attorney had alienated the judge.

"But Your Honor, if I can call Jayne Stoneworthy to the stand, there won't be any need for these proceedings to continue."

Youngblood, damn it. She was his wife!

Wilcox laughed contemptuously. "He's her husband. Naturally, she'll lie to protect him. Her testimony is worthless."

"Because she's married to the defendant?" Larimer challenged.

The gavel sounded. "That will do, gentlemen. Mr. Larimer, if you continue in this vein, I will find you in contempt. As much as Mr. Wilcox's unsolicited remarks annoy me, he is correct. Anything Mrs. Youngblood says is bound to be biased."

"But that's just it, she isn't his wife."

Burke shot to his feet. "The hell she isn't!"

Conversations erupted throughout the courtroom. This time Pinegar wielded the gavel as if it were a sledgehammer. "Order in the court. If I have to arrest every man and woman present, there will be order in this court. Sit down, Mr. Youngblood, or I'll have the bailiff escort you from this chamber, in shackles."

Burke returned to his chair and scowled at his attorney. Competent, hell. The man was a blithering idiot.

"Mr. Larimer, I will give you one sentence to clarify your statement."

"No legal wedding occurred between my client and Miss Stoneworthy."

Burke had to grit his teeth to keep from assaulting his own lawyer.

"You have another sentence to elaborate. Stand and deliver it." The judge waved the gavel at the audience. "I remind you this is a court of law, and you will show proper respect. *You will be quiet.*"

Looking amazingly unperturbed, Larimer rose. "The fraudulent ceremony was performed by Erastus Lowder, purportedly an ordained minister, who is an imposter and *not* a member of any recognized clergy. Mr. Lowder has no legal authority to marry anyone."

"Meaning that there is no Mrs. Youngblood," Judge Pinegar observed. "By the way, that was two sentences. You owe the court five dollars." He turned to the bailiff. "See that he pays it before he leaves. So now, where were we?"

"There is no Mrs. Youngblood."

"And, it's your claim that Miss Stoneworthy's testimony will prevent the necessity of a trial?"

Larimer nodded. "Also correct, Your Honor. Had Sheriff Donner taken a statement from her about my client's whereabouts on the night in question, charges never would have been brought against him."

Numbed by the sudden turn of events, Burke tried to cope with the frigid emptiness expanding inside him. He hadn't bound Jayne to him in marriage. A woman might dig deep within herself to forgive her husband for an unpardonable sin, but how far would she exert herself to forgive a man who had no legal claim on her?

The judge lapsed into deep reflection. A thick hush settled over the room. Minutes passed before Pinegar set aside the papers in front of him.

"And in light of this information, you're requesting Miss Stoneworthy speak now?"

"After you hear her testimony, I believe you'll dismiss the case."

"As for that, it's up to the jury to decide whether or not the woman is telling the truth and, after hearing all the evidence, render their verdict."

"That's just it, Your Honor. There *is* no evidence against my client. No one saw him at Sutton's place. Other than some words spoken in anger, *nothing* connects him to Mr. Dilicar's murder. Every person in this room has voiced an intemperate statement when overcome by emotion. That hardly makes them killers."

"A persuasive argument. Is Miss Stoneworthy present?"

"Yes, Your Honor, I am."

At the sweet sound of Jayne's voice, Burke bowed his head. His mind raced ahead to the testimony she might offer on his behalf. The thought of her opening herself to public ridicule clawed at the fragments of his weakening self-control.

"Your Honor." Wilcox sputtered. "Surely you're not going to be taken in by defense council's theatrics?"

The gavel fell. "You will speak when spoken to, is that clear, Mr. Wilcox?"

The attorney shot a lethal glance at Larimer. "Yes, Your Honor."

In short order, Jayne was sworn in and seated in the witness chair. She appeared pale, but calm.

Burke's heart hammered in his chest.

"Miss Stoneworthy, according to the defense, you're willing to testify as to Mr. Youngblood's whereabouts on the night in question, is that correct?"

"Yes."

"Considering your...uh...close relationship with the defendant, how can I be sure you aren't lying in order to save him from a hangman's noose?"

Any remaining color she possessed bled from her face. "I admit I don't wish for Mr. Youngblood to be executed. There isn't any way I can prove I'm speaking the truth. All I can do is—" she raised her eyes to the judge "—tell you that I was with Mr. Youngblood when the murder took place. You'll have to decide whether or not to believe me."

Her gentle courageousness filled Burke with an unexpected surge of pride. No one hearing her steady voice or gazing into her guileless features could doubt her utter sincerity, except a fool such as himself.

"Proceed, Miss Stoneworthy." Obviously the judge reached the same conclusion.

She clasped her hands together. "According to the transcripts Mr. Larimer showed me, Mr. Dilicar's servants said that the last time they saw him alive was sometime after midnight. As you probably realize, I'm going to swear that I was with Mr. Youngblood in the hours before midnight." She paused and cleared her throat. The unnatural silence gripping the courtroom pounded in Burke's ears. "I was also with him in the hours *after* midnight." Her pallid cheeks blazed with sudden color. "Until dawn, actually."

The judge briefly pondered her statement. "And he couldn't have slipped away for a short span of time during that period, without you noticing?"

The flags of color decorating her cheeks blazed crimson. "I would have definitely noticed."

"Why is that?"

"We were…uh…in bed. Together."

There was no stifling the low throb of excited whispers. Evidently the judge was so riveted by Jayne's testimony, he chose to ignore the minor hum. "But if you were asleep, he could have easily removed himself without you being aware of it."

"I wasn't asleep," she murmured quietly.

The animated comments rose in volume. The judge employed the gavel vigorously. With obvious reluctance, the spectators subdued their desire to exchange opinions on Jayne's statement.

"During the entire stretch of time?" he asked gently.

"We thought we'd just been married. It seemed the natural thing to do."

Gasps and chuckles broke out from the gallery. Pinegar raised his head and visually wrung compliance for decorum. After a moment, he redirected his attention to a visibly shaken Jayne.

Burke tried to surge to his feet and demand this public exhibition be ended. Larimer grabbed his coat and jerked roughly. "Sit down. You're a minute from walking out of this court a free man."

Burke ignored his attorney's savage whisper. The price of Jayne's humiliation was too great, even if his life hung in the balance.

"Young lady, under the circumstances, it took a lot of courage for you to come forward, and—"

Burke and his wrestling attorney finally gained the judge's attention.

"Ah, good, you anticipated my order to stand."

Obviously startled, Larimer loosened his hold.

Burke straightened. "I don't know about that, but—"

"Mr. Larimer, you will instruct your client to hold his tongue until invited to speak."

"For hell's sake, shut up, Burke. Listen to what the judge has to say."

"Hardly the orthodox instruction I expected, but I suppose it will do," Judge Pinegar said repressively.

Burke clamped his jaw tight. If Jayne was forced to make another embarrassing statement, there definitely wouldn't be order in the court.

"As I was saying, Miss Stoneworthy, I admire your bravery in publicly testifying about such private matters. Considering the sensitive nature of that testimony and what it obviously cost you to offer it, I'm inclined to believe its veracity."

"Your Honor, you can't be serious," Wilcox shouted in frustration. "You can't take the word of an immoral woman in a matter as serious as this."

"I've warned you about such outbursts. Bailiff, escort Mr. Wilcox to the sheriff's office where he will held under arrest for the next fourteen days."

A man built along Newton White's mammoth proportions stepped forward and took the attorney by his arm. "This is preposterous! I refuse to be treated like a common criminal."

"Make that thirty days."

Wilcox prudently fell silent.

"You may step down from the witness stand, Miss Stoneworthy. Mr. Youngblood, the court extends some latitude in exercising my judgment in cases such as this. On the basis of Miss Stoneworthy's obviously sincere testimony, I choose to apply my discretionary privilege in your favor. You are a free man." His gavel thundered. "Case dismissed."

Burke strode forward. "Just a minute, Your Honor."

"Yes?"

"Do you have a spare minute to legally join me and Miss Stoneworthy as husband and wife?"

A gleam appeared in the judge's formerly austere expression. "I have the time to conduct such a ceremony, providing Miss Stoneworthy is willing."

Enthusiastic murmurs flooded the room. Halfway back to her seat, Jayne turned and looked at Burke in disbelief. She couldn't have heard him correctly. After the horrible things he'd said in his office the day he was arrested, it was inconceivable he would want to be tied to her.

"*Are* you willing, Miss Stoneworthy?" the judge inquired.

"Uh, I'm not sure this is a good time," she replied weakly. "Burke, I mean Mr. Youngblood, is probably trying to show his gratitude for my testimony. That's not a very good reason to get married."

"I see your point. Well, Mr. Youngblood, don't stand there like a stump. Is your proposal a way to repay the woman for saving your neck?"

"No, sir. I happen to love her."

She gazed at Burke in bewilderment. "That's impossible. You aren't capable of loving anyone. You told me so yourself."

"Can't you overlook my monumental stupidity?" he asked with mesmerizing sincerity. "Your aunt was right. As a gender, men can be dumber than fence posts. The good news is we're capable of being trained."

Laughter rang out. The judge joined in. "What do you say, are you going to overlook the man's deficiencies and marry him anyway?"

Tears blurred her vision. "If Mr. Youngblood will swear under oath that he loves me, I'll be his wife."

A Bible was presented to Burke. He put one hand on it, raised the other and stared into Jayne's eyes. "I do solemnly swear that I love you with every fiber of my being."

How she wanted to believe him!

A great, collective sigh was followed by cheers.

The gavel pounded. "If you folks will shut up, I'll perform a wedding so this couple can cease being a public spectacle."

Judge Pinegar proved more proficient in pronouncing their vows than Erastus Lowder. This time when Jayne said "I do," it was with the burning hope that Burke truly did love her.

"You may kiss the bride."

Burke's mouth covered hers with a gentle warmth that loosened more tears. Gradually he deepened the pressure, as if resealing their earlier vows. She surrendered to the inexorable power he exerted over her. Dimly, she heard more cheers. She opened her eyes and saw the judge toss his gavel over his shoulder.

"I said to kiss the bride, not make love to her in the courtroom." His sonorous voice held no reprimand.

What captured Jayne's attention was a tear's solitary path down Burke's lean cheek.

Since they shared the carriage to Burke's home with his parents and brother, there was no opportunity for private conversation. Actually, there was no conversation. Neither Burke, nor his brother nor his parents seemed inclined to break the uncomfortable silence.

Her new husband appeared uninterested in ending the estrangement from his family. His assumed indifference wavered, however, whenever he looked at Logan. Jayne sensed he was searching for a way to overcome the awkwardness between himself and his brother but didn't know how to proceed. She considered it her wifely duty to help reconcile the stubborn family.

"I suggest we adjourn to the parlor," she announced brightly as they entered Burke's foyer. "I would like to…uh…" *What?* she wondered desperately.

Burke regarded her with a raised eyebrow. "Yes, dear?"

"Exchange a toast," she blurted, euphoric with her inspired answer. Not everyone could think under the kind of pressure the taciturn Youngblood clan generated. "We have your release to celebrate, as well as our wedding."

Her husband shrugged. "I don't suppose a drink would do any harm."

Such enthusiasm. The five of them entered the parlor. No friendly conversation ensued. Jayne sighed. With everyone standing around staring at one another, it would be an interminable afternoon.

Burke performed the honors of pouring the claret and presenting each person with a glass.

"Mr. Youngblood." The butler stepped into the room. "You have visitors."

The servant moved aside, and Hunter and Gideon, along with his wife, Emma, entered the parlor.

"Excuse us for intruding," Emma said. "We just had to give you our good-wishes and congratulations."

Jayne set down her glass and went to her friend. "Don't spoil things by apologizing." They exchanged hugs. Jayne felt the roundness of Emma's expanding figure. It occurred to her that soon she might be carrying a babe. A wellspring of emotion choked her. "I'm so glad you're here."

They stepped apart. Gideon eyed their affectionate outburst, then grinned at Burke. "I'll to drink to your future, but that's as far as it goes."

Everyone, including Burke's parents, laughed.

More drinks were poured. Hunter proposed the first toast. "Damn..." He coughed. "Excuse me, ladies. I mean, darn your hide, Burke. What happened to your famous rules about never falling in love and getting married?"

"What kind of toast is that?" Emma demanded.

Hunter smiled. "All right, here it is. Let's raise our glasses to the newly wedded couple. May they live long and have a passel of younguns."

"Hear, hear, I'll drink to that," Burke's father said.

At the obviously heartfelt sentiment, Burke glanced speculatively at the gray-haired man. "Thank you, sir."

Glasses were raised and spirits imbibed.

"To the bride and groom," Gideon announced. "May they be as blissfully happy as Emma and I. And may Burke never make another rule."

The traditional ritual continued with Emma speaking next. "To my best friend and her new husband. May they be as in love on their fiftieth anniversary as they are today."

"To my brother," Logan said, his voice rich with emotion, "who, though older than me, wisely followed my example and married a good woman—the only one who would probably have you. May your decision bring you as much happiness as mine has brought me."

Jayne saw that his brother's banter touched Burke. He raised his glass. "You have the soul of a banker, Logan. Don't ever try your hand at poetry."

Laughing at the brotherly exchange, everyone joined in the toast.

"I resent that," Burke's father said in the same gruff voice his son often used. "A banker is capable of writing decent poetry. I remember writing a few romantic lines to your mother when I was courting her."

Mrs. Youngblood, looking less tense than earlier, shook her head. "I was charmed by your love notes, Warren, but I don't recall anything rhyming."

Flushing, the senior Mr. Youngblood raised his glass. "That's hardly the point, Cora. It's the sentiment that's important." He cleared his throat and harrumphed. "In a more serious vein, I'd like to say that it sometimes takes years for a man to recognize his...er...mistakes."

"The same is true for a woman." Mrs. Youngblood wiped a tear from her eye as she looked longingly between her two sons.

Jayne dabbed at her own tears.

"My toast is to letting the past remain where it belongs and concentrating on new beginnings," the older man said. "To the future and every promise it holds."

Jayne found it impossible to swallow past the lump in

her throat, and sensed her husband faced the same challenge.

They went around the circle several more times, each person's toast becoming more outrageous than the previous one.

When the mantel clock chimed the hour and Hunter straightened, the buoyant mood sobered. "As much fun as this has been, I'd better be on my way. It's a long ride to the ranch."

"Why don't you stay with Emma and me?" Gideon suggested.

"I wouldn't want to impose."

"You wouldn't be imposing," Emma quickly assured him.

The handsome rancher looked out the window. "In case something happens, it's better that I'm there."

Burke's gaze sharpened. "You mean more rustling?"

Hunter nodded. "I figure Sutton's behind it."

"And most likely he had Dilicar murdered," Gideon said. "Too bad we probably won't be able to prove it."

Hunter retrieved his hat from a green brocade cushion. "I'll just have to watch my back."

Burke's father stepped forward. "I appreciate the way you've supported my son. I owe you a debt of gratitude for standing by him during this mess. If money is ever a problem, I'd be honored to loan you whatever you need."

Hunter grinned. "That's quite an offer. What if I said I wanted a million dollars?"

The older man didn't smile. "I've sized you up, cowpoke. After looking out for my son's interests, I'd gladly give you any funds you needed. You're too proud, though, to accept a gift like that. You'd call it charity. The loan's a standing offer. Any time you're strapped for cash, send me a telegraph, and I'll see you get what you need."

"Your father's a shrewd man," Gideon observed. "And, as I assumed he'd be, he's a lot snappier dresser than Pappy."

Burke threw back his head and laughed. No one but he and Gideon appeared to get the jest.

"I'm with my father on this," Logan interjected. "You and Gideon were there for Burke. I'd be insulted if you needed help and didn't contact me."

"You know you can count on me," Gideon said quietly.

"And me," Burke added.

Jayne was overwhelmed by the strong feelings of loyalty the five radiated toward one another. Though he was substantially older than the younger men pledging their mutual support, Burke's father's hawkish demeanor was just as unyielding. They only lacked gleaming swords to complete the picture of battle-ready warriors.

Burke swirled the claret that remained in his goblet. "Before you go, I would like to offer a toast to my new bride," he continued, "To the former Miss Jayne Stoneworthy, niece of the august female philosopher, Euphemia Stoneworthy, may I never give you cause to regret becoming my wife. I pledge my love, my loyalty and my life to you, darling." A fire burned in his eyes as he stared at her. "I'll share the rest of the toast when we're alone."

"Hear! Hear!"

Later, after an unexpectedly congenial dinner, Burke showed his parents to their room and bade them good-night. He and Logan continued down the hall to the next bed chamber.

Logan whistled softly as he stepped through the doorway. "You've done pretty well since you left Boston."

"From what I hear, you've done just as well in Trinit Falls."

Logan grinned. "Face it, we Youngbloods might need two-by-four to get our attention, but we sure know how t make money."

Burke's thoughts flashed back to that highly charged encounter with Jayne in her bedchamber. Absently, he rubbe his forehead. "I couldn't have said it better myself."

"What do you think of Father's idea to merge our separate banking networks into a single entity?"

"I think," Burke began thoughtfully, "that both our parents have changed so much I hardly recognize them as the people who raised us."

Logan's expression became reflective. "I was surprised by the difference in them, too. When Jayne's telegraph arrived, saying that you were being put on trial for murder, she mentioned that she was also notifying our parents about your arrest. Considering the fireworks the last time we were all together, I was wondering if they'd even acknowledge the wire."

Burke felt a familiar grief squeeze his heart. Part of him wanted to forever extinguish the memory of that night. Another part realized that the devastating episode had to be exhumed before it could be buried.

"About what happened with Robeena," Burke began carefully, "we've never resolved that…misunderstanding."

Logan looked him square in the eye. "I'm sorry I ever doubted you."

Dumbstruck by his brother's apology, Burke didn't know what to say.

"It took me years," Logan continued. "but I finally figured out that, not only had Robeena slipped into your room, she'd also set me up to discover her in your bed. Looking back, I can see that she'd been using me to make you jealous. I don't know how you managed to resist her, but there's not a doubt in my mind. You never betrayed me."

Staggered that the bitter memory no longer tainted Logan's feelings toward him, Burke's heart expanded, "I didn't think I would ever hear those words from you."

"They've been a long time coming. I guess I had to grow up, experience life and meet Victoria before I learned that appearances aren't always what they seem." He held out his hand. "Am I forgiven?"

Burke clasped his brother's hand. "There's nothing to forgive."

"Thank you, big brother," Logan said unsteadily.

"What for?"

"Being a silent partner when I started the Territorial Bank. For hiring a personal bodyguard to watch over me during the war." Logan chuckled. "On a couple occasions, he saved my neck. Thank you for encouraging Martin Pritchert to come west and coach me on the intricacies of setting up a bank."

"You would have done the same for me."

Logan shook his head. "No, I wouldn't. At the time I was a hotheaded fool who thought he had an answer for everything." He grimaced. "I'm glad I outgrew that bit of arrogant self-righteousness."

"There's nothing I'd rather do than let bygones be bygones."

"I'm not done thanking you, big brother."

"Having you *not* hate me is all the thanks I need," Burke said gruffly.

"Two more things, and I've had my say. Thank you for arranging for Victoria to become Madison's tutor. I don't know why you ever thought a prissy Bostonian bluestocking would make me the perfect wife, but you were right."

"It was Pritchert who drew my attention to her. I was tired of reading his reports about you catting around. Hell, you even moved in with a tribe of Indians for a while. I decided Miss Amory had enough fire and vinegar to wet your interest."

A grin slashed Logan's face. "I got a taste of the vinegar when she let me out of the stockade at that abandoned fort. Besides getting a wagonload of books to Trinity Falls, her main mission became reforming me."

"Pritchert wrote that she saved your life."

"She did more than that. She saved my soul."

A shiver slid down Burke's spine. He felt exactly the same way about Jayne. "I'm glad she was the one."

Logan's features remained serious. "My final thank-you is for the way you accepted my apology. It was wrong of me to pronounce you guilty without hearing your side of the story. Seeing Robeena in your bed like that, though, and knowing it was you she really wanted... I guess it was easier to blame you than face the truth.'' He shook his head. ''By forgiving my stupidity without any recriminations or blame, you've proved yourself to be the older brother I've always admired. Thank you.''

Another handshake wasn't enough. As Burke fiercely hugged the man who'd once been his tagalong brother, he realized he'd been wrong. Things could be the way they'd once been between them. Better. It was as if an amputated limb had been restored.

Alone in her husband's bedchamber, Jayne pushed aside green velvet draperies and peered into the night. There was nothing to see, other than the faint mist of her breath upon the darkened pane of glass.

She was on edge, she realized, wrapping her arms around herself. Burke's subtly shifting moods during dinner left her uncertain about what to expect when he finally joined her. It was scary to know she was married to such a complex man, a man who often held his most intense emotions beneath a layer of iron control. She sought solace from the times when, after some prodding on her part, he did share his feelings.

He loved her—had sworn it so upon a Bible, before a judge, a gallery of spectators and the Great Almighty.

A sound drew her gaze to the bedchamber door. The brass knob turned. Her heart fluttered. She was about to discover her new husband's mood.

He entered the room quietly. The door clicked shut behind him. Her breath caught. To her, he seemed a powerful, masculine force of unfathomable depths, similar to a bottomless sea of dangerous, uncharted currents.

There was no reason for the trepidation that made breathing difficult. Burke Youngblood *was* powerful. But the raw strength at his command would never be used against her. Euphemia had believed a woman gave away her power when she loved. The opposite was true. In some mysterious way she was just beginning to comprehend, Burke's strength had become hers—just as he had absorbed a portion of her softness.

Together they completed each other. Perhaps the uneasiness she experienced was the sudden understanding that she would never again be whole—without him.

"Why didn't you answer the letters I sent from jail?" he growled softly. "Why didn't you visit me?"

"I was afraid to," she confessed.

"Afraid?" He moved closer. "Of me?"

It was uncanny how his questions mirrored her thoughts moments before he'd arrived. "Not physically."

"Then how?"

Tell the truth. "I was frightened you would want a divorce."

He closed his eyes. When he opened them, they were filled with stark ferocity. "It seems a night for apologies. I'm sorry, Jayne. When I found out that bank draft was worthless, my anger made me forget something important."

"What?"

"That you're a woman of superior integrity who hasn't a larcenous bone in her beautifully formed body."

She flushed. Burke's mood seemed...promising.

"I should have guessed," he continued, "there was probably a good reason that your uncle was the black sheep of the family."

"While you were in jail, I read Aunt Euphemia's journal. Her entries about her brother were enlightening. Evidently he was incapable of telling the truth, even when lying offered no benefit. He's served time in prison for defrauding widows of their life savings. Euphemia called him a charlatan and grand deceiver. She suspected he often believed his own outlandish lies. When he contacted me, he might have convinced himself that the bank draft *was* real and not just a figment of his imagination."

"I've run across a few people like that."

"I wonder if part of Euphemia's problems with men stemmed from having an older brother who could not be trusted."

"At least you're admitting she had problems."

Jayne flushed as she recalled several pithy passages in the woman's journal about what part of their anatomy men used for brains. "Well, yes, she was a bit biased in her unflattering assessments about the male gender."

"A *bit?*"

"All right, she was completely closed-minded on the topic."

Burke caressed her cheek with the pad of his callused fingertip. She tilted her face to better savor the gently abrasive contact.

"Tonight also seems to be a night for thank-yous."

She lost herself in his gaze. "For what do you want me to thank you?"

"You've got it wrong. *I* want to thank *you.*"

"For?" She was melting from the inside out.

"Sending telegraph messages to my family, helping me discover that my parents aren't the unfeeling creatures my memory painted them and making it possible to heal the wound between Logan and me." He paused. "For giving me back the brother I thought I'd lost."

"Oh, Burke, you're the one who ended the estrangement between yourself and your family."

"It never would have happened without you."

"Given enough time, I'm sure you would have worked things out."

"Not in a million years." He cradled her face in his strong hands. "There's three more things I want to thank you for."

"So many thank-yous..." she breathed.

"I told you, it's a night for them."

"Do go on." Standing on tiptoe, she twined her arms round his neck.

"Thank you for having enough love in your heart to forgive me and for being willing to sacrifice your reputation to keep me alive."

"That's only two things," she said, her fingers luxuriating in the thick hair that had gone uncut for more than a month and now brushed his shirt collar. "You said there were three."

"I was saving the most important for last." He nibbled the sensitive skin at her throat. "Thank you for becoming my wife. I do love you, Jayne. Tonight and forever."

Hot tears brimmed and fell. She couldn't speak.

He gave her a slight shake. "Well?"

Well what? Didn't he realize she was a teary, aching blob of emotion, incapable of anything save sniffling?

"Come on, honey. Tell me that you love me."

"Oh, Burke..." She pulled his head down and brushed her lips against his jaw. "Of course, I love you. How could I not?" She struggled to speak coherently. "You're everything a man should be—honorable, brave, strong, tender... My aunt was wrong. They may be somewhat rare, but good men do exist. And the woman lucky enough to find such a mate thanks God every night of her life that she's been so blessed."

"I'm the one who's blessed," he countered. "Before you entered it, my world had shrunk to a colorless void. You made me come alive again." A slow smile curved his mouth. "As Hunter's top ranch hand would say, you showed me my rules weren't 'worth a bucket of spit.'"

She returned his smile. "The less said about those wretched rules, the better."

"They're gone." He stepped back and snapped his fingers. "Just like that, they went up in a puff of smoke."

She giggled softly. "Just like that, hmm?"

He scooped her into his arms and strode toward the bed. "The same way we're going to in a little while."

One moment she was locked in his embrace, and the next he dropped her onto the mattress. As she oriented herself to the abrupt change in position, another bout of tingling déjà vu stirred. "This reminds me of the afternoon you barged into the tavern and tried to teach that obscure lesson."

He whipped off his jacket and tossed it to the floor. "It was a cathouse, honey." He unbuttoned his shirt with startling speed and shrugged it aside. "And the lesson wasn't obscure. It was direct and to the point."

He tugged off his boots and socks. The belt went next. When his fingers went to the front closure of his trousers, he paused. "Still squeamish about seeing me without my pants on?"

She blushed. "Umm, I seem to have a lot more clothes on than you. Perhaps we could even things out before you…"

"What?"

"Reveal your total naked splendor to my innocent eyes?"

His laughter was deep and incredibly stimulating. "Not so innocent now, my sweet wife." He leaned over and began unfastening the buttons holding her bodice together. "I just thought of something."

She trembled. "What's that?"

He managed to pull her opened gown over her shoulders and down her hips in a single movement. "I bet I'm the only man to have two wedding nights with the same woman."

"The first one wasn't real."

"It felt real." He whisked away her petticoats, then quickly vanquished the corset, leaving nothing but her sheer undergarments. "Though I admit the surroundings left something to be desired."

"I meant the ceremony," she explained. He joined her on the bed and leaned over her. Having his powerful, darkly furred chest pressed against her had an alarming effect on her heartbeat. His hot skin burned through the fragile material of her chemise, just as his muscular thighs scorched through her pantalettes. "The lovemaking was very real."

He kissed her deeply, then raised his head. "It will only get better."

"Becoming your wife is the most beautiful thing that's ever happened to me." She bit her lip. "I don't need my academy to make me happy."

His expression darkened. "What are you talking about? Of course, you'll have your school."

"After what happened in court today?" She shook her head. "No one's going to place their daughter under my care."

"*Mrs. Youngblood,* I've invested a small fortune in that venture."

"You can afford to lose a small fortune. After all, you've still got your federal charter, and you recovered the stolen gold and cash."

"You're talking to a banker, honey. As far as I'm concerned, no one's rich enough to be blasé about losing a small fortune."

"But my reputation is destroyed!"

"*Was* destroyed," he corrected softly. "Temporarily."

"But—"

He kissed her, no doubt to shut her up. Though unfair, his tactics were effective. She surrendered to his mastery with a sigh.

It wasn't long before she lay limply beneath him. "The minute Pinegar pronounced us man and wife, our fraudulent ceremony became irrelevant."

"It did?"

"You're a respectably married woman. There'll be no problem acquiring students."

"Truly?"

"Truly." He tugged the pink ribbon holding her chemise together. "Jayne, have I mentioned that the sight of you takes my breath away?"

She touched the small indentation in his chin. "Funny, I have the same reaction to you."

The chemise was of insufficient strength to survive his tender assault. The sounds of tearing fabric, her indrawn breath and Burke's labored breathing set a torch to the fire smoldering between them.

Later as she lay cradled in her husband's embrace, in the seconds before sleep claimed her, she realized that both she and Burke had seen love as a weakness. They'd been wrong. Love was so powerful it could change peoples' lives, if they let it.

Oh, Euphemia, I'm sorry you never found your true mate. It's a glorious experience I wish you could have known....

Epilogue

As Burke made his way along the crowded Denver boardwalk, he paid little attention to the people brushing past him. Gone were the days of being forced to scan the faces of passersby for potential bank robbers. Dilicar's death had brought a cessation to the armed men trying to empty the First National of its gold and cash.

Aware of the lateness of the hour, Burke hastened his step. The special class Jayne conducted Thursday afternoons would be finishing soon. Now that she was expecting their baby, he found himself wanting to spend as much time with her as he could. His chest tightened. He didn't want to miss a moment of the magic. He shook his head. For a man who hadn't believed in love, he'd certainly changed his tune.

From the corner of his eyes, a flash of red drew Burke's gaze. Disbelievingly, he caught sight of a…humpbacked man. The gentle warmth he'd been experiencing vanished. Damn it, Pappy Pickman must have escaped. When it came time to elect a new sheriff, Burke wouldn't be voting for Donner.

It took only two strides to catch up with the aging criminal. "All right, Pappy, hold it right there."

The man squealed. "Let me go. I ain't done nothing wrong."

Burke strong-armed Pappy to the side of the boardwalk and pushed him up against a wall. "What did you do, break out of jail?"

"No, sir, I did not," came the emphatic denial. "I done got released."

"Now why would anyone want to do that?"

"On account of I got real sick, and nobody wanted to take care of me."

"Right."

"It's true," Pappy protested. "I got me a long-lost granddaughter. When she showed up, the authorities decided to let her take care of me. I'm a free man." He coughed. "As long as I don't go robbing any banks."

"Let's see what you've got in your pockets."

"Ain't got nothing, 'cept this."

A big, red, lint-covered sucker came into sight.

Burke blinked. The mauled confectionary wasn't what he'd expected.

"Don't be afraid," Pappy said snidely. "It ain't likely to go off."

Burke didn't appreciate the older man's attempt at humor. "There was a sizable reward for your capture."

"My granddaughter paid back the money I was accused of taking. I'm a respectable citizen now. Reformed, they call it."

Reluctantly, Burke relaxed his hold. Pappy's tone was so self-satisfied that Burke tended to believe the old coot. "I don't care what the law says. Keep your sorry carcass out of the First National."

"Don't be worrying about that."

Burke leveled a hard look at the gratingly smug man. "See that you remember what I said."

"Right. Stay away from your precious bank."

Without further comment, Burke turned from the grinning thief. Let Sheriff Donner keep Denver's streets safe.

A few minutes later Burke stood before floral-etched glass doors and a circumspect sign framed in polished mahogany that read Jayne Youngblood's School of Tutoring for Young Ladies.

He stepped into the building and was embraced by the mysterious, beckoning warmth he associated with Jayne. The parlor area with its papered walls. Oriental carpets, settees and lamps seemed an invitation to linger. The clusters of earnestly talking schoolgirls who filled the room accepted that unspoken invitation as they waited for their families to pick them up. In less than twenty minutes the girls would be on their way home.

At the entrance, he became the focal point of their inquiring stares. He never was quite so aware of his masculinity as when he crossed the threshold of Jayne's school, or their bedchamber.

"Hello, Mr. Youngblood."

He acknowledged the chorus of greetings and steeled himself against the giggles that accompanied all encounters with Jayne's students, then consulted his timepiece before moving down the hall. Knowing Jayne would still be with her afternoon class, he would wait in her office. Again he entered a chamber of quiet, feminine warmth. His gaze went automatically to the plank of wood propped in a place of honor on the desk. That Jayne had kept Newt's sign lifted Burke's spirits. His wife—how he loved calling her that—was a sentimental woman, cherishing inherently flawed keepsakes that were of value to her.

Since he was far from perfect, he counted her sentimental streak as one of her most treasured virtues. He figured as long as she kept the sign, she'd keep him, too.

The door opened.

Laughter in her eyes, a smile lighting her face, stood Jayne.

"Am I late?"

His throat muscles tightened. "I'd say you were just in time."

He opened his arms, and she flew to him. It no longer terrified him that he'd surrendered his heart to her, though sometimes it did keep him awake at night knowing he was responsible for safeguarding her against an often brutal world. Feeling the ripening fullness that cradled their unborn baby inspired him to want to battle dragons on her behalf.

A firm tap against the door frame and someone clearing his throat had Burke smothering an oath. It was *his* turn to be alone with Jayne.

"'Scuse me, but them girls pointed me to this here office."

At the disagreeable sound of Pappy Pickman's voice, Burke's head snapped up. "What the hell are you doing here? Did you follow me?"

"No, sir," the man answered. "I'm here on account of the lady. I got business with her."

Burke's eyes narrowed. "Wrong answer, Pappy. You don't have any business at all with my wife."

Surprised by Burke's hostility toward the older man, Jayne rested a restraining hand on her husband's arm. "I believe Mr. Pickman is interested in signing up for my Thursday class."

"That's right! I heard tell you were teaching readin' and writin'. My granddaughter says I ain't too old to learn some of that."

"Son of a—"

"Burke," Jayne interrupted hastily. She smiled at their visitor. "Today's class is finished, but you're more than welcome to come next week. The class starts at three o'clock."

"No, you're not welcome," Burke contradicted. He turned to Jayne. "You don't want anything to do with Pappy Pickman. He's a crook. He even tried to rob my bank."

"Oh dear, is that true, Mr. Pickman?"

The man blushed. "You couldn't hardly call it a robbery. I didn't even have a gun."

"You had a stick of dynamite," Burke pointed out coldly.

"A really old one. It probably wouldn't have gone off."

As excuses went, Jayne didn't think Pickman's had much merit. "I'm afraid I can't open my class to criminals. Think how disruptive it would be for the other students to have the sheriff show up and arrest you."

"But I ain't a criminal anymore. I done got reformed. Nobody's going to arrest me."

Jayne looked at Burke. "Is that true?"

"So Pappy says."

"Well, if he's paid his debt to society—"

"Don't even think it, Jayne. There's no way I'm going to let you consort with known bank robbers."

Burke had had that same implacable look on his face the unforgettable afternoon at the stream when they'd almost made love and he'd refused to find Baldwin's widow and girlfriend. Months later, both women and their children were being supported by her husband's generosity.

She faced Mr. Pickman. "It appears my husband and I need to discuss this."

"I'll come back next week at three to see what you decided."

"Don't bother," Burke snapped.

The man ducked his head and turned away. It was impossible not to feel a smidgen of sympathy for someone wanting to improve his life.

Burke slammed shut the door. "Forget it, Jayne. Pappy Pickman isn't going to worm his way into our lives."

"He doesn't appear all that dangerous."

"The man carries dynamite in his pockets!"

"Only very old dynamite."

"That's the most dangerous kind!"

Jayne reached up and touched Burke's cheek. She loved being his wife and having the freedom to touch him. "Then he hasn't truly reformed, and we certainly won't allow him in our school."

Burke frowned. "Damn it, Jayne."

Perplexed, she tilted her head. "What's wrong? I just agreed with you. The man shouldn't be allowed on the premises."

Burke sighed. "He's given up toting sticks of dynamite. He's got lollipops packed in his pockets now. But that doesn't change anything."

It did, of course, but they would discuss it later. She wound her arms around his neck and stood on tiptoe, nudging his hips provocatively.

"So, what are you packing, mister, dynamite or lollipops?"

Sensual heat glinted in his dark eyes. "Honey, I'm dying to show you, but this is hardly the place."

"Isn't it?"

He leaned forward and covered her mouth with his. His kisses intensified. Heat gathered.

Ending the torrid kiss, he reached out and bolted the door shut.

"On second thought, any woman who's been immortalized in marble as a Greek goddess can handle a little afternoon romancing."

"I've told you before that the statue my aunt made of me is a runner, not a goddess."

His low chuckle vibrated in her heart. "Darling, any man worth his salt recognizes a goddess when he's lucky enough to catch one."

* * * * *

Author Note

Burke's Rules is set in Denver, Colorado, in a magical time period accessible to authors of fiction. My next book will also take place in Denver during this period. Hunter Moran is the hero. As with all my stories, I blend elements of reality and creativity to build a ''let's pretend'' world of romance and adventure where my heros and heroines resist falling in love all the way to paradise. The Guardmen of Denver are purely fictional creations. Sigh....

MEN at WORK

All work and no play?
Not these men!

January 1999
SOMETHING WORTH KEEPING by Kathleen Eagle
He worked with iron and steel, and was as wild as the mustangs that were his passion. She was a high-class horse trainer from the East. Was her gentle touch enough to tame his unruly heart?

MEN OF **STEEL**

February 1999
HANDSOME DEVIL by Joan Hohl
His roguish good looks and intelligence drew women like magnets, but Luke Branson was having too much fun to marry again. Then Selena McInnes strolled before him and turned his life upside down!

TALL, DARK AND SMART
$E=MC^2$

March 1999
STARK LIGHTNING by Elaine Barbieri
The boss's daughter was ornery, stubborn and off-limits for cowboy Branch Walker! But Valentine was also nearly impossible to resist. Could they negotiate a truce...or a surrender?

MEN OF THE WEST

Available at your favorite retail outlet!

MEN AT WORK™

HARLEQUIN®   Silhouette®

My Secret Admirer

Savor the magic of love
with three new romances
from top-selling authors
**Anne Stuart,
Vicki Lewis Thompson and
Marisa Carroll.**

My Secret Admirer is a unique collection
of three brand-new stories featuring passionate
secret admirers. Celebrate Valentine's Day with
these wonderfully romantic tales that are
ideally suited for this special time!

Available in February 1999 at your favorite retail outlet.

HARLEQUIN®
*M*akes any time special ™

Look us up on-line at: http://www.romance.net   PHSECRET

COMING NEXT MONTH FROM

HARLEQUIN HISTORICALS